Grammar & Writing Practice

Let's See Grammar

The Passive
被動語態

The coffee is brewed fresh every morning.

Intermediate 1

彩圖中級英文文法 三版

written by Alex Rath Ph.D.

Relative Clauses With Prepositions
搭配介系詞的關係子句

This is my pet mouse's favorite book, at which she can look for hours.

Verbs Followed by Infinitives
要接不定詞的動詞

Don't attempt to persuade me to get rid of my favorite armchair.

Unreal Present Conditionals
與現在事實相反的條件句

If his travel agent offered tourist trips to the moon, Jim would book tickets right away.

Intermediate 1 Contents

Intermediate 2

Part 1 Nouns 名詞

Unit 1

Singular and Plural Nouns: Regular
單數與複數名詞：規則名詞

單數名詞要用**單數動詞**，
複數名詞要用**複數動詞**。

- That book is **on the shelf.**
  那本書在架子上。
- Those books are **on the shelves.**
  那些書在架子上。

1 可數名詞具有單數與複數形態。大多數**規則名詞**直接加上 s，即構成**複數名詞**。

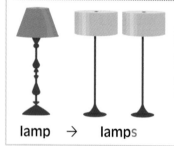

bed → bed**s**
table → table**s**
chair → chair**s**

lamp → lamp**s**

2 字尾是 ch、sh、s、x、z 的名詞，要加上 es。

crutch → crutch**es**
flush → flush**es**
kiss → kiss**es**
box → box**es**
buzz → buzz**es**

例外
這兩個字尾的 **ch** 都發 /k/ 的音，只加 s。
- stomach → stomach**s**
- monarch → monarch**s**

3 特殊字尾的名詞：

y
子音 + **y** → 去 y 加 **ies**
baby → bab**ies**
lady → lad**ies**

母音 + **y** → 加 s
key → key**s**
holiday → holiday**s**

例外
「子音 + **o**」只加 s
- cello → cello**s**
- piano → piano**s**
- photo → photo**s**

o
子音 + **o** → 加 **es**
tomato → tomato**es**
potato → potato**es**

母音 + **o** → 加 s
radio → radio**s**
kangaroo → kangaroo
→ kangaroo**s**

有兩種複數形式，加 -s 或與單數同形

例外
兩種拼寫都有
- buffalo → buffalo**s**/buffalo**es**
- volcano → volcano**s**/volcano**es**
- mosquito → mosquito**s**/mosquito**es**

f
字尾 **f/fe** → 去 f/fe 加 **ves**
leaf → lea**ves**
thief → thie**ves**
wife → wi**ves**

字尾 **ff** → 加 s
cliff → cliff**s**
sheriff → sheriff**s**

例外
兩種拼寫都有
- hoof → hoof**s**/hoo**ves**
- scarf → scarf**s**/scar**ves**
- dwarf → dwarf**s**/dwar**ves**

例外
字尾 **f/fe** 只加 s
- giraffe → giraffe**s**
- belief → belief**s**
- safe → safe**s**
- roof → roof**s**
- chief → chief**s**

1

請將括弧內的名詞以「複數形態」填空，完成句子。

1. Eliot saw dozens of _____ (frog) in the pond.
2. Since I cooked, you need to wash the _____ (dish).
3. Real life _____ (hero) are much better than those in comic books.
4. Our company has _____ (factory) all over the world.
5. Gary sharpens his _____ (knife) with a wet stone.
6. There are six _____ (galley) on this cruise ship.
7. Laura rented two _____ (safe) for storing her jewelry.
8. We need three _____ (loaf) of bread and two _____ (carton) of milk.
9. The government caught two _____ (spy) last week and will bring them to trial.
10. *Hamlet* and *Macbeth* are Shakespeare's famous _____ (play).

2

請勾選正確的答案。

1. I visited many ☐ churchs ☐ churches during my trip around Europe.
2. A man cannot have two ☐ wives ☐ wifes at the same time in Taiwan.
3. Electric ☐ toothbrushes ☐ toothbrushs can clean your teeth better.
4. Do you know a story about a poor girl selling ☐ matches ☐ matchs on the street?
5. If I had had two ☐ stomachs ☐ stomaches, I could have eaten more cake.
6. Most ☐ babies ☐ babys start to say simple words by the time they are 12 ☐ months ☐ monthes old.
7. Keith told me he put the ☐ keies ☐ keys on the washing machine.
8. I can get you some more ☐ boxs ☐ boxes from the supermarket if you need them.

3

o 與 f 是兩個麻煩的字尾，字尾是 o 或 f 的名詞，其複數形態的構成方式經常不只一種。請試著將左欄的名詞改寫為「複數形態」，填入右欄正確的空格內（可參考字典）。

1	子音 + o		-es	-s	-s/-es
mango	hero	zero			*mangos/mangoes*
cargo	potato	memo			
kilo	solo	tomato			

2	-f/-fe/-ff		-ves	-s
puff	knife	brief		
half	roof	gulf		
chief	calf	tariff		

Part 1 Nouns 名詞

Unit 2

Singular and Plural Nouns: Irregular
單數與複數名詞：不規則名詞

1 不規則名詞的複數形態，構成方式雖然沒有規則，某些依然有跡可循。第一種方法是變換其中的「**母音**」。

a → e	ou → i
man → men	mouse → mice
woman → women	louse → lice

oo → ee
foot → feet
tooth → teeth
goose → geese

2 第二種不規則名詞是字尾加上 en 或 ren。

child → children   ox → oxen

3 第三種不規則名詞是「**單複數同形**」，不論數量多少都不變化形式。

 sheep   reindeer

 bison   moose

 deer   aircraft

· species
· series

4 源自**希臘文**或**拉丁文**的名詞，其複數形態也沿用希臘文或拉丁文之拼法。

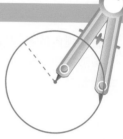

-us → -i
alumnus → alumni 校友
stimulus → stimuli 刺激物
radius → radii 半徑
syllabus → syllabi 教學大綱
fungus → fungi 菌類

-on → -a
phenomenon → phenomena 現象
criterion → criteria 標準

-is → es
analysis → analyses 分析
crisis → crises 危機
basis → bases 基礎
oasis → oases 綠洲
thesis → theses 論點

-x → -ces（或規則）
index → indices/indexes 索引
appendix → appendices/appendixes 附錄

-um → -a（或規則）
memorandum → memoranda/memorandums 備忘錄
referendum → referenda/referendums 公投

5 關於魚類名詞的複數形：

1 如果指「**同類魚**」或「**泛指魚**」，不論幾隻都是單複數同形，**不加 s/es**；

2 如果指「**不同類**」的好幾隻，可以加 s/es 也可以不加 s/es，但**以不加較常見**；

3 當它們指「**魚肉**」時，則為**不可數名詞**，不能加 s/es。

I bought three salmon. 我買了三隻鮭魚。
  ↳ 三隻一樣品種的鮭魚

Scientists are working hard to protect many types of salmon from extinction.
科學家致力於保護許多種類的鮭魚，以免牠們絕種。

I love to eat fried cod. 我愛吃煎鱈魚。
  ↳ 鱈魚肉

Practice

1　請將括弧內的名詞以正確的「單複數形態」填空，完成句子。

1. The dentist insisted that I floss my _____ (tooth) every day.

2. There are 22 _____ (child) in each class.

3. There are many _____ (species) of waterfowls in the USA.

4. A shepherd dog can manage hundreds of _____ (sheep) alone.

5. On Christmas Eve, Santa Claus will ride a sleigh pulled by eight _____ (reindeer) to give out gifts.

6. Frontline Plus is used to kill _____ (louse) that bite dogs and cats.

7. _____ (bison) are large animals that live on the plains in North America and Europe.

8. Molds and mushrooms are considered two members of the _____ (fungus) family.

9. Auroras are special atmospheric _____ (phenomenon) occurring in the polar regions.

10. Marvel's *Spiderman* comic book _____ (series) is the source of several movies.

11. The government has called on every citizen to work together to get through this economic _____ (crisis).

2　請從圖片中選出符合說明的詞彙，並以適當的「複數形態」填空，完成句子。

1. _____ are born in fresh water. They grow up in the ocean but swim back up the rivers to lay their eggs in the breeding season.

2. _____ is low fat and nutritious. It is a common source of fish fillets.

3. Goldfish and koi are two famous ornamental _____. They are popular aquarium and pond fish.

4. Clams, mussels, and shrimp are all described as _____.

cod

salmon

carp

shellfish

Part 1 Nouns 名詞

Unit 3

Countable and Uncountable Nouns
可數與不可數名詞

1 名詞可分為可數名詞和不可數名詞。
可數名詞的數量可以計算,並且有**單複數之分**。

可數	不可數
spoon	rice
spoons	rice
湯匙	米

one bowl	two bowls	碗
one highchair	two highchairs	兒童用餐椅
one child	two children	小孩

2 可數名詞的前面,通常會加不定冠詞 a/an 或「**數量**」,不能完全不加修飾詞單獨使用。

a stove 一個火爐
an icebox 一台冰箱
two washing machines 兩台洗衣機

3 可數名詞可以搭配單數或複數動詞。**單數名詞用單數動詞,複數名詞用複數動詞**。

This tree is **beautiful**. 這棵樹很美。
These trees are **beautiful**. 這些樹很美。
That flower is **fragrant**. 那朵花很香。
Those flowers are **fragrant**. 那些花很香。

4 不可數名詞的數量不可以計算,並且**沒有複數形態**。

milk 牛奶

beer 啤酒

5 不可數名詞前面,通常不能加**不定冠詞 a 或 an**,也不會直接用**數字**來計算。

✗ Dolphins show signs of a cognition and language use.

✓ Dolphins show signs of cognition and language use.
跡象顯示海豚有認知與使用語言的能力。

比較

在某些情況下,不可數名詞之前可以加 a/an 和「**數量**」,例如在咖啡館、酒吧或餐廳「點飲料」時。

• We would like one wine, one beer, and one coffee.
我們要一瓶葡萄酒、一瓶啤酒和一杯咖啡。

6 不可數名詞沒有複數形態,只能搭配**單數動詞**使用。
(常見的不可數名詞,請見 Unit 4。)

✗ Accurate informations are hard to find.
✓ Accurate information is hard to find.
精確的訊息不容易找到。
✗ Intuitions are the basis of a guess.
✓ Intuition is the basis of a guess.
「直覺」是猜測的基礎。

7 可數名詞和不可數名詞都可以用 some 或 any 來修飾。

→ some 用於肯定句
I'm going to cook some peas tonight.
我今晚要來煮一些豆子。
I'd like to have some fried rice.
我想吃一些炒飯。

→ any 用於疑問句和否定句
Is there any green tea in the refrigerator?
冰箱裡還有沒有綠茶?
I don't have any coins in my pocket.
我的口袋裡沒有零錢。

Practice

1 請從框內選出正確的名詞填空，並註明其為 C（可數）或 U（不可數）。

cherry

typhoon

sugar

lamp

anger

soda

block

soup

1　　　soda　　U/C

2

3

4

5

6

7

8

2

請將句子中的錯誤劃去，並寫出正確的用語。

1. Sandy and Trent went to ~~store~~ to buy new home furnishings.
   a store

2. They bought sofa, four dining chair, and a nightstands for their new apartment.

3. Trent isn't satisfied with the sofa. The sofa are too dark.

4. There is not enough dining chairs, because Trent always invites his friends and relatives to their house.

5. The nightstand do not fit their bedroom decor, either.

6. They had argument over the newly bought furnitures.

7. Trent thought Sandy should take an advice or two from him.

8. But Sandy doesn't like any of Trent's opinion.

9. Now, Trent has convinced himself that the dark sofa are easy to maintain. He has stopped inviting so many friends and relatives to their house, and he repainted the bedroom to match the nightstand.

Unit **4**

List of Common Uncountable Nouns
常見不可數名詞表

有些名詞同時具有**可數**和**不可數**的形態，但是**兩者的意義不同**。

事物的整體

baggage
clothing
equipment
food
furniture
fruit
garbage
jewelry
luggage
machinery
mail
money
scenery
silverware
traffic

氣體

air
ammonia
carbon dioxide
hydrogen
nitrogen
oxygen
pollution
smog
smoke
steam

oxygen

抽象名詞

advice	intelligence
anger	knowledge
attention	love
beauty	music
confidence	patience
courage	peace
education	progress
evidence	recreation
happiness	sadness
health	significance
honesty	truth
importance	violence
information	wealth

顆粒

corn	rice
dirt	salt
dust	sand
chalk	sugar
flour	wheat
pepper	

軟物

bacon	meat
beef	mud
bread	pork
butter	seafood
chocolate	skin
cheese	toast
cream	tofu
jam	toothpaste
jelly	

glass	
C 杯子	a glass of water 一杯水
U 玻璃	stained glass 彩繪玻璃

hair	
C 一根一根的毛髮	a hair in my soup 我的湯裡的一根頭髮
U 毛髮的總稱	red hair 紅頭髮

paper	
C 報紙	a paper 一份報紙
U 紙張	some paper 一些紙

iron	
C 熨斗	an iron 一台熨斗
U 鐵	the Iron Age 鐵器時代

potato	
C 一顆顆的馬鈴薯	two potatoes 兩顆馬鈴薯
U 食用的一份	some potato 一些馬鈴薯

液體

beer	perfume
blood	sauce
coffee	shampoo
cologne	soda
gasoline	soup
juice	syrup
ketchup	tea
milk	vinegar
oil	water
paint	wine

固體

aluminum	plastic
copper	silver
cotton	steel
glass	tin
gold	wax
ice	wood
iron	wool

語言

Arabic	German
Chinese	Japanese
English	Russian
French	Spanish

學科

biology
chemistry
geography
geometry
history
literature
mathematics
physics
psychology
science

自然

electricity
fire
fog
hail
heat
lightning
rain
snow
sunshine
thunder
weather
wind

Practice

1

請將各個名詞與對應
的圖片連起來。

jewelry

pepper

perfume

wheat

cheese

copper

hail

mud

2

請依據題意與提示，
以正確的「不可數
名詞」填空，完成
句子。

1. Tony speaks C_____e and F_____h.
   He is a professional interpreter.

2. Living things cannot survive without w_____ and
   o_____.

3. Artificial i_____e will greatly improve human life in the near
   future.

4. I had b_____n, t_____t, and hot c_____e
   for breakfast this morning.

5. Ada studied b_____y and c_____y in college.
   After graduation, she worked in the research department at a
   biotechnology company.

6. The eruption of the volcano released many types of toxic
   g_____s and heavy s_____e. If you breathe them,
   they will endanger your health.

7. Louis lacks c_____e in himself. He doesn't believe he can
   achieve anything.

8. This coin is made of c_____r and tin.

Unit **5**

Nouns Always in Plural Forms
只以複數形態出現的名詞

1 有些名詞永遠只以**複數形態**出現。其中有一種是具有「**成雙、成對**」的特性，要搭配**複數動詞**來使用。在計算的時候，可以使用 a pair of、two pairs of 等來修飾。

Your new trousers are fashionable.
你的新褲子真時髦。
Where are my glasses?
我的眼鏡呢？
Please pass a pair of chopsticks to me.
請拿一雙筷子給我。

glasses

trousers/pants

shorts

jeans

scissors

socks   underpants

chopsticks

gloves   briefs

panties
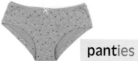

2 某些學科類的名詞永遠以**複數形態**出現，但它們的意義其實是「**單數**」的，要搭配**單數動詞**來使用。

The news is shocking. 這則新聞震驚社會。
I studied economics and politics in college.
我大學時修了經濟學與政治學。

- **news** 新聞
- **politics** 政治學
- **economics** 經濟學
- **physics** 物理學
- **mathematics** 數學
- **statistics** 統計學
- **optics** 光學
- **athletics** 體育
- **gymnastics** 體操
- **civics** 公民學

比較

statistics 指「統計數字」時，則是**複數意義**，要搭配**複數動詞**。

Our company's statistics are promising.
我們公司的經營數據顯示前景看好。

politics 這類的詞指「觀念」時，也是**複數意義**。

We differ in our politics.
我們的政治立場不同。

3 某些表示「疾病」的名詞，也都以**複數形態**出現，但它們卻也是「**單數意義**」，要搭配**單數動詞**來使用。

- **rabies** 狂犬病
- **measles** 麻疹
- **mumps** 腮腺炎

Rabies is a dangerous disease.
狂犬病是一種很危險的疾病。

Practice

1

請勾選正確的答案。

1. The newspaper ☐ is ☐ are on the sofa. Today's news ☐ is ☐ are so bad that I don't want to read the newspaper.

2. Are you looking for your ☐ sunglass ☐ sunglasses?
☐ It is ☐ They are on your desk.

3. I'm looking for ☐ a pair of ☐ a piece of gloves. Do you sell gloves?

4. Mumps ☐ is ☐ are a common disease among children.

5. Statistics ☐ indicate ☐ indicates that the crime rate is decreasing.

6. Billiards ☐ is ☐ are one of my favorite games.

7. What ☐ is ☐ are your monthly earnings?

8. I'd like to express my special ☐ thank ☐ thanks to Mr. John Hogan for his support.

2

請從框內選出正確的名詞填空，完成句子。

shoes
ruins
pajamas
gymnastics
shears
tights

We will see the Roman .... on the trip.

Father is pruning the bushes with a pair of ....

Lisa has practiced .... since childhood.

Mary loves pink ....

Judy got a new pair of ballet ....

Tutus and .... are important for ballet dancers.

Unit 6

Counting Uncountable Nouns
不可數名詞的計算

1 計算不可數名詞，很常見的一種方法是使用量詞（quantifier）。

> 可數名詞也適用於這種 of 片語。

a bottle of

 water  beer wine

a jar of

 honey  tomatoes jam

a can of

 soda sardines beer

a slice of

 pizza lime ham

a bowl of

 rice soup porridge

a piece of

 cake broccoli bread

a package/packet of

 crackers nuts

a carton of

 milk  juice

a bar of

 chocolate soap

a tube of

 toothpaste hand cream

a pot of

 coffee tea

a box of

 macaroons chocolate

2 另一種計算不可數名詞的方法，是以同義的可數名詞來代替。

a slice of bread		a roll 一條麵包捲
a piece of bread	→	a bun 一個圓麵包
a loaf of bread		a loaf 一條麵包
a sum of money		a coin 一枚硬幣
an amount of money	→	a 50-dollar bill 一張 50 美元的鈔票
		a 10-pound note 一張 10 英鎊的鈔票

Practice

1 請將各項物品名稱搭配適當的「量詞」，以「of 片語」填入空格中。

1 mustard
2 cheese
3 luggage
4 melon
5 toast
6 mussels
7 soap
8 liquor
9 bath salt
10 cookies
11 tea
12 spices
13 shower gel
14 peach lotion

1. *a jar of mustard*	8.
2.	9.
3.	10.
4.	11.
5.	12.
6.	13.
7.	14.

Unit 7

Proper Nouns and Collective Nouns
專有名詞與集合名詞

1 專有名詞用來指一個特定的人、事物或地點，字首要大寫。

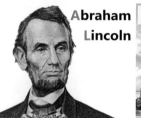 Abraham Lincoln

 Madrid

 the Bible

 the Mediterranean

2 大部分的專有名詞都不需要加 **the**。

Uncle Lee has gone to Cairo on vacation.
李叔叔去開羅度假了。

Halloween **falls on the 31st of October.**
10 月 31 日是萬聖節。

Mt. Fuji **is the highest mountain in** Japan.
富士山是日本第一高山。

3 集合名詞用來指「一個整體」或「一個團體」，屬於可數名詞。

- family
- company
- audience
- class
- army
- committee
- crowd
- mob
- team
- police

4 集合名詞可以搭配單數動詞，也可以搭配複數動詞。

1 當它指「整體」時，要用單數動詞；
2 如果指「組成這個整體的一個個成員」，就用複數動詞；
3 美式英語的集合名詞要用單數動詞搭配。如果要強調成員，美式英語用 members 與複數動詞搭配。

英式 My family are **from Canada.**
美式 My family is **from Canada.**
我的家人來自加拿大。

Family is **the bedrock of community.**
家庭是社群的基石。

英式 The government are **taxing the poor and giving the rich tax breaks.**
美式 The government is **taxing the poor and giving the rich tax breaks.**
政府對窮人課稅，卻給予富人賦稅優惠。

Government is **the main provider of social services for the poor.**
政府是為窮人提供社會福利的主要來源。

5 「特定的數量」、「數目的總和」也屬於集合名詞，但這時要搭配**單數動詞**。

Thirty thousand tons is **a lot of food aid. That is a lot of rice and wheat.** 三萬噸是為數不小的糧食援助，有大量的稻米和小麥。
Six thousand dollars is **not a great amount of money.** 六千塊美金不是太可觀的數目。
The United States is **going to take part in the G20 conference.**
美國將出席二十國高峰會。

6 集合名詞 people、police 和 cattle 則要使用**複數動詞**。

When people act **like cattle, we describe that behavior as the herd instinct.**
當人類的行為像牛群一樣時，我們描述這種行為是一種「群起效尤」的本能。
Like everybody else, police are **only human.**
就像其他人一樣，警察也只是凡人。

Practice

1 請勾選正確的答案。如果句子的美式用法和英式用法不同，請以美式用法為準。

1. One hundred thousand yen ☐ is ☐ are a lot of money for tuition.

2. Family ☐ is ☐ are more important than school in shaping values.

3. People ☐ needs ☐ need jobs to pay for daily necessities.

4. The cattle ☐ is ☐ are eating grass on the meadow.

5. Has Kenny already gone to ☐ the Beijing ☐ Beijing?

6. The whole class ☐ was ☐ were fascinated by his loud and clear voice.

7. His concert had ☐ a large audience ☐ large audience.

8. The crowd in front of the city hall ☐ was ☐ were dispersed by the police.

9. The army ☐ is ☐ are essential for a country's self-defense.

10. The mob ☐ has ☐ have occupied the airport for over three weeks.

11. The police said ☐ they were ☐ it was coming in five minutes.

2 請將句中的「專有名詞」標上 P（proper），「集合名詞」標上 C（collective）。

1. My <u>class</u> elected <u>Mark</u> to be the class leader.
             C   P

2. An army of five thousand men assembled at the border of India.

3. The criminal ran into the crowd in Federation Square.

4. *La Traviata* attracted an audience of thousands to the City Theater.

5. Half of the staff of KPMG International Limited got a pay raise.

6. The mob occupied hospitals and airports, causing chaos and wreaking havoc.

7. Football teams from 32 countries gathered in Russia to compete in the 2018 World Cup.

8. The government has come up with several solutions to prevent the unemployment level from getting worse.

Unit **8**

Compound Nouns
複合名詞

---

1 複合名詞是由**兩個或兩個以上的名詞**組成的**一個或一組名詞**。

bathroom 浴室
keyboard 鍵盤
jet fuel 噴射推進飛行器專用之航空燃油
sheep dog 牧羊犬
low fat milk 低脂牛奶

---

2 複合名詞中，第一個名詞往往被視為**修飾語**，用來修飾第二個名詞。因此，不管整個複合名詞是單數還是複數，**第一個名詞通常只作單數形態**，不隨之變化。

a plastic **bag** 一個塑膠袋
two apple **pies** 兩個蘋果派
the town **hall** 鎮公所
　　　↳ 修飾語

比較

有些名詞因為本來就固定用**複數形**，因此當作複合名詞裡的修飾語時，也採用**複數形態**。
• a sports **team** 一支運動隊伍
• the clothes **closet** 衣櫥

---

3 複合名詞的構成方式有三種，第一種是由**兩個或兩個以上的名詞組成的詞組**，是分開的兩個或三個單字。

ice cream 冰淇淋
music store 唱片行
oxygen mask 氧氣罩
key card 鑰匙卡
vacuum cleaner 吸塵器
tomato salad 番茄沙拉
chicken soup 雞湯

bus stop 公車站

---

4 複合名詞的第二種構成方式，是將**兩個名詞連在一起變成一個字**，中間**沒有連字號**。

shoeshine 鞋油
newspaper 報紙
wastebasket 廢紙簍
rainbow 彩虹
earthquake 地震
bedroom 房間
baseball 棒球
lifestyle 生活方式
battleground 戰場

armchair 扶手椅

---

5 複合名詞的第三種構成方式，是將**兩個或三個名詞連在一起**，中間**有連字號**。

mother-in-law 岳母；婆婆
runner-up 亞軍

---

6 複合名詞的複數形，通常是把「**最後一個字**」變成**複數形**。

computer virus → computer viruses
電腦病毒
cruise ship → cruise ships 遊輪
bookstore → bookstores 書店
weekend → weekends 週末

---

7 也有許多複合名詞的複數形並不是把最後一個字變成複數。因此比較標準的說法，是把複合名詞中的「**主要名詞**」改成**複數**。

father-in-law → fathers-in-law 岳父；公公
passer-by → passers-by 路人
attorney general → attorneys general
首席檢察官
editor-in-chief → editors-in-chief 主編

Practice

1 圖中物品名稱為何？請分別從 A 框和 B 框內選出適當的名詞，組成「複合名詞」，來說明圖中的物品名稱。注意要用正確的格式（可參考字典）。

A
coffee　fax
screw　star
cotton　drug
camp

B
fire　abuse
grinder　fruit
machine　driver
field

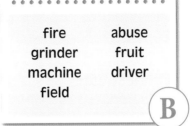

1. *fax machine*
2. ....
3. ....
4. ....

5. ....
6. ....
7. ....

2 請從框內選出適當的「複合名詞」，以正確的「單複數形態」填空，完成句子。

tissue paper
coffee milk
brother-in-law
passer-by
animal right
football
tool box
rock music

1. When Dave has the flu, he uses a lot of *tissue paper* to blow his nose.

2. Some pet owners have strong opinions about ....

3. Geraldine doesn't like to listen to ....

4. Archie likes to kick the .... around the field.

5. My extended family includes three ....

6. When Denny was being pushed around by three gangsters, the .... did nothing to help him.

7. Chester has two .... full of hammers, wrenches, and screwdrivers.

8. I feel like having a cheeseburger and some .... for breakfast today.

Unit 9

Possessive 's: Forms
所有格「's」的形式

---

1 用來表示名詞所有格的符號是「's」。

Hal's map 海爾的地圖
Vicky's AI watch 薇琪的人工智慧手錶

Form 形式

2 單數名詞 +「's」→ 所有格

Amy's recording contract
艾美的錄音合約
my little sister's favorite stuffed animal
我妹妹最喜歡的動物填充娃娃
the teacher's glasses 老師的眼鏡

3 字尾是 s 的複數名詞 +「'」→ 所有格

my parents' house 我父母的房子
states' rights
州權（美國憲法所賦予各州的權利）
birds' nest 鳥巢

4 字尾非 s 的不規則複數名詞 +「's」
→ 所有格

men's room 男廁
children's play area 兒童遊戲區
people's imagination 人的想像力

5 字尾是 s 的單數人名，經常要加「's」
成為所有格，也有人主張只加「'」。

Levi Strauss's original blue jeans
= Levi Strauss' original blue jeans
李維・史特勞斯原創的牛仔褲
Santa Claus's sleigh and reindeer
= Santa Claus' sleigh and reindeer
聖誕老人的雪橇和馴鹿

6 用 and 連接的兩個名詞，如果共同擁
有某物，則在**最後一個名詞**加上所有
格即可。

Ben and Jenny's
ice cream
班和珍妮的冰淇淋

7 用 and 連接的兩個名詞，如果分別都
擁有某物，則**兩個名詞**都要加上所有
格。

Jane's bicycle and Joe's bicycle
珍的腳踏車和喬的腳踏車
Stephanie's lunch box and Susie's lunch
box
史蒂芬妮的午餐盒和蘇西的午餐盒

比較

Sam and Chris's house
↳ 兩人共同擁有的房子
山姆和克里斯的房子

Sam's and Chris's houses
↳ 兩人各自擁有的房子
山姆的房子和克里斯的房子

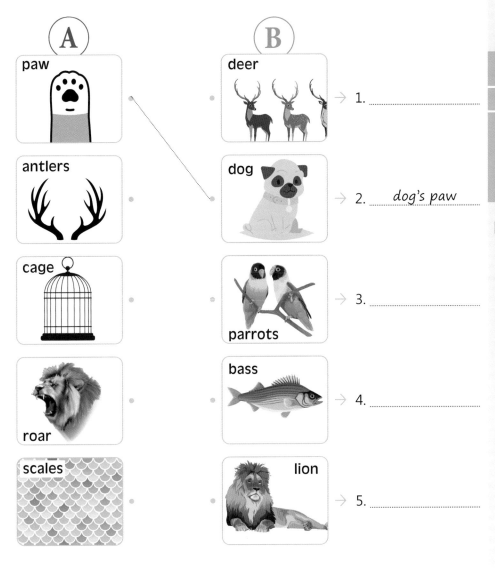

Practice

1

請將 A 欄的詞彙與 B 欄的詞彙配對，以「所有格's」的形式，寫出它們的關係。

A

paw

antlers

cage

roar

scales

B

deer → 1. _____

dog → 2. *dog's paw*

parrots → 3. _____

bass → 4. _____

lion → 5. _____

2 請依圖示，寫出表示「共同擁有」或「分別擁有」的所有格。

1 John
Amy
apartment

John and Amy's apartment

2 Edward
Betty
kitchen

_____

3 Selina
Christine
teddy bears

_____

4 Ken
Lynn
laptops

_____

Unit 10

Possessive 's: Use
所有格「's」的用法

---

1 所有格「's」通常用於「人」。

Sam's wallet
山姆的皮夾
Melissa's purse
梅莉莎的皮包

Amanda's suitcase
亞曼達的皮箱

---

2 所有格「's」可以用於「人」，也可以用於「動物」、「地點」、「時間」或「度量」。

動物

the horse's bridle 　　a cow's bell
馬匹的籠頭 　　　　　牛鈴

地點 Brazil's soccer team
巴西的足球隊

the concert hall's sound system
　　　↳ 不常用
= the sound system of the concert
hall 　↳ 常用
音樂廳的音響系統

時間 yesterday's dishes 昨天的菜
next month's program 下個月的節目

度量 an hour's walk 一小時的步行
ten dollars' worth 10 元美金的價值

---

3 所有格後面的**名詞**如果在前面已經提過，在聽者可以清楚判斷的情況下，經常**可以省略**。

I have my sandwich. Where is Bart's?
= Bart's sandwich ↵
我自己有三明治，巴特的呢？

Claire's compact car is red, and Claudia's
is blue. 　　　= Claudia's compact car ↵
克萊兒的小車是紅色的，克勞蒂亞的則是藍色的。

---

4 所有格**省略名詞**的用法，經常拿來表示「商店」、「工作地點」。

I went to McDonald's for lunch.
我到麥當勞吃午餐。
I'm going to the dentist's this afternoon.
我今天下午要去看牙醫。
Can you go to the baker's and get me
some bread?
你去麵包店幫我買一些麵包好嗎？

---

5 所有格**省略名詞**的用法，也常拿來指「某人的家」。

How about going to Janet's this
weekend? 　　↳ = Janet's
house/home
這個週末去珍妮家好不好？
I was at David's yesterday.
　　↳ = David's house/home
我昨天在大衛家。

Practice

1 請依圖示，從框內選出適當的名詞，以「the + 所有格」的形式填空，完成句子。

dentist

barber

doctor

hairdresser

baker

1 I am going to have a perm at __the hairdresser's__ .

2 Father usually gets his hair cut at _____.

3 Gill went to _____ yesterday.

4 Jacky often needs to go to _____.

5 I love to buy cinnamon rolls at _____.

2 請將括弧內的詞彙以「所有格」的形式填空，完成句子。

1. This is the spare tire from __Paul's car__ (Paul / car).

2. I was walking down Third Street and I found _____ (someone / keys).

3. Put the _____ (dog / bone) back on his bed.

4. The _____ (company / office) is closed after 5 p.m.

5. I am going to the newsstand to buy _____ (today / newspaper) so I can read the sports section.

6. After a _____ (week / vacation), I am ready to get back to work.

7. These are my _____ (grandparents / bicycles), but we can ride them.

8. These are _____ (Mick and Jeri / wedding photos) and shots of their honeymoon.

9. You must get a _____ (driver / license) before you borrow my car.

27

Unit 11

"The . . . Of . . ." for Possession
「The . . . Of . . .」表示「所有權」的用法

1 「無生物」的所有格，通常不用「**'s**」，而要用「**the . . . of . . .**」的形式。

the door of the house
房子的門

the time of the party 派對的時間

2 「無生物」中，除了 Unit 10 所提到的「地點」、「時間」、「度量」常用「**'s**」而不用「**the . . . of . . .**」之外，「擬人化」的用法也可用「**'s**」來構成所有格。

the moon's halo 月暈
for heaven's sake 天呀
the company's crisis 公司的危機

3 「the . . . of . . .」常用於**較長的句子裡**。

✗ I met the Japanese distributor who handles our product line's director.
✓ I met the director of the Japanese distributor who handles our product line.
我遇見管理我們日本生產線的經銷商主管。

4 太複雜的「**複合名詞**」，也適合用「the . . . of . . .」來表示所有格，避免拗口。

the opinions of the editors-in-chief
= the editors-in-chief's opinions
主編們的意見
the daughters-in-law of the boss
= the boss's daughters-in-law
老闆的眾媳婦

5 在雙重所有格中，有時可以用「the . . . of . . .」，使句子更順暢。

Peter's father's hat
= the hat of Peter's father
彼得的父親的帽子
Sally's dog's beautiful hair
= the beautiful hair of Sally's dog
莎莉的狗的一身漂亮狗毛

6 「the . . . of . . .」的用法也可用於「**生物**」，例如「**人**」或「**動物**」。

a cat's life = the life of a cat
貓的一生
Jude and Mary's marriage
= the marriage of Jude and Mary
裘德和瑪麗的婚姻

7 有時，我們常用複合名詞來表示兩物的「**附屬關係**」，而不用**所有格**。

the bathroom window 廁所的窗戶
the dog house 狗屋

比較

- Tony's juice 東尼的果汁
  ↳ 人的所有格用「's」。
- the juice of these watermelon
  ↳ 物的所有格用「the . . . of . . .」。
  這些西瓜的榨汁
- watermelon juice 西瓜汁
  ↳ 用複合名詞不強調所有權

Practice

1

請將括弧內的詞彙以最適當的「所有格」（「's」或「the . . . of . . .」）填空，完成句子。

1. There is going to be a performance at _____Nelly's school_____ (Nelly / school).

2. What is the _____ (name / ballet) they will perform?

3. _____ (Nancy / dance teacher) is Tracy Deville.

4. The _____ (address / theater) where the show will be performed is on the tickets.

5. The _____ (price / the tickets) is low.

6. _____ (Norma / part) in the ballet is small.

7. The bereaved were comforted by the _____ (jury / judgment).

8. Jeff joined the _____ (workers / movement) to demand higher salaries.

9. Do you think I can borrow _____ (Veasna / VIP card) to shop in this store?

10. The _____ (building / facade) is spectacular.

2

請用「the . . . of . . .」的句型改寫句子。

1. The lotion's cap is missing.

   → _The cap of the lotion is missing._

2. The United Electric Company's vice president will visit our new factory next week.

   → _____

   _____

3. Audrey and Lucas's grocery store is going to open next month.

   → _____

   _____

4. The Empire Hotel's Chinese restaurant's waiters are well trained.

   → _____

   _____

5. My mother-in-law's birthday is coming soon.

   → _____

   _____

Part 2 Articles 冠詞

Unit 12

A, An
不定冠詞 A、An

1 a 和 an 是不定冠詞，意指「**一個**」。**非特指的單數可數名詞**前面要加 a 或 an。

a raincoat 一件雨衣
a basketball 一顆籃球
an umbrella 一把雨傘
an ear ring 一只耳環

不定冠詞 a/an 不能用來修飾**複數可數名詞**和**不可數名詞**。

✗ a trucks　　✓ two trucks 兩輛卡車
✗ an employees　✓ some employees 一些員工
✗ a snow　　　✓ lots of snow 很多白雪

2 一個字的發音若是「**子音**」開頭，則用 a。

a buffalo
一頭水牛

a notebook
一本筆記本

3 一個字的發音若是「**母音**」開頭（通常是字母 a、e、i、o、u），則用 an。

an oral practice class
一堂口語練習課

an elephant
一頭大象

4 有些字看起來像是母音開頭，實際發音卻是「**子音**」，此時也要用 a。

a university [ˏjunəˋvɝsətɪ] 一所大學
a Euro [ˋjuro] 一塊歐元
a unique [juˋnik] design 獨一無二的設計

5 有些字看起來像是子音開頭，實際上**開頭的子音卻不發音**，實際發音是「**母音**」開頭，此時則要用 an。

an hour [aur] 一個小時
 ↳ h 不發音
an honest [ˋɑnɪst] man 一個誠實的人
an heir [ɛr] 一名繼承人

6 以 f、h、l、m、n、r、s、x 為字首的縮寫詞，都是「**母音**」發音開頭，前面要用 an。

an FBI [ˏɛf bi ˋaɪ] agent 一名 FBI 探員
an RNA [ˏɑr ɛn ˋe] molecule 一個 RNA 分子

an LED [ˏɛl i ˋdi] light bulb
一顆 LED 燈泡

7 通常當讀者或聽者**不需要清楚知道所指的是哪一個人或物**時，就用 a/an 作限定詞。

There is a truck in the parking lot.
 ↳ 我們只知道裡面有一輛卡車，但不需要知道是哪一輛。
停車場有一輛卡車。
She has a grandchild.
 ↳ 我們不知道她有沒有其他孫子，或這個孫子是誰。
她有一個孫子。

Practice

1 請依圖示，從框內選出對應的名詞，並加上 **a** 或 **an**，填入空格中。

UFO
SUV
astronaut
one-way road
eagle
volleyball
onion
heir
whale
meatball
first-aid kit
idea

1. _____
2. _____
3. _____
4. _____
5. _____
6. _____
7. _____
8. _____
9. _____
10. _____
11. _____
12. _____

2 請在框內填上 **a** 或 **an**，完成下列「非特指某個人或物」的句子。

1. I went to _____ bakery downtown and bought these buns.

2. Jack's father gave him _____ unicycle on his birthday.

3. I saw _____ lioness at a distance when we drove through the zoo.

4. Is he filling in _____ online application form?

5. There is _____ backpack on the floor. Whose is it?

6. I'm meeting _____ sales rep from the Bobson Company.

7. It's going to rain in any minute. Did you bring _____ umbrella?

8. Are you _____ early bird or do you often sleep late?

9. I'm writing _____ email to my teacher.

Unit 13

The
定冠詞 The

1 the 是定冠詞，可修飾**單複數**的**可數名詞**，也可修飾**不可數名詞**。

the **trash bag** 這個垃圾袋
↳ 單數可數名詞

the **cans and bottles** 這些瓶瓶罐罐
↳ 複數可數名詞

the **recycling of paper products**
↳ 不可數名詞

紙類產品資源回收

2 「**特定的人、事物**」前面，要用 the 來修飾，我們稱這種用法為「**特指**」的用法。

Is this the **bag of old clothes** that needs to be taken to the church's drop-off box?

這是要拿到回收箱的那袋舊衣服嗎？

Do you see the **black hairy dog** in front of the fire hydrant? What breed is it?

你有看到消防栓前面那隻毛茸茸的黑狗嗎？牠是什麼品種？

3 「**再次提及某個人或事物**」時，也要用 the。

There is only one restaurant around here. The **restaurant** is near the highway.

這附近只有一間餐廳，那間餐廳離高速公路不遠。

4 當「**對方清楚知道你講的是哪個人或事物**」時，則可以用 the 來修飾。

The pickup of recyclable material is on Tuesdays. At 3:30 p.m., the **truck** parks where Brownstone Alley meets Third Street.
↳ 我們都知道 the truck 就是回收車。

資源回收日是星期二，回收車會在下午 3 點 30 分停在布朗史東巷和第三大街的交叉口。

What time is it? It's time to take out the **recyclable material**.
↳ 我們都知道回收物指的是一袋瓶瓶罐罐。

現在幾點了？
應該把回收物拿出去了吧！

I handed the bag to the **guy** by the truck. The **guy** told me that they didn't accept cartons used for beverages.
↳ 我們知道 the guy 就是指垃圾車旁的人。

我把袋子交給垃圾車旁的那個人，他跟我說他們不收飲料紙盒。

5 of 的介系詞片語也一定要搭配 the 來使用，句型為「the . . . of . . .」。

the **music** of Franz Schubert
舒伯特的音樂

the **war** of words 唇槍舌戰；筆戰

the **player** of the year 年度最佳球員

Practice

1　請用 a、an 或 the 填空，完成句子。若該句不需要加冠詞，
　　則在空格內劃上「/」。

1. Ken went to the store to buy _____ book to read on his trip.

2. His wife asked if she could read _____ book when he finished it.

3. Do you have _____ information on the new policy?

4. I saw two houses, but I didn't like _____ second one very much.

5. Did you see _____ metal box I put on the coffee table?

6. Please pass me _____ napkin.

7. Colin wants to be _____ epidemiologist in the future.

8. _____ king and queen live in the palace.

9. Lindsay is _____ athlete.

10. _____ man at the door is Mr. Robertson.

11. Since it's so hot in here, I will turn on _____ air conditioner.

12. His latest album has won _____ album of the year.

13. Can you hear _____ words they're whispering?

14. Do you like _____ paintings by Johannes Vermeer?

15. How about going to _____ newly-opened tea shop across the street and have a glass of lemon tea?

16. Good idea! But I think I'll have _____ milk tea instead.

Unit 14

Talking in General
「泛指」的用法

1 通常，我們會以不加 the 的複數可數名詞或不可數名詞，來**泛指「一般的人或事物」**。

Chili peppers come in many shapes and sizes. ↳ 一般通稱的辣椒

辣椒有很多種形狀和大小。

Salsa is always hot and spicy.
↳ 一般的莎莎醬

莎莎醬都很辣，味道又重。

2 「a/an + 單數可數名詞」也常用來**泛指「一般的人或事物」**，通常意味著該人或事物的「**大部分、任一、全部**」是如此。

An Airedale is a large black terrier with a wiry, tan coat.
↳ 這種類型的所有萬能梗犬

萬能梗是一種有著又硬又黑毛髮的大型犬種。

3 而「the + 名詞」則用來指「**特定的人或事物**」，是**特指**的用法。

The chili peppers from your garden are
↳ 指特定的辣椒
mild and sweet.

你花園裡種的辣椒味道很溫和，還有甜味呢。

The salsa at this restaurant will burn your
↳ 特定的莎莎醬
mouth.

這家餐廳的莎莎醬會讓你的嘴巴冒火。

4 「the + 單數可數名詞」經常用來**泛指「一般的事物」**。動物、花卉、植物名稱經常以這種形式出現。

The hawk has the keenest eyesight of all birds. ↳ 泛指所有的老鷹

在所有鳥類中，老鷹的視覺最銳利。

The sparrow hawk is the smallest member of the hawk family.
↳ 泛指所有的松雀鷹

松雀鷹的體型在所有老鷹之中最嬌小。

5 「the + 形容詞」經常用來**泛指「某一類型的人」**。

the **poor** 窮人
the **middle class** 中產階級
the **rich** 富人
the **middle aged** 中年人
the **old** 老人
the **blind** 盲人
the **deaf** 聾人
the **young** 年輕人

Tax cuts help the rich and hurt the poor
　　　　　　　↳ = the rich　　　↳ = the poor
　　　　　　　　 people　　　　　　 people
and the middle class.
　　　　↳ = the middle class people

節稅的作法對富人有益，卻損及窮人和中產階級。

6 「the + 國家名稱／民族名稱」可**泛指該國或該民族的「人民」**。

The Hmong are people living in highland areas of Southeast Asia.

蒙族人是住在東南亞山區的人民。

The Amish don't believe in using electricity or cars. 門諾教派信徒不用電也不開車。

Practice

1

在要加 **the** 的空格內填上 **the**，不需要加 **the** 的空格內劃「/」。

1. Elle likes to drink _____ coffee.

2. Richard asked his wife where she had put _____ coffee.

3. _____ Coffee is grown all over the world.

4. There are the three brands of _____ coffee I like to drink.

5. Arlene only buys _____ French roast coffee.

6. Raymond says _____ Italian roast coffee at this café is superb.

7. _____ Penguins are birds that can't fly.

8. _____ vulture is a bird that will eat dead animals.

9. _____ blind are people that can't see.

10 _____ rich can afford gas no matter what the price is.

11. _____ Lebanese live in a country with a Mediterranean climate.

12. People from the ancient empire located in what is now Italy were called _____ Romans.

13. The largest mammal in the world is _____ blue whale.

14. My son is in first grade and is learning how to play _____ recorder.

2

請將下列使用「形容詞 + 名詞」的句子，改寫為使用「the + 形容詞」來泛指的句子。

1. <u>The poor people</u> need national health insurance more than <u>the middle class people</u> and <u>the rich people</u>.

   → *The poor need national health insurance more than the middle class and the rich.*

2. The city council has approved several proposals for the welfare of <u>the elderly people</u>.

   → _____

   _____

3 The excavation of these sites has revealed the life and culture of <u>the Maya people</u>.

   → _____

   _____

4. Opportunities go to <u>the strong people</u>, not <u>the weak people</u>.

   → _____

Unit 15

Expressions With "The" (1)
要加 The 的情況（I）

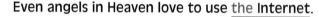
the sun

1 獨一無二的事物，要加 the。

Even angels in Heaven love to use <u>the Internet</u>.
連天使都愛用網路。

the earth

the stars

the President

the world

2 彈奏樂器，要加 the。

J. S. Bach played several musical instruments, including <u>the harpsichord</u>.
巴哈會演奏好幾種樂器，包括大鍵琴。

the piano

the guitar

the harmonica

3 一般性地點，要加 the。

Frank is going to spend the weekend at <u>the shore</u>.
法蘭克將到海邊度週末。

the suburbs   the countryside

the ocean/sea   the mountain

the city

4 政府、政治機構，要加 the。

- the FBI 聯邦調查局
- the Ministry of Finance 財政部
- the White House 白宮

5 發明物，要加 the。

Leo Fender invented <u>the electric guitar</u>.
李奧·凡德發明了電吉他。
Several people, including Alexander Graham Bell and Antonio Meucci, were credited for the invention of <u>the telephone</u>. 包含貝爾和穆齊等幾個人，被認為是電話的發明者。

Practice

1

請從框內選出適當的名詞，加上 the 填空，完成句子。

Moon

mayor

airplane

cello

President

lion

countryside

beach

stars

king

city

1. Let's go for a trip in _____ and get some fresh air this weekend. I'm tired of _____.

2. Katherine is going to play _____ at the National Concert Hall next month.

3. _____ of the city will show up at the opening of the exhibition on Friday morning.

4. Liz is building sand castles on _____.

5. _____ is going to build a golden palace as a birthday present for the queen.

6. There are many impact craters on the near side and the far side of _____.

7. _____ of Guatemala is going to visit us in June.

8. The Wright brothers are credited with the invention of _____.

9. _____ is the king of the beasts.

10. Nothing makes you feel smaller than looking into the night sky and seeing _____.

2

請將 A 欄與 B 欄的用語搭配，造出具有意義的句子。

A
• Bill is climbing
• Lee commutes between his downtown office and
• Larry is working for
• In 1990, NASA launched
• John is swimming laps in
• Caterina learned to play

B
• the pool.
• the Hubble Telescope into orbit.
• his home in the suburbs.
• the flute when she was 12.
• the Ministry of Education.
• the mountain.

1. _Bill is climbing the mountain._

2. _____

3. _____

4. _____

5. _____

6. _____

Unit **16**

Expressions With "The" (2)
要加 The 的情況（2）

1 報刊名稱，要加 the。

- *the China Post* 中國郵報
- *the New York Times* 紐約時報
- *the Washington Post* 華盛頓郵報

2 某些時間慣用語，要加 the。

- in the morning
- in the afternoon
- in the evening

3 某特定時刻的**天氣狀況**，要加 the。

The typhoon has passed the island.
颱風已經通過小島。

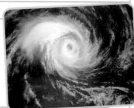

the hurricane

the **rain**

the **snow**

the **wind**

the **tornado**

4 娛樂活動或場所，要加 the 或 a。

Lorna is going to the movie theater tonight.
蘿娜今晚要去電影院（看電影）。

the **movies**

the **concert**

the **circus**

the **fair**

the **theater**

the **symphony**

the **performance**

the **fashion show**

Practice

1

請用 the、a 或 an 填空，完成句子。

1. The weather forecast said there will be ＿＿＿＿＿ big storm coming this weekend.

2. The traffic was held up by ＿＿＿＿＿ heavy snow.

3. Can I clip ＿＿＿＿＿ article from the front page of ＿＿＿＿＿ *Washington Post* after you finish reading it?

4. Can you buy me ＿＿＿＿＿ *Time* magazine on your way to the office?

5. ＿＿＿＿＿ book exhibition is held annually in February.

6. Are you going to sell these chickens at ＿＿＿＿＿ fair?

7. I'd rather go to ＿＿＿＿＿ symphony than listen to CDs at home.

8. His dream is to play in ＿＿＿＿＿ concert at the National Concert Hall.

9. ＿＿＿＿＿ wind is blowing hard outside.

10. I usually read newspapers in ＿＿＿＿＿ morning.

11. Cinema International Inc. is planning to build ＿＿＿＿＿ IMAX theater in the neighborhood.

12. Stanley has gone to ＿＿＿＿＿ movies with his friends.

13. Did you think ＿＿＿＿＿ fashion show in the Crystal Hall last week was a big success?

2

請勾選正確的答案。

1. ☐ Snow ☐ The snow is formed when the temperature drops below zero and the humidity is high.

2. ☐ Tornadoes ☐ The tornadoes are violent natural phenomena. They often cause great damage along their path.

3. Even though I had an umbrella with me, I got all wet when I walked home in ☐ rain ☐ the rain.

4. I've got two tickets to ☐ circuses ☐ the circus. Are you going with me? You'll love ☐ performance ☐ the performance.

5. I watch soap operas in ☐ the evening ☐ an evening after I finish eating dinner and washing dishes.

6. Every time I lit a match ☐ the wind ☐ a wind blew it out, so I waited until I found an alley between two buildings.

7. Harry reads ☐ *the Taipei Times* ☐ *Taipei Times* every morning before going to work.

Unit **17**

Expressions Without "The" (1)
不加 **The** 的情況（I）

1 星期幾不加 the。但是「**週末**」要加 the。

Phil goes to the gym on Saturdays.
菲爾每星期六上健身房。

• **on the weekend**
在週末

MONDAY
TUESDAY
~~WEDNESDAY~~
THURSDAY
FRIDAY
SATURDAY
SUNDAY

2 **月分**不加 the。

The exhibition will take place in June.
這場展覽將於 6 月展開。

Months of the Year

January	February	March
April	May	June
July	August	September
October	November	December

3 某些時間慣用語，不加 the。

Jerry went home at midnight.
傑瑞半夜才回家。

• **at night** • **by night**
• **at noon** • **by day**

4 **季節**不加 the。「**秋天**」如果用 the fall，就一定要加 the。

spring

summer

autumn / the fall

winter

5 **節日**不加 the，但如果和 festival 連用，則通常會加 the。

New Year's Eve

Christmas Day

Halloween

Thanksgiving

• **the Mid-Autumn** Festival 中秋節
• **the Dragon Boat** Festival 端午節

Practice

1　請從圖片中選出適當的詞彙，並視情況加上 the 或 s 等填空，完成句子。

| night | noon | summer | autumn |

| Dragon Boat Festival | Valentine's Day | Father's Day | Songkran Festival |

| Saturday | Sunday | February | June |

1. _____ falls on the fifth day of the fifth lunar month.

2. Typhoons usually hit Taiwan during _____ and _____.

3. _____ is a unique festival in northern Thailand. People celebrate it by splashing water on one another.

4. Jim was born on the third of _____, so he is a Gemini.

5. Where does your family plan to take your father on _____?

6. I have to finish this project by _____, because I'm taking this afternoon off.

7. Would you like to go out with me on _____? I know a romantic French restaurant.

8. The weekend includes _____ and _____.

9. I go to work from 9 a.m. to 6 p.m. I don't work at _____.

Unit **18**

Expressions Without "The" (2)
不加 The 的情況（2）

1　學科名稱，不加 the。

I am good at geography.

地理是我擅長的科目。

- math
- music
- physics
- history
- chemistry
- literature

2　工作地點、家，不加 the。

Lester said he was going to work.

萊斯特說他要去上班了。

I called Toby's house and he was not at home. 我打電話到托比家，但是他不在家。

3　體育活動，不加 the。

I love playing soccer. 我喜歡踢足球。

He is playing badminton. 他正在打羽毛球。

play basketball

play baseball

play football

play golf

play tennis

4　「**by** + 交通工具」及 **on foot** 片語，不加 the。

Are you going by bus? 你要搭公車去嗎？

We are traveling by train.

我們要坐火車旅行。

by car

by plane

by motorcycle

by bicycle

on foot

5　社會機構、學術單位，不加 the。

Phillip's cousin is not at school today.

菲利普的表哥今天沒有來上學。

Myna goes to college. 米娜去唸大學了。

go to church

go to jail

go to school

go to court

這些社會機構、學術單位，如果指的是建築物本身，則可以加 the。

請見 Unit 20 說明。

Practice

1　請仔細分辨下列句子是否屬於前述「不需要加 **the**」的狀況。
在空格內填上 the、a、an，或劃上「/」表示不需要冠詞。

1. My daughter rides her bicycle to _____ school.

2. Irene wants to study accounting at _____ university.

3. My son just started _____ school.

4. There's a small fountain in front of _____ school.

5. It is much more pleasant to see the garden on _____ foot than by _____ car.

6. Are you going to travel by _____ plane or _____ train?

7. Put this box in _____ car that is parked in the driveway.

8. Everyone got off _____ bus to take photos of the beautiful canyon.

9. Randy had a friend that almost went to _____ prison.

10. Lacking evidence, the police released Joe from _____ jail last week.

11. He kept complaining about food in _____ prison cafeteria.

12. After we had gathered enough evidence, we finally brought this case to _____ court.

13. Elaine didn't go to _____ work today, but she was not at _____ home, either. Where did she go?

14. Johnny stayed in _____ office until midnight.

15. _____ Math is my favorite subject.

16. I studied _____ literature at college.

17. Susie loves to read stories about _____ history of China.

18. Rebecca has no idea how to compete in _____ bobsleigh races.

19. Team members on _____ bobsleigh have to be well-trained, or it could be extremely dangerous.

20. Who left _____ baseball bat on the floor? Someone could trip over it.

Unit **19**

Place Names With or Without "The"
專有地名加 The 或不加 The

要加 the 的專有地名

1 海洋名，要加 the。
- the **Pacific Ocean** 太平洋
- the **Indian Ocean** 印度洋
- the **Red Sea** 紅海
- the **Mediterranean** 地中海

2 河川、流域、海灣名，要加 the。
- the **Danube** 多瑙河
- the **Seine** 塞納河
- the **Amazon Basin** 亞馬遜河流域
- the **Persian Gulf** 波斯灣

3 運河、海峽名，要加 the。
- the **Panama Canal** 巴拿馬運河
- the **Intracoastal Waterway** 海灣沿岸航道
- the **Victoria Strait** 維多利亞海峽

4 群島名，要加 the。
- the **San Juans** 聖胡安群島
- the **Florida Keys** 佛羅里達礁島群
- the **West Indies** 西印度群島

↳ 參看後面「獨立島嶼名，不加 the」。

5 山脈名，要加 the。
- the **Himalayas** 喜馬拉雅山脈
- the **Alps** 阿爾卑斯山脈
- the **Rocky Mountains** 落磯山脈

↳ 參看後面「獨立山岳名，不加 the」。

6 沙漠名，要加 the。
- the **Gobi Desert** 戈壁沙漠
- the **Sahara** 撒哈拉沙漠

7 各種大型建築物、公設，要加 the。

the **Statue of Liberty**
自由女神像

the **Taj Mahal**
泰姬瑪哈陵

the **Great Wall**
萬里長城

the **Milan Cathedral**
米蘭大教堂

the **London Eye**
倫敦眼

8	橋樑、塔名，要加 the。	• the **Tower Bridge** 倫敦塔橋
		• the **Golden Gate Bridge** 金門大橋
		• the **Great Pyramid of Giza** 吉薩大金字塔
		• the **Eiffel Tower** 艾菲爾鐵塔

| 9 | 博物館、紀念館、畫廊，要加 the。 | • the **Andy Warhol Museum** 安迪‧沃荷博物館 |
| | | • the **Lincoln Memorial** 林肯紀念館 |

| 10 | 電影院、劇院名，要加 the。 | • the **Central City Opera House** 中央城歌劇院 |
| | | • the **Carré Theater** 卡列劇院 |

11	飯店、餐廳、酒吧、俱樂部，要加 the。以「人名所有格」構成的地名、建築名，都不加 **the**。	• the **Hotel Royal** 老爺酒店	• Jack O'Sullivan's **Tavern** 傑克蘇利文酒館
		• the **Deer Path Inn** 迪爾佩斯餐廳	• McDonald's 麥當勞
		• the **Brass Monkey** 銅猴子酒吧	• St. Paul's **Cathedral** 聖保羅大教堂

不加 **the** 的專有地名

1	洲名，不加 **the**。	• **Asia** 亞洲
		• **Europe** 歐洲
	但是一些**大區域名稱**，則慣用 the。	• **Africa** 非洲
		• **Australia** 澳洲
	• the **Middle East** 中東 • the **West** 西方	

4	鄉村、城鎮名，不加 **the**。	• **Florence** 佛羅倫斯
		• **Canterbury** 坎特伯里
		• **Nagasaki** 長崎

2	國家名，不加 **the**。	• **Mexico** 墨西哥
		• **Canada** 加拿大
	國家名稱中若含 kingdom、republic、states 等「可數名詞」，則要加 the。	• **Korea** 韓國
		• **Malaysia** 馬來西亞

• the **Netherlands** 荷蘭   • the **Philippines** 菲律賓
• the **United** Kingdom 英國
• the **Republic of Congo** 剛果共和國
• the **United States of America** 美利堅合眾國

| 5 | 湖泊名，不加 **the**。 |

Sun Moon Lake 日月潭

Lake Victoria 維多利亞湖

| 3 | 州名、省名，不加 **the**。 | • **California** 加州 |
| | | • **Ontario** 安大略省 |

6 獨立島嶼名，不加 **the**。

Orchid Island 蘭嶼

Santorini 聖托里尼島

↳ 參看前面「群島名，要加 the」。

7 獨立山岳名，不加 **the**。

K2 喬戈里峰

Mount Jade 玉山

↳ 參看前面「山脈名，要加 the」。

---

8 街道名、廣場名，不加 **the**。

- Elm Street
  艾姆街
- Davis Street
  戴維斯街
- Times Square
  時代廣場
- Trafalgar Square
  特拉法加廣場

- the Gulf of Mexico
  墨西哥灣
- the Statue of Liberty
  自由女神像
- the Rock of Gibraltar
  直布羅陀巨岩
- the University of California
  加州大學

> 但是任何以 of 片語構成的**地名、建築名**，都要加 the。

---

9 公園名、學校名，不加 **the**。

- Central Park 中央公園
- Seattle University 西雅圖大學

---

10 機場名，不加 **the**。

- Taiwan Taoyuan International Airport 臺灣桃園國際機場
- JFK International Airport 甘迺迪國際機場

Practice

1

請勾選正確的答案。

1. Ukraine is located in ☐ **Europe** ☐ **the Europe**.

2. Northern Ireland is a part of ☐ **the United Kingdom** ☐ **United Kingdom**.

3. Manila is the capital of ☐ **Philippines** ☐ **the Philippines**.

4. The longest river in Africa is ☐ **the Nile** ☐ **Nile**.

5. ☐ **The Colosseum** ☐ **Colosseum** is an ancient amphitheater in the center of Rome.

6. ☐ **Metropolitan Museum of Art** ☐ **The Metropolitan Museum of Art** has the largest collection of European art in New York.

7. The trees on ☐ **Ridge Street** ☐ **the Ridge Street** are beautiful this time of year.

2

請在需要 **the** 的空格內填上 the，不需要的則劃「/」。

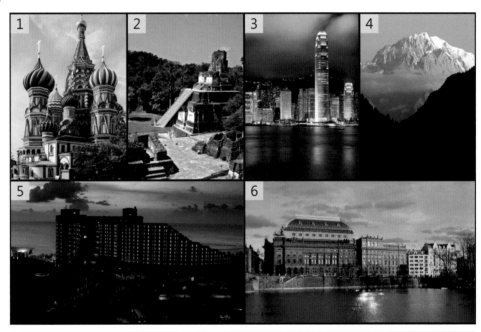

1. ＿＿＿＿＿ St. Basil's Cathedral is located on ＿＿＿＿＿ Red Square in ＿＿＿＿＿ Moscow.

2. ＿＿＿＿＿ Tikal National Park in ＿＿＿＿＿ Guatemala has preserved many sites of the Mayan civilization.

3. After we finished lunch, we walked along ＿＿＿＿＿ Victoria Harbor back to our hotel.

4. ＿＿＿＿＿ Mont Blanc is the highest mountain in France and Italy.

5. I stayed in ＿＿＿＿＿ Hotel Nikko when I was vacationing in ＿＿＿＿＿ Guam.

6. What is playing at ＿＿＿＿＿ National Theater tonight?

Unit **20**

Expressions With or Without "The" With Different Meanings

加 **The** 或不加 **The** 意義不同的用語

三餐

1 三餐通常不加**冠詞**。

Let's meet for breakfast in the hotel dining room at 8:00. 我們 8 點在飯店的餐廳見面，一起吃早餐吧！

Do you want to have dinner in the Rooftop Restaurant?

想要一起到屋頂餐廳吃晚餐嗎？

2 指「**特定的一餐**」，則要加上冠詞 the。比如，表示三餐的單字後面如果有**介系詞片語**、**分詞片語**或**形容詞子句**修飾，則需要加 the。

The lunch provided during the conference wasn't too bad.

會議上提供的午餐其實不算太糟。

3 breakfast、lunch、dinner 前面如果還有**形容詞**，則需要加 a/an。

They gave us a quick lunch and hurried us onto the bus. 他們讓我們匆匆地吃了午餐，接著就催我們上巴士。

4 meal 這個字可加 a 或 the。

A meal is included in the trip.

旅遊行程中會提供一餐。

地點

5 ■ 一些**地點名稱**若表示「**功能、目的**」，則不加 **the**；
■ 若單純表示「**地點**」、「**建築物**」，則**要加** the。

Adrian went to school.
↳ go to school 指的是「學校的功能」、「去學校的目的」。

亞德里安去上學了。

This morning Wilfred went to the school to talk to the principal.
↳ the school 指學校「這個地點」、「這棟建築物」。

今天早上威爾福前往學校找校長說話。

Vivian had to go to church.
↳ 目的是去做禮拜。

薇薇安得上教堂。

Nicole is applying for a job at the church.
↳ the church 指「工作的地點」、「這棟建築物」。

妮可在應徵那座教堂裡的一份工作。

It's time to go to bed.
↳ 目的是上床去睡覺。

該去睡覺了。

Mom laid out your clothes on the bed.
the bed 指衣服放置的「地點」。

媽媽把你的衣服放在床上。

lying on the bed

Practice

1 請在空格內填上 the、a 或 an，如果不需要冠詞，請劃上「/」。

1. Did you eat _____ breakfast offered by the hotel?

2. We had _____ breakfast at a local coffee shop.

3. After Carl drops his wife at work, he has _____ breakfast at a café.

4. Please tell your sister _____ dinner is served.

5. _____ dinner in that French restaurant is famous.

6. Grandma made _____ delicious dinner for Lisa and me.

7. We went for _____ meal after shopping.

8. Does this price include _____ meals?

9. We went to the fishing harbor for _____ fish meal yesterday.

2 請在空格內填上 the、a 或 an，如果不需要冠詞，請劃上「/」。

1. I am tired and I am going to _____ bed.

2. Who left the books, toys, dolls, and pajamas on _____ bed in my room?

3. Your slippers are under _____ bed.

4. Is there _____ church nearby?

5. Dad should be out of _____ church in a few minutes.

6. When I arrived at _____ church, he had already left.

7. Is that _____ nursing home where Mrs. Finch stayed after her stroke?

8. Although Grandpa has retired, he is never at _____ home in the morning.

Unit 21

Personal Pronouns:
Subject and Object Pronouns

人稱代名詞：
「主格代名詞」與「受格代名詞」

How to use object pronoun for thing

one thing

I like **it**.

many things

I like **them**.

1 人稱代名詞可分為三類：主格代名詞、受格代名詞和所有格代名詞。

		主格代名詞	受格代名詞	所有格代名詞
第一人稱	單數	I	me	mine
	複數	we	us	ours
第二人稱	單數	you	you	yours
	複數	you	you	yours
第三人稱	單數	he/she/it	him/her/it	his/hers/its
	複數	they	them	theirs

2 主格代名詞用來當作句子中**主要動詞**的「主詞」。

Where is Dad? He is in the garage.
爸爸在哪裡？他在車庫裡。

Mom didn't take us to school.
She is in New York.
媽媽沒有送我們到學校，她目前人在紐約。

3 受格代名詞用來作為句子中**動詞或介系詞**的「受詞」。

Can you call me tomorrow?
你可以明天打電話給我嗎？

Please ask him to help us.
請他幫忙我們。

I'll talk to him.
我會跟他談談。

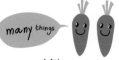

Call and ask for him.
打電話找他。

I will ask him all about it.
我會向他問清楚一切。

4 be 動詞的後面，要接主格代名詞。但在電話用語中，**第一人稱**通常用 me。

Don't you recognize my voice? It's me.
你聽不出我的聲音嗎？是我啊！

It is I, your beloved King.
是我，你深愛的國王。

It was I who broke the window.
打破窗戶的是我。

5 「比較的句型」中，as 和 than 的後面經常接受格代名詞。
但如果在正式用語裡，as 和 than 後面還是以「主格代名詞 + 動詞」的形式為佳。

She is taller than him.
= **She is taller** than he is.
她比他高。

I am as short as him.
= **I am as short** as he is.
我和他一樣矮。

6 口語中，受格代名詞可以在**簡答句**中代替**主詞**。

Peter: I'm very thirsty.
Sam: Me too. / I am, too.
彼德：我的口好渴。
山姆：我也是。

1

請勾選正確的答案。

1. Wally called to say ☐ he ☐ him is coming soon.
2. Charlotte has a great sense of humor. I like ☐ her ☐ she very much.
3. Your grandparents gave you a nice gift, but you have not said "thank you" to ☐ they ☐ them.
4. ☐ They ☐ Them are giving out tickets for speeding.
5. Why don't ☐ us ☐ we go to the night market together?
6. Marian didn't go to her office. ☐ She ☐ Her stayed at home.
7. Would you help ☐ me ☐ I doing the housework this afternoon?
8. Ivan's girlfriend is in Puerto Rico. He says he has called ☐ her ☐ she several times.
9. A boy and a girl compared their heights. He was taller than ☐ she ☐ her.
10. You are smarter than ☐ I ☐ I am.
11. Betty can't climb a tree. ☐ I ☐ I can't, either.
12. It is ☐ us ☐ we that cleaned the house before our guests arrived.

2

請以正確的「人稱代名詞」填空，完成句子。

1. Jenny got up early this morning. _____ practiced the piano after breakfast.
2. James got up too early today. _____ felt sleepy when playing baseball with his friends.
3. Sandy is not in the office. Do you know where _____ is?
4. I don't know how to sing. Can you teach _____?
5. Maybe that snake is sick or dead. _____ is not moving.
6. I saw Sam sneaking out of the room. It must be _____ who took the diamond ring.
7. Lisa and Helen are free tomorrow. You can ask _____ to help you move to your new apartment.
8. We're going to the beach this Sunday. Would you like to go with _____?
9. Nick has broken his ankle. Can you help carry _____ to the health center?
10. Aren't you having a meeting tomorrow morning? Shall I give _____ a wake-up call?

Unit 22

Common Usages of Subject Pronouns and Pronoun "It"

「主格代名詞」與代名詞 It 的常見用法

1 主格代名詞 we 有時包含聽者，有時不包含，視說話的情況而定。

Why don't we go to the Indian
↳ we 包括說話者和聽者。
restaurant tonight?
今晚我們何不去印度餐廳吃飯？

We are going out on the town tonight. Do you want to join us?
↳ We 包括說話者，但不包括聽者。
我們今晚要到城裡，你要和我們一起去嗎？

2 主格代名詞 you 可拿來指「包含你我的所有人」。這種情況在非常正式的用語中須用 one。

You can waste a lot of time staring into space.
你大可以浪費很多時間發呆。

You can send emails around the world almost instantly.
你幾乎可以瞬間將電子郵件傳到世界各地。

One must support one's country.
一個人必須支持自己的國家。

3 主格代名詞 they 也可拿來指「包含你我的所有人」。

They say 1.5 million people ride the transit system each day.
據說每天有一百五十萬人搭乘運輸系統。

4 主格代名詞 they 經常拿來指「政府或權威人士」。

They have new laws to allow them to spy on you. 政府制訂了新法，讓他們可以監視你。

They are watching you at this very moment.
此時此刻他們正在監視著你。

5 代名詞 it 也可以指「人」，尤其在「詢問或告知身分」的時候。

Who is on the phone? Ask who it is.
是誰打電話來？問問到底是誰。

Who is it? 是誰啊？

It's Ed on the phone. 是艾德打電話來。

6 代名詞 it 在某些句中並沒有特殊的意義，也就是所謂的虛主詞，這種用法常見於說明「時間」、「距離」、「天氣」和「溫度」的句型中。

I'd guess it is about 9:00. 我猜現在大概9點左右。

It is about ten kilometers to the town.
這邊離城裡大約10公里。

Bring in the laundry because it's going to rain tonight. 把衣服收進來吧，因為今晚會下雨。

It's so hot you could fry an egg on the blacktop.
天氣熱得要命，都可以在柏油路上煎蛋了。

7 代名詞 it 作為虛主詞的時候，後面經常接「加 to 的不定詞」或者 that 子句。

It is interesting to travel in South America.
= To travel in South America is interesting.
去南美洲旅遊很有趣。

It is a good idea that we avoid the tourist spots.
= That we avoid the tourist spots is a good idea.
避開那些知名景點，是個不錯的主意。

Practice

1

請勾選正確的答案。

1. Who is □ him □ it at the door?

2. Why don't □ we □ us stay at home and play the Nintendo Switch games?

3. □ We □ Us should hang out together sometime.

4. □ It □ She is Janet on the phone.

5. Have □ you □ your been to Honolulu before?

6. □ They □ It say sharks do not attack humans for fun.

7. □ Them □ They have brought up a proposal of building a community center in every administrative district.

2

請依圖示，從框內選出適當的用語，搭配 it 作為「虛主詞」，填空完成句子。

| was cold outside | is 200 meters from here |
| is going to rain | was 10 p.m. |

1

....
....,
so I put on my jacket.

2

....
....
when Jake went to bed.

3

....
....
Let's bring in the laundry.

4

....
....
to the mountain peak.

3

請用 it 當「虛主詞」，改寫下列句子。

1. To go down a water slide is exciting.

   → ....

2. To drink soy milk every day is good for your health.

   → ....

3. That we follow the traffic rules is important.

   → ....

Unit 23

Possessive Pronouns and Possessive Adjectives
「所有格代名詞」與「所有格形容詞」

1 所有格代名詞和所有格形容詞的形式非常類似，經常在句子中搭配使用。

		所有格代名詞	所有格形容詞
第一人稱	單數	mine	my
	複數	ours	our
第二人稱	單數	yours	your
	複數	yours	your
第三人稱	單數	his/hers/ -	his/her/its
	複數	theirs	their

2 所有格形容詞要接**名詞**，用來說明該名詞的「**所有權**」。

Jack can't buy his new car until next month. 傑克下個月才能買新車。

Andrea traded in her SUV for an electric car. 安德麗把她的休旅車換成了電動車。

3 所有格代名詞要**單獨使用**，後面不需要接名詞。

I thought I saw Wayne's new gas-electric hybrid vehicle, but it wasn't his. 我以為我看到的是韋恩的油電混合車，不過那輛車並不是他的。

Patsy's new electric car takes only three hours to charge, which is better than mine. 佩希的新電動車只要花三小時充電，比我的還要好。

4 my own、your own、his own 這類的用語放在**名詞前面**，用來強調某事物的「**專屬權**」。our own、their own 則是「**共同擁有權**」。

This is my office computer.
這是我辦公室的電腦。

I've got my own computer now. I don't share it with anybody else in my department anymore.
我現在有自己的電腦，不再和部門裡的其他人共用電腦了。

That isn't my email address. That is the general address for customer support.
那不是我的電子郵件，那是開放給一般顧客服務的電子郵件位址。

This is my own email address.
這是我專用的電子郵件位址。

5 my own、your own 這類的用語之前，也可以加 of。此時 of my own、of your own 等，會放在**名詞後面**。

I use a personalized email address of my own for my side business.
我用私人的信箱接收和副業相關的電子郵件。

6 my own、your own 等用語，也可以用來強調「**某人自己的事，與他人無關**」。

Do your job. 做你的工作。

Do your own job, and stop telling me what to do. 做你自己的工作，別一直指揮我做事。

7 (do something) on my own、on your own 這類的用語，則表示「**獨立從事某件事，不靠外人幫助**」。

I can't solve this problem on my own because it involves another department. 我沒辦法自己解決這個問題，因為這牽涉到其他部門。

Nobody knows what to do, so you are on your own. 沒有人知道該怎麼做，所以你得靠自己了。

Practice

1

請勾選正確的答案。

1. That is ☐ her ☐ hers villa.

2. He drives ☐ him ☐ his car to work.

3. I was eating ☐ my ☐ mine lunch box at that time.

4. They're going to sell ☐ their ☐ theirs refrigerator.

5. ☐ We ☐ Our garden needs weeding.

6. Do you see that apartment? That's ☐ my ☐ mine.

7. Your house is more expensive than ☐ our ☐ ours.

8. This is the first time I have had ☐ my own ☐ on my own house.

9. Louise doesn't have ☐ her own ☐ she own house.

10. I can't do it ☐ on my own ☐ my own, and I need some help.

11. I can't find ☐ my ☐ mine cell phone.

12. Howard has his cell phone, but Amy can't find ☐ her ☐ hers.

13. I used to drive my father's old scooter, but I have a scooter ☐ my own ☐ of my own now.

14. It's ☐ his own ☐ on his own idea.

15. This is ☐ mine ☐ my apple pie.

16. He crossed the desert ☐ of his own ☐ on his own.

2

請用正確的「所有格代名詞」填空，完成句子。

1. This is David's computer. This is Helen's computer, too. So, this computer is ___theirs___.

2. Sonia owns the shop alone. The shop is _____.

3. Your car is an SUV. My car is a compact. _____ is smaller than _____.

4. I wanted to borrow Andy's bicycle, but he said the bicycle was not _____.

5. We have paid off the mortgage on the apartment. Now the apartment is _____.

6. I'm doing my job. You should be doing _____.

Unit 24

Reflexive Pronouns (1)
反身代名詞（I）

I Love myself!

1 反身代名詞用來指涉「自己」。

反身代名詞		
	單數	複數
第一人稱	myself	ourselves
第二人稱	yourself	yourselves
第三人稱	himself herself itself	themselves

2 當句子的**主詞和受詞是同一人或同一事物**時，為了避免重複，會使用反身代名詞。

I bought myself a bottle of champagne.
我給自己買了一瓶香檳。

The old man trusts nobody but himself.
那位老人家除了他自己，誰也不信任。

3 反身代名詞經常用來「**加強語氣**」，強調是「**某人親自**」做了某事。

Dean drew everything in the comic book himself. 漫畫書是迪恩自己畫的。

Hank and Bernice started selling their games themselves.
漢克和柏尼斯開始自行販賣他們的遊戲。

I myself prefer to work alone, but I will take on a partner if I have to.
我個人是偏好獨力作業，但如果必要，我還是會找個合作夥伴。

4 有時，反身代名詞是用來強調「**獨自**」做了某事，沒有其他任何人介入。

Adam washed, dried, and folded all the laundry himself, even though Marvin was supposed to help him.
原本梅爾文應該要幫忙的，不過亞當卻獨自洗好、烘乾並摺好所有的衣服。

Bobby needs to finish the job himself, and nobody is supposed to help him.
巴比得自己完成工作，別人不應該幫忙他。

5 by myself、by yourself 等是反身代名詞的慣用語，說明「**某事由某人獨力完成，不靠他人幫助**」。

He did the job all by himself.
這項工作完全是由他獨力完成的。

Earl can't keep the comic book store open all day and all night by himself.
只靠厄爾獨自一人，根本不可能讓漫畫店整天營業。

He tried to do it by himself, but he couldn't do it.
他嘗試過自己做，但是沒成功。

6 help yourself、enjoy yourself 等也是反身代名詞的慣用語。

Please help yourself to soft drinks while reading the comics.
看漫畫的時候，請自行取用飲料。

Enjoy yourself at the Game Designers Workshop.
在「遊戲設計家」工作坊裡好好享受吧。

Practice

1

請勾選正確的答案。

1. Harry bought □ herself □ himself a new camera for his birthday.
2. Peter lacks self-confidence. He doesn't believe in □ he □ himself.
3. We sailed across the Strait of Magellan □ myself □ ourselves.
4. I translated the novel □ my own □ by myself.
5. You don't have to do your homework □ all by yourself □ yours.
6. They completed the experiment □ by □ on themselves.
7. Please help □ you □ yourself to the dessert.
8. Johnny bought some wrapping paper and ribbons. He wanted to wrap the present □ him □ himself.
9. Sandy made □ she □ herself a scarf.

2

請用正確的「反身代名詞」填空，完成句子。

I painted the picture
....

Lily forgets things all the time, so she often writes .... a note.

Please help ....
at the salad bar.

Henry assembled the bookshelf by
....

Emma traveled around Europe
by .... last
month.

Sarah and Jimmy cooked the
dinner all by ....

Unit **25**

Reflexive Pronouns (2)
反身代名詞（2）

1 有些詞彙不能跟反身代名詞連用。

• feel
• relax
• concentrate

✗ Hannah feels herself young and energetic.

✓ Hannah feels young and energetic.

漢娜感到年輕有活力。

✗ When Jess wants to relax herself, she listens to Celtic music.

✓ When Jess wants to relax, she listens to Celtic music.

潔思想要放鬆的時候，就會聽凱爾特音樂。

✗ Patrick can't concentrate himself when the TV is on.

✓ Patrick can't concentrate when the TV is on.

只要電視開著，派屈克就沒辦法專心。

2 片語 each other 的意義經常和反身代名詞混淆。each other 意指「**兩個人彼此、互相**」。

We are videotaping ourselves.
↳ 大家都在影片裡。
我們自己幫自己錄影。

We are photographing each other.
兩個人各自幫彼此拍照。↵
我們正在幫彼此拍照。

3 另一個與 each other 意義相近的片語 one another，也不能和反身代名詞的用法混淆。

one another 也是「**彼此、互相**」的意思，但 one another 只能用於「**三個人以上**」。

When playing doubles, you and your partner must always keep an eye on each other.
↳ 兩個人；這裡不能用 watch yourselves。
進行雙打的時候，
你和你的夥伴應該
要不斷彼此注意。

Everybody on the team must help one another if we are to win the game.
↳ 人數超過兩名
如果我們想贏得比賽，每一名隊員都應該彼此幫助。

Practice

1 請從框內選出正確的詞彙或片語填空，完成句子。不需要填任何詞彙的地方，請劃上「/」。

| me |
| myself |
| himself |
| by herself |
| ourselves |
| each other |
| one another |
| themselves |

1. I am going to take my camera with ....

2. Nobody taught Isabelle how to swim. She learned ....

3. Kent is relaxing .... on the back porch.

4. We didn't hire anybody. We painted our house ....

5. When my sister and I go swimming, we look out for ....

6. With the economy being so bad, we need to help ....

7. I feel .... strong and healthy.

8. You must concentrate .... on the book.

9. Craig didn't shave .... this morning.

10. My dog Lou always dries .... in front of the fan.

11. Brenda was dressed .... quickly and left her apartment.

12. They are still in love with ....

2 請依圖示，從框內選出適當的用語填空，完成句子。

| herself |
| themselves |
| each other |
| one another |

Lily and Nana are chasing
....

To win the race, everyone on the yacht must help ....

They are photographing
....

Cathy is putting together the puzzle by ....

Unit 26

Expressions for Quantity
表示「數量」的用語

1 a number of 意指「一些」，常用來修飾**複數可數名詞**，動詞也要用**複數動詞**。

A large number of customers have gathered in the shoe department for their refunds.

很多消費者聚集到鞋子部門要求退費。

比較

the number of 則表示「某物的數量」，須用**單數動詞**。

• The number of unemployed teachers in this city keeps rising.

這個城市的失業教師人數持續增加。

2 a group of 意指「一群」，用來修飾**複數可數名詞**，動詞也要用**複數動詞**。

A group of unemployed teachers are marching on New York City Hall, demanding teaching jobs. 一群失業教師在紐約市政府前遊行，要求教職。

3 plenty of 意指「大量的」、「比剛好還要多一點」。可修飾**複數可數名詞**，也可修飾**不可數名詞**。

We still have plenty of time. Why don't we drop by Mary's before we return to Phoenix? 我們的時間還很多，何不在返回鳳凰城之前，繞去瑪莉家一下？

plenty of lamb
很多羊肉

plenty of lamb chops
很多羊排

4 a great deal of 意指「大量的」，可修飾**複數可數名詞**，也可修飾**不可數名詞**。搭配的動詞視其修飾何種名詞而定。

A great deal of work needs to be done by tomorrow.

有許多工作要在明天之前完成。

Jenny has a great deal of toys. Please do not buy her any more toys.

珍妮的玩具已經很多了，請不要再買給她了。

5 a lot of 或 lots of 意指「很多」、「比剛好多很多」。可修飾**複數可數名詞**，也可修飾**不可數名詞**。

a lot of pork
大量豬肉

a lot of sausages
大量香腸

lots of beef
大量牛肉

lots of steaks
很多牛排

Practice

1　請勾選正確的答案。

1. We've got □ a plenty of □ plenty of fruit in our refrigerator.

2. □ A plenty of □ Plenty of juice □ was □ were made for the party.

3. Plenty of shops □ is □ are open if we need more supplies for the party.

4. We have plenty of □ people □ person with cars to pick up the guests at the train station and drive them to the clubhouse.

5. The company is prepared to spend □ a great deal of □ great deals of money on the new production facility in China.

6. A great deal of □ planning □ a planning has gone into this new facility.

7. A great deal of money □ was □ were required to get the land for the factory.

8. As we enter the construction phase for this project, a great deal of □ time □ the time will be required for management to complete this expansion.

9. □ A number of □ The number of the pictures we took □ is □ are astonishing.

10. □ A number of □ The number of pictures □ has □ have been ruined.

11. A number of □ problem □ problems reduced the number of usable photos.

12. Therefore, □ a number of □ numbers of pictures have to be deleted.

13. There is □ lot of □ lots of sand on this beach.

14. A lot of □ sand □ sands went into my sneakers.

15. Are you going to build a lot of □ a sand castle □ sand castles today?

16. A lot of beaches □ is □ are so rocky.

Part 4 Quantity 數量

Unit 27

Indefinite Pronouns for Quantity
表示「數量」的不定代名詞

不定代名詞的個別用法，請見 Units 29-38 說明。

1 不定代名詞用來指「**不特定的人、事、物**」，經常帶有**數量**的含意。

- a few 一些
- all 全部
- a little 一些
- some 一些
- any 任何
- both 兩者
- either 兩者之一
- neither 兩者皆非
- another 另一個
- each 每個
- half 一半
- many 很多
- much 很多
- more 更多
- most 大多數
- none 完全沒有

2 不定代名詞當語意清楚時，它們**可以單獨存在**，後面不需要加名詞。

If you want some donuts, I will go buy some.
如果你想吃甜甜圈，我就去買一點回來。
I didn't count the number of no-shows, but there weren't many.
我沒算缺席的人數，但是不太多就是了。

3 上述這些詞彙，有許多都常作「限定詞」使用，可以直接放在**名詞前面**修飾名詞。

The fruit stand has some watermelons.
水果攤上有一些西瓜。
They have many types of grapes.
他們有很多不同品種的葡萄。
All the fruit is fresh. 所有的水果都很新鮮。
The fruit stand has more bananas than the grocery store. 水果攤的香蕉比雜貨店的多。

這些詞彙如果**單獨使用**，或者**先接 of** 再接名詞，它們就是代名詞；如果**後面直接加名詞**，就是限定詞。

4 不定代名詞後面接的名詞，如果已經是加了所有格或 the/these 的名詞（the room、her key 等），則不定代名詞後面要先接 of，再接這些帶有修飾語的名詞。

Does this store sell any of the English newspapers? 這間店裡有賣任何英文報紙嗎？
The mini-mart has a lot of your favorite soft drinks.
這間小型超市有很多你喜歡喝的飲料。
None of these soft drinks are caffeine-free. 這些飲料沒有一種是不含咖啡因的。

5 all、half 和 both 後面如果接加了**所有格代名詞或 the/these** 的名詞（the room、her key 等），則**可加 of 也可以不加**。
如果接**受格代名詞**（them、us 等），就一定要加 of。

I bought all (of) the groceries on the shopping list.
我把購物單上所有的物品都買齊了。
Half (of) the gifts have been wrapped.
一半的禮物都包裝好了。

✗ It would be helpful if you could move some of the boxes, but it is not necessary to move all them.

✓ It would be helpful if you could move some of the boxes, but it is not necessary to move all of them.
要是你能幫我搬一些箱子，就算是幫了我的忙了，不過不用搬全部的箱子。

✗ I told Sue I couldn't attend the party unless she invited both us.

✓ I told Sue I couldn't attend the party unless she invited both of us.
我告訴蘇除非我們兩個都受邀，不然我就不能去派對。

Practice

1

請勾選正確的答案，有些句子可能兩個答案皆適用。

1. There are ☐ some ☐ some of markers in the drawer.
2. ☐ Both ☐ Both of tissue bags are empty.
3. ☐ A few of ☐ A few your friends sent you birthday cards.
4. There were two phone calls, but ☐ neither of ☐ neither was for you.
5. ☐ All ☐ All of the boxes you left here are stored in the garage.
6. I only bought ☐ a few ☐ a few of apples.
7. I bought a new type of tea. I'll make you ☐ some ☐ some of.
8. I only finished ☐ half ☐ half of the spaghetti.
9. I threw out ☐ some ☐ some of them.
10. ☐ Most ☐ Most of the tourists are Chinese.
11. ☐ Many ☐ Many of them came here for the first time.

2

請將句中可省略的名詞劃除，精簡句子；必要處可以用其他代名詞替代。

1. I need some crayons. Do you have any ~~crayons~~?
2. I bought some soy milk. Would you like to drink some soy milk?
3. I ate some cherries, but not all of the cherries.
4. I borrowed some books from the library, but not very many books.
5. I've read a few articles in the newspaper, but not all of the articles.
6. I've run out of printing paper. I need more printing paper.
7. I dropped the spoon. Please give me another spoon.
8. There're five singers in the band. Each singer has his or her own fans.
9. I can't decide which shirt to buy. I think I'll take both shirts.
10. I took the whole box of grapes out of the fridge and found out half of the grapes had gone bad.
11. I can't lend you much money. I have only a little money.
12. Over two hundred students have joined our dance club. Most of the students are college students.

Part 4 Quantity 數量

Unit 28

Indefinite Pronouns With Singular or Plural Verbs
不定代名詞搭配單數動詞或複數動詞

1 應該搭配**單數動詞**的不定代名詞：

- each
- either
- neither
- another
- much
- every (one)
- everyone
- everybody
- everything
- anyone
- anybody
- anything
- someone
- somebody
- something
- no one
- nobody
- nothing

No one believes his story.

沒人相信他說的事情。

Someone is knocking on the door.

有人在敲門。

Neither of the dogs has a skin problem.

兩隻狗都沒有皮膚病。

Each of the rooms is decorated in a different theme.

每個房間各自以不同的主題做裝潢。

單數意義的不定代名詞，除了動詞要使用**單數**之外，如有需要使用相對應的其他代名詞，也要使用**單數**，例如**人稱代名詞**要用 he/she/it，**所有格代名詞**要用 his/her/its。

- Everyone is writing his or her research paper carefully.

  每個人都全神貫注在寫自己的研究論文。

- If anything has to be done, it has to be done quickly.

  如果還有任何待辦事項，都得盡快完成。

2 應該搭配**複數動詞**的不定代名詞：

- both
- many
- (a) few
- several

Both of the clerks wear black hats. 兩名店員都戴著黑帽子。

A few vases were broken when they were transported.

有些花瓶在運送途中破損了。

Several days have passed.

已經過了好幾天。

Many of them have been to Tokyo two or three times.

他們之中，許多人已經去過東京兩、三次。

3 同時可修飾**複數可數名詞**和**不可數名詞**的不定代名詞，則要視其搭配的名詞而定。

當後面接**複數可數名詞**的時候，就要用**複數動詞**；當後面接**不可數名詞**的時候，就要用**單數動詞**。

- all
- most
- some

Some fresh blueberries are added to the fruit tea. 水果茶裡加了一些新鮮藍莓。

Most of the work is going to be done today. 大部分工作會在今天完成。

All the furniture in the store is handmade.

這家店裡賣的家具全都是手工製作的。

All the fruit tarts were sold in two hours.

所有水果塔在兩個小時內銷售一空。

Practice

1

請將括弧內的動詞以正確的形式填空，完成句子。

Most of the pieces left on the board _____ (be) white.

Some of the peppers _____ (be) red.

All of the fish _____ (be swimming) in the same direction.

Each dog _____ (have) its own personality.

Both racing cars _____ (be) fast.

Everyone _____ (work) hard in the office.

2

請勾選正確的答案。

1. □ Does □ Do anybody know when the bus will arrive?

2. Nothing □ was □ were achieved today.

3. Everybody □ was □ were yelling her name.

4. Neither of the children has □ their □ his or her cell phone.

5. Several students lost □ their □ his or her coats.

6. There □ isn't □ aren't much time left.

7. I left my cell phone on the kitchen table. I'll go and get □ it □ them.

8. Only a few of the rings □ cost □ costs a lot.

Part 4 Quantity 數量

Unit 29

"Some" and "Any"
Some 與 Any

1 some 和 any 可用來修飾**複數可數名詞**和**不可數名詞**，表達「**不確定的數量**」。

some messages 一些訊息
any messages 任何訊息
some food 一些食物
any food 任何食物

2 一般來說，some 用於**肯定句**；any 用於**否定句**和**疑問句**。

Christy has some job offers.
克莉絲蒂有一些職缺機會。
Christy doesn't have any job offers.
克莉絲蒂沒有獲得任何的職缺機會。
Do you have any milk?
你有牛奶嗎？
Do you have any small plastic tubing?
你有小的塑膠管線嗎？
There were some phone calls for you.
有幾通電話打來找你。
There weren't any phone calls for you.
沒有打給你的電話。

3 如果一個問句「**希望得到肯定的回答**」，也就是期待對方回答 yes，那麼就可以在**疑問句**中使用 some。

Do you have some black electrical tape?
↳ 提問的人認為對方有黑色的絕緣膠帶。
你有黑色的絕緣膠帶可以借我用嗎？
Jason, can I have some of the cookies on the table?
傑森，我可以拿一些桌上的餅乾嗎？

4 如果 any 表示「**無論哪一個都可以**」、「**隨意選擇一個**」的時候，就可以用於**肯定句**。

Take any of those PVC pipes if you need one. ↳ 你要拿哪一個都可以。

如果需要的話，你可以從那些塑膠管中拿一個去用。

5 any 可以和 never、seldom、rarely、hardly 和 without 等單字連用，強調這些單字的**否定意義**。

Fran never helps any of her colleagues in her office.
法蘭從來不幫助辦公室裡的任何同事。
Nelson seldom calls any of his relatives.
奈爾森很少打電話給親戚。

6 some 經常用於「**比較**」的句子裡，以強調「**差異性**」。

Some of these new water heaters use a lot less electricity than the older models.
這些新型熱水器裡，有些比舊型的省電很多。

Practice

1

請用 some 或 any 填空，完成句子。有些句子可以同時使用 **some** 和 **any**。

1. I received _____ interesting emails from an old friend.

2. I haven't received _____ messages from Mom.

3. Louis found Mary's phone number without _____ trouble.

4. If you need _____ letters of reference, I will write one for you.

5. Do you have _____ books to help me get ready for civil service examinations?

6. I don't have _____ paperclips in my drawer.

7. You can get staples from _____ business supply stores.

8. _____ people like plastic folders, but I like the paper ones.

9. Could you make me _____ coffee?

2

請用 any 將右列句子改寫為「否定句」和「疑問句」。

1. We can take some plums from the box.
   → _____
   → _____

2. I have some lip balm.
   → _____
   → _____

3. She made some strawberry milkshake in the morning.
   → _____
   → _____

3

請用括弧裡提供的詞彙改寫句子。

1. Sue doesn't buy any diamonds. (never)
   → _____

2. Tanya doesn't play any online games. (rarely)
   → _____

3. Sunny doesn't cook any fish. (hardly)
   → _____

4. We don't watch any horror movies. (seldom)
   → _____

Part 4 Quantity 數量

Unit 30

"Many" and "Much"
Many 與 Much

1 many 和 much 是**代名詞**，也是**形容詞**，意指「**大量的**」。

We don't have many free tickets for the circus performance. 我們沒有很多馬戲團表演的免費入場券。

Is there any orange juice left?
還有柳橙汁嗎？

Yes, but not much.
有，但是所剩不多。

2 many 用來修飾**複數可數名詞**；much 用來修飾**不可數名詞**。

many bricks
許多磚塊

much concrete
大量的混凝土

I didn't take many photos in Spain because I didn't have much free time.
我在西班牙的時候沒拍很多照片，因為我沒多少空閒時間。

3 many 和 much 多用於**疑問句**和**否定句**，少用於**肯定句**。

How much gas is in the car?
車子還有多少油？
We don't have much gas in the car.
我們車裡的油不多了。
Is there much time left?
還剩下很多時間嗎？
There isn't much time left.
剩下的時間不多了。

4 如果要在**肯定句**表示「**大量的**」，通常會用 a lot of、lots of 或 plenty of 這類的量詞，而不用 **many** 或 **much**。

✗ Cathy always has many questions.
✓ Cathy always has a lot of questions.
凱西總是有很多問題。
✗ There is much space to add another desk.
✓ There is plenty of space to add another desk.
還有足夠的空間可以增加一張書桌。
✗ The room has much light.
✓ The room has lots of light.
房間裡的光線充足。

5 many 和 much 如果搭配 too、so、as、very，就可以用於**肯定句**。

The department has too much boxes of copier paper. 部門裡的影印紙太多箱啦。
Put as much copier paper as you can in the storage room.
盡可能把影印紙放到儲藏室裡。
The secretary has so many things to do that we need to help her move the boxes. 秘書要做的事實在太多了，所以我們得幫她搬那些紙箱。
Your help is very much appreciated.
非常感謝您的幫忙。

Practice

1

請勾選正確的答案。

1. There are ☐ many ☐ much cars on the road.

2. There is ☐ a lot of ☐ many sand in my shoes.

3. How ☐ much ☐ many oatmeal is in the pot?

4. He has ☐ plenty of ☐ many clothing.

5. Do you have ☐ so many ☐ many handbags?

6. The agency doesn't have ☐ much ☐ many work this week.

7. There isn't ☐ much ☐ many time before the bus leaves.

8. There is still ☐ much ☐ a lot of room in the trunk.

9. I drank ☐ much ☐ too much tea tonight.

10. I've found ☐ many ☐ much mistakes in this proposal.

2

請從框內選用適當的用語填空，完成句子。

plenty of

many

too many

as many

much

too much

There isn't _____ wine in the decanter.

She poured _____ wine into the glass.

She is eating _____ sandwiches as she can.

We've made _____ sandwiches.

They collected _____ grapes this year.

I don't have _____ grapes to eat.

Part 4 Quantity 數量

Unit 31

"Few" and "Little"
Few 與 Little

1 few 和 little 是**代名詞**，也是**形容詞**，兩者都指「**幾乎沒有**」，帶有**否定**的口氣。

few 用於**可數名詞**，little 用於**不可數名詞**。

There is little relevant information on this topic in the briefing book.

重點手冊裡幾乎沒有和這個主題相關的資訊。

Few customers have purchased the deluxe spa services since they were introduced.

在聽過介紹後，還是沒什麼人購買豪華 SPA 服務。

2 a few 和 a little 也是**代名詞**兼**形容詞**，表示「**一些**」，通常用於**肯定句**中。a few 用於**可數名詞**，a little 用於**不可數名詞**。

The application takes a little work so plan your time accordingly.

申請要花一點功夫，所以你要好好安排時間。

There were a few applicants for the position. 這個職位有一些應徵者。

3 few、little、a few、a little 都可不接名詞，單獨存在，作為**代名詞**使用。

Everybody complained, but few of us failed the exam.

雖然大家都在抱怨，但我們之中只有少數幾個考試沒過。

Little of my homework has been finished. 我的作業都還沒做完。

Is there any apple juice left?
還有蘋果汁嗎？

There is a little left. 剩下一些。

Just a few will do. Thanks.
只要幾個就好，謝謝。

How many bags do you need?
妳需要幾個袋子？

4 few 和 little（不加 a）屬於較正式的用語，口語中，多用 not much、not many、only a little、only a few 和 hardly any 來表達「**不多**」、「**只有一點點**」。

如果要表示「**極少**」，較常用 very little 或 very few。

There is not much tea in the pot.

茶壺裡沒有多少茶了。

Not many people have shown up.

出席的人不怎麼多。

The typhoon knocked over very few trees. 颱風只吹倒了少數幾棵樹。

The refrigerator has very little food in it.

冰箱裡的食物少得可憐。

Practice

1

請勾選正確的答案。

1. It's raining heavily. There are ☐ few ☐ little people on the streets.

2. The chicken soup was so delicious. There is ☐ few ☐ little left.

3. Could you pull the curtain? We need ☐ little ☐ a little light in the room.

4. ☐ A few ☐ A little of us have come to the conference.

5. ☐ Few of ☐ Few of the runners could finish the marathon.

6. Jack put ☐ a few ☐ a little sugar in his coffee.

7. He also poured some cream into the coffee, but just ☐ little ☐ a little.

8. We still have ☐ little ☐ a little time. Let's get some souvenirs at the duty-free shop.

9. ☐ A few ☐ A few of the passengers are sitting in the transit lounge.

2

請將括弧內的動詞以正確的形式填空，完成句子。

Very little vinegar _____ (be poured) on the salad.

Very few students _____ (have solved) this math question.

Not many chickens _____ (be) able to fly.

There _____ (be) not much preservative in this hot sauce.

Only a little light _____ (penetrate) through the leaves.

Only a few plants _____ (survive) in a desert.

Unit 32

Both
Both

1 both 是**形容詞**,也是**代名詞**,意指「**兩者皆是**」,是一個具有複數意義的詞彙。both 作為**形容詞**時,會接**複數可數名詞**。

Both employees won awards for their performance.
兩名員工都因為工作表現良好獲得獎賞。
The boss had a picture taken with both winners of the contest.
老闆和比賽的兩名獲獎者都合拍了照片。

2 both 可以單獨使用,作為**代名詞**。此時,動詞要用**複數動詞**。

Peter and Clive were fighting in the hallway. Both were punished by the teacher.
彼德和克里夫因為在走廊打架,雙雙被老師處罰。
The orchestra is going to play the works of Beethoven and Bach. Both are my favorite musicians.
這個管弦樂團將演奏貝多芬和巴哈的作品,兩位都是我最喜愛的音樂家。

3 both 經常放在**主詞或受詞的後面**。

The two Australian players both entered the semifinals.
兩名澳洲選手雙雙挺進四強賽。
The human resources department required them both to take an aptitude test.
人事部要求他們兩位都要做性向測驗。

4 如果句中有助動詞或 be 動詞,則 both 會放在**助動詞或 be 動詞後面**。

They will both graduate this year.
他們兩個都將於今年畢業。
Rondo and Nick are both workaholics.
朗道和尼克都是工作狂。

5 both of 後面常接**帶有 the/these/my/your 等修飾詞的複數名詞**,這種情況下,**of** 也可以省略。

Both (of) the applicants have arrived.
兩位應徵者都已經到了。
Both (of) the vice presidents are being considered for the presidency of the company.
兩位副總裁都被列入考慮擔任公司的總裁。

6 both of 後面如果接的是 **you、us、them** 等複數代名詞,則 **of** 不可省略。

✗ The company invited both them for interviews.
✓ The company invited both of them for interviews.
公司請他們兩位都來面試。

7 「both . . . and . . .」這個用法,常用來**連結兩個詞彙或詞組**。

Grace contacted both the general manager and the executive director of the agency.
機關裡的總經理和執行長兩位,葛麗絲都聯絡了。

Practice

1

請勾選正確的答案，有些句子可能兩個答案皆適用。

1. My cousin has two boys, and ☐ both ☐ both of them love basketball.

2. I already asked ☐ both ☐ both of your aunt and uncle to come.

3. My parents ☐ both are ☐ are both teaching in secondary schools.

4. Both Jenny and Keith ☐ is athlete ☐ are athletes.

5. ☐ Both you ☐ Both of you should respect your parents.

6. ☐ Both ☐ Both of the ideas are wonderful.

7. ☐ Both concerts ☐ Concerts both will attract many people.

8. Both volleyball ☐ and ☐ or swimming are my favorite sports.

9. ☐ Both ☐ Both of my cousins are studying at law school.

10. Sandra and Chris are best friends. You should invite ☐ both them ☐ them both.

2

請依圖示，從框內選出適當的動詞，搭配 both，以正確的形式和語序填空，完成句子。

be violinists

have passed the exam

love fishing

be Russian Blue cats

be the best friends of human beings

can do the freestyle

Mike and James _____.

Wendy and Rita _____.

Mumu and Lulu _____.

Roger and Janet _____.

Ken and Tom _____.

Dogs and cats _____.

Unit 33

"Either" and "Neither"
Either 與 Neither

1 either 意指「**兩者之一**」，neither 意指「**兩者皆不**」，都是**形容詞**，也是**代名詞**。當形容詞時，後面都接**單數可數名詞**。

Either size **will work.** 兩種尺寸都可以用。
If neither scanner **can make five mega-pixel images, then find a different one.**

如果兩台掃描器都沒辦法掃出五百萬畫素的圖，那就再選別的。

2 either 和 neither 作為**代名詞**時，經常用 either of 和 neither of。它們後面都會接**帶有 the/these/my/your** 等修飾詞的複數可數名詞。

Will either of your **children be willing to help me plant flowers?**

你的兩個小孩有誰要幫我種花嗎？
Neither of the chairs **was comfortable.**

這兩張椅子都不好坐。

3 either of 和 neither of 後面也常接 **you、us、them** 等複數代名詞。

Can either of you **fix the washing machine?**

你們兩個人有誰可以把洗衣機修好嗎？
Neither of us **are repairmen.**

我們兩個都不是維修人員。

neither 的發音有兩種：[`ˈniðɚ]〔美式〕和 [`ˈnaɪðɚ]〔英式〕，但是並沒有規定何時要發哪一個音。選定一種發音後可以大膽說出來，不要將兩種發音混合使用，便可避免引起誤解。

4 either 不管是單獨使用，或者接**單數名詞**，或者「either of + 複數名詞」，動詞都用**單數動詞**。

Either was **possible in the beginning, but not now.**

兩種可能性一開始都有，但現在沒了。
Either of the writers has **the skill to do the job. Call one of them.**

兩位作者都能勝任這份工作，打電話給他們其中一個。

5 neither 如果單獨使用，或者接**單數名詞**，也是使用**單數動詞**。

但 neither of 接**複數可數名詞**時，可以用**單數動詞**，也可以用**複數動詞**，**單數動詞**多用於正式用語。

Neither is **strong enough to beat the boxing champion.**

兩位選手都不夠強壯，難以挑戰拳擊冠軍。
Neither machine **works.**

那兩台機器沒有一台是好的。
Neither of us know/knows **the answer.**

我們兩個都不知道答案。

6 常用句型：
either . . . or . . .（不是……就是……）
neither . . . nor . . .（不是……也不是……）

Herman indicated that either the order should be filled or the payment should be refunded. 赫曼指示，要不把訂單完成，要不就必須退費。
Neither getting a refund nor receiving the product **will address the underlying issues.**

不管是獲得退費或是收到產品，都不能解決潛在的問題。

Practice

1

請用 either、either of、neither 或 neither of 填空，完成句子。

1. My husband and I want to join you, but _____ us have the time.

2. We can leave on _____ Monday or Tuesday.

3. Can _____ your parents chaperone the school dance?

4. _____ withdraw the money from the ATM machine or write a check.

5. _____ us is hungry because we already ate.

6. _____ you pay now or you lose the chance.

7. _____ outbound nor inbound flights are going anywhere because of the typhoon.

2

請將括弧內的動詞以正確的形式填空，完成句子。

1. Neither of the fire lanterns _____ (be flying) high enough.

2. Neither book _____ (be) easy to read.

3. Most of the time the ducks _____ (be) either swimming or walking.

4. Neither of the tennis players _____ (have made) six double faults in this match.

5. Neither the Petronas Twin Towers nor the Taipei 101 _____ (be) taller than the Burj Khalifa.

6. Either espresso machine _____ (can make) good coffee.

7. You can choose between these two tables. Either of them _____ (be) fine with me.

None   All

1 all 指「所有的」，可作為**形容詞**，也可當**代名詞**。all 可修飾**複數可數名詞**和**不可數名詞**。
1 當 all 修飾**複數可數名詞**的時候，要用**複數動詞**；
2 當 all 修飾**不可數名詞**的時候，要用**單數動詞**。

All coins are stamped with a mint date.
所有的錢幣上面都刻有鑄幣日期。
All old money has some value to collectors.
對收藏家來說，所有的舊錢都有價值。

2 all 作為**代名詞**時，常搭配**關係子句**，意義等於 **everything** 或 **the only thing**。此時 all 如果作為**主詞**，要使用**單數動詞**。

The company has all (that) it needs to make money.
= The company has everything (that) it needs to make money.
公司要用來生財的東西都有了。
All I need is the address, not the phone number.
= The only thing I need is the address, not the phone number.
我需要的就只有地址，不要電話號碼。

3 all 經常放在**主詞或受詞的後面**。

Those sports cars all belong to Derek.
那些跑車都是德瑞克的。
I asked them all to go home.
我要他們全部都回家。

4 如果句中有助動詞或 be 動詞，則 all 會放在**助動詞或 be 動詞的後面**。

We must all finish our homework before we go to the party.
我們去參加派對之前，得都先寫完作業。
The tableware they sell is all silver.
他們賣的餐具全都是銀製品。

5 all of 後面常接**帶有 the/these/my/your 等修飾詞的複數名詞**，這種情況下，**of** 也可以省略。all (of) 後面也可接**不可數名詞**。

All (of) the people got on the bus.
所有人都上了公車。
Do you have all (of) the books I need?
你有我要的那些書嗎？

all of the books

6 all of 後面如果接的是 **you**、**us**、**them**、**it** 等代名詞，則 **of** 不可以省略。

Where is the chocolate milk? Did you drink all of it?
巧克力牛奶在哪裡？你全部喝光了嗎？
Janet told all of us about the procedures at the customs office. 珍娜把海關的所有程序都告訴我們每一個人了。

Practice

1

請勾選正確的答案，
有些句子可能兩個答
案皆適用。

1. Almost all kids ☐ love ☐ loves to visit the zoo.

2. ☐ Do ☐ Does women all love diamonds?

3. I put some cherries on the table. Have you eaten ☐ all them ☐ them all?

4. ☐ All ☐ All of pigeons can tell directions by instinct.

5. All I have ☐ is ☐ are three hundred dollars.

6. You ☐ should all ☐ all should arrive at the station by five.

7. ☐ All ☐ All of the developed countries have begun to make an effort to explore sustainable energy.

8. All wealth ☐ is ☐ are temporary.

9. Sammi bought all ☐ that was ☐ that were on the shelf.

10. Our effort ☐ all was ☐ was all in vain.

11. All ☐ is ☐ are good that ends well.

12. I gave you one hundred dollars. Did you spend ☐ it all ☐ all it?

2

請用 all 改寫句子。

1. I've sold everything I had.
   → ....

2. This lamb chop is the only one left.
   → ....

3. Do you have every book I requested?
   → ....

4. The only thing you've done right is marrying that woman.
   → ....

5. You will find everything you need in this outlet.
   → ....

6. Did you eat everything in the refrigerator?
   → ....

7. I looked up every word I didn't know in the dictionary.
   → ....

8. The only thing I read last week was *The Stolen Bicycle*.
   → ....

Unit 35

"All," "Every," and "Whole"
All、Every、Whole

1 all 和 every 都用來指「**一整個群體**」，同時意指「**全體裡的每一個成員**」。all 可以當**形容詞**，也可以當**代名詞**。every 則是只能當**形容詞**。

Mr. Smith bought all the roses in the flower shop.
史密斯先生買下花店裡所有的玫瑰花。

Derek bought every rose in the flower shop. 德瑞克買下花店裡的每一朵玫瑰花。

2 every 只用來修飾**單數可數名詞**，並且使用**單數動詞**。

I checked the date on every coin.
我查看了每一枚錢幣上面的日期。

Every citizen has his or her responsibility.
每位市民都有責任。

3 如果要指「**所有的人**」或「**所有的東西**」，會用 everybody 或 everything，而不常用單獨的 **all**。

✗ All got on the bus.
✓ All the people got on the bus. /
They all got on the bus.
所有的人都上了公車。／他們全都上了公車。

✗ All got off the train.
✓ Everybody got off the train. /
They all got off the train.
每一個人都下火車了。／他們全都下火車了。

✗ Did you get all on the list?
✓ Did you get everything on the list?
單子上列的所有東西你都準備好了嗎？

4 whole 表示「**事物的整體**」、「**事物的每一個部分**」，可以修飾**單數可數名詞**或**不可數名詞**。

The distributor shipped the whole order to the customer.
經銷商將所有的訂貨都運送給客戶。

Jill had to stay at the trade show the whole time. 吉兒得從頭到尾一直待在貿易展。

5 whole 的前面要加上 **the/this/my** 等修飾語，後面再接**名詞**。

Did you buy the whole set, or just part of it? 你買了一整套，還是只單買一部分？

I spent my whole vacation babysitting my sister's kids.
我整個假期都花在幫我姐姐帶孩子。

6 a whole 後面只能接**單數可數名詞**。

This is my first time to write a whole novel by myself.
這是我第一次獨力寫一整本小說。

7 all、every 和 whole 的意義比較：

all 表示「**整體**」	all day 整天 all morning 整個早上
every 表示「**頻率**」	every day 每天 every morning 每個早上
whole 強調「**完整**」，比 all 更具強調語氣。	the whole day 一整天 the whole morning 一整個早上

I like to listen to the radio all day.
我喜歡整天聽廣播。　　↳ 聽一整天

I like to listen to music every day.
我喜歡每天聽音樂。　　↳ 每天至少聽一次

I keep the TV on the whole day.
我讓電視一整天開著。　↳ 比 all day 強調

Practice

1

請勾選正確的答案。

1. ☐ All ☐ Every student likes vacation.
2. Matt loves ☐ all ☐ every classical music.
3. ☐ Everybody ☐ All enjoyed the concert tonight.
4. After ☐ everything ☐ all the help I gave you, you still didn't finish it.
5. Did you complete ☐ the whole ☐ all job?
6. I sent ☐ all the ☐ the whole thank-you letters.
7. Yesterday I spent ☐ all ☐ every day working on a book review.
8. My bowling league plays ☐ every ☐ all Wednesday night at 7:00.
9. ☐ Every one of ☐ Every your old friends has moved away.

2

請從框內選用適當的用語填空，完成句子。

all
every
whole

1. Have you changed the sheets and towels in _____ guest room?
2. The police searched the _____ building but found nothing.
3. _____ the strawberry milk on the rack has been sold out. Let's go to another supermarket.
4. I checked the expiration date on _____ bottle of milk and then picked the freshest one.
5. Did you write down _____ word I said?
6. Janice spent her _____ winter vacation taking driving lessons.
7. Dawn checked the _____ house, but she couldn't find her passport.
8. After I read _____ message on my cell phone, I deleted _____ of them.
9. Can you eat a _____ pizza by yourself?
10. I've bought _____ the items I need. Let's go home.

Unit 36

"No" and "None"
No 與 None

1 no 是**形容詞**，可以修飾**名詞**，表示「**沒有**」，等同於 not a 或 not any，但語氣更強烈。

There is no room in the trunk of the car.

= There is not any room in the trunk of the car.

後車廂已經沒有空間了。

There are no seats available on the 11:00 flight.

= There are not any seats available on the 11:00 flight.

11 點起飛的班機已經沒有座位了。

No appointments are available until July 5.

= There aren't any appointments available until July 5.

7 月 5 日之前的預約都滿了。

2 no 可以修飾**單數可數名詞**、**複數可數名詞**和**不可數名詞**。

Today Brian has no handkerchief in his pocket. 今天布萊恩口袋裡沒有放手帕。

Betty has no shoes under her bed.

貝蒂的床鋪底下沒有鞋子。

Anna has no space in her closet.

安娜的衣櫥裡已經沒有空間了。

3 none 是**代名詞**，意指「**沒有**」。none 不能當作**形容詞**，所以後面不能接名詞。

I checked to see if we had basil, but we had none.

我檢查了一下看我們還有沒有羅勒，不過一點都不剩了。

I will go buy some cumin if there is none in the spice rack.

如果放調味罐的架上沒有孜然了，我會去買一點回來。

4 none 後面如果需要接**名詞**，要使用 none of，同時後面的名詞要有**修飾語 the/this** 或 **my/your/his/her** 等所有格。

None of these cold medicines have helped. 這些感冒藥沒有一種有用。

None of my friends caught my cold.

我沒有朋友被我傳染感冒。

5 none of 後面如果接**不可數名詞**，那麼動詞就要用**單數動詞**。

None of the bread tastes good.

這些麵包都不好吃。

None of the sauce is spicy enough to go with the chicken.

這些醬料對這道雞肉來說都不夠辣。

6 none of 後面如果接**複數名詞**，那麼動詞可以用**單數**，也可以用**複數**。

None of my grandmother's home remedies have/has worked. 我外婆的那些家傳療法，沒有一種是有效的。

7 none 單獨使用時，如果是代替**複數名詞**（not any people or things），可以用**單數**或**複數動詞**。

Most of my classmates can speak good English, but none speaks/speak Spanish.

我班上大部分同學英語都講得很好，但是沒有人會說西班牙文。

cumin

Practice

1

請用 no 或 none 填空，完成句子。

1. We have _____ carry-on luggage.

2. _____ of my friends are on the trip.

3. There are _____ connecting flights.

4. I checked for taxies and _____ were available.

5. If there are _____ taxies, then we will have to rent a car.

2

請勾選正確的答案，有些句子可能有兩個適用的答案。

1. We have ☐ no ☐ none soy sauce left.

2. I was looking for coffee beans to make an espresso, but there were ☐ none ☐ none coffee beans.

3. ☐ None of plates ☐ None of the plates ☐ None plates are clean.

4. None of today's news ☐ is ☐ are exciting.

5. None of the books ☐ is ☐ are informative.

6. She gave me lots of excuses, but none ☐ was ☐ were acceptable.

7. No one ☐ want ☐ wants to go into the water first.

8. The sign says ☐ None Smoking ☐ No Smoking.

9. None of his ideas ☐ was ☐ were accepted.

3

請用 no 的句型改寫句子。

1. There isn't any milk in the refrigerator.
   → _____

2. She doesn't trust anyone but her sister.
   → _____

3. I don't have any money with me.
   → _____

4. There aren't any rooms available today in this hotel.
   → _____

5. There isn't any room for negotiation.
   → _____

Unit 37

"One" and "Ones"
One 與 Ones

1 為了避免重複使用兩次相同的名詞，可以在語意清楚的情況下，用 one/ones 取代**第二次出現的名詞**。one 用來取代**單數可數名詞**，ones 用來取代**複數可數名詞**。

The new boss is much nicer than the old one.
新老闆比以前的老闆和善多了。　= boss ↵

Which office is yours? Is it the one by the window?　↳ = office

你的辦公室是哪一間？窗戶旁邊的那一間嗎？

Bonnie likes her new coworkers more than the last ones. 邦妮喜歡她的新同事勝於之前的同事。
　↳ = coworkers

one/ones 不能代替**不可數名詞**。不可數名詞只能**重複出現**或**省略不用**。

• We have classical music, but we don't have any Baroque.
　↳ = Baroque music
我們有古典音樂，但是沒有任何巴洛克時代的音樂。

2 one 的前面除非有**形容詞**修飾，否則不能與 **a/an** 連用。

✗ I'm looking for a job, but not just any job. I'm looking for a one.

✓ I'm looking for a job, but not just any job. I'm looking for a good one.
我在找工作，但不是什麼工作都行，我要一份好工作。

✗ Are you going to take that job? I'm waiting for a one with a high salary.

✓ Are you going to take that job? I'm waiting for one with a higher salary.
你要接受那份工作嗎？
我在等薪水好一點的工作。

3 one 的前面常加 this、that，形成 this one 或 that one。但是 ones 的前面卻不能加 **these** 或 **those**，除非 ones 的前面還有**形容詞**。

You can have this one here or that one over there. 你可以拿這邊的這一個，或是那邊的那一個。

✗ I like these red apples more than those ones.

✓ I like these red apples more than those green ones.
我喜歡這些紅蘋果勝過那些青蘋果。

✗ I like those ties more than these ones.

✓ I like those ties more than these.
我比較喜歡那些領帶，比較不喜歡這些領帶。

4 which one 或 which ones 可以構成**疑問句**，用來詢問「**哪一個**」、「**哪一些**」。

There are two trails in the botanical garden. Which one do you want to take?

植物園裡有兩條路，你想走哪一條？

There are lots of books on this shelf. Which ones are yours?

這個架子上有很多書，哪些是你的？

5 each one of 用來強調「**個別性**」。

There are ten cacti on sale. Let's look at each one of them.

有十棵仙人掌在特價拍賣，我們每一棵都來看看吧。

Practice

1 請用 one 或 ones 填空，完成句子。

We have some extra sandwiches.
Would you like ....?

I like the hat with the chin strap more
than the other ....

Get the green grapes. They look better
than the purple ....

I don't want a large fish. Can you give
me a small ....?

My apartment is the largest ....
on the third floor.

I like those white plates more than the
colorful ....

Which shoes are yours?
Are yours the yellow ....?

Which puppy do you prefer? How about
the second .... from the left?

Unit 38

Indefinite Pronouns With Some-, Any-, Every-, No-
以 Some-、Any-、Every-、No- 開頭的不定代名詞

1 以 some-、any-、every-、no- 開頭的複合代名詞，是不定代名詞的大宗。

	some-	any-	every-	no-
-thing	something	anything	everything	nothing
-body	somebody	anybody	everybody	nobody
-one	someone	anyone	everyone	no one
-where	somewhere	anywhere	everywhere	nowhere

2 以 some- 和 any- 開頭的不定代名詞，在用法上的差別，和 **some**、**any** 完全一樣。

1 something/somebody/someone/somewhere 用於**肯定句**；

2 anything/anybody/anyone/anywhere 用於**否定句**和**疑問句**。

I want you to do something for me.
我想要你為我做一件事。

I do not want you to do anything for me.
我不要你為我做任何事。

Is there anywhere you want to go?
你想去什麼地方嗎？

3 如果一個問句「希望得到肯定的回答」，也就是期待對方回答 yes，就可以在**疑問句**中使用 something/somebody/someone/somewhere。

Are you looking for someone?
你在找什麼人嗎？

Would you like something to drink?
你要不要喝點什麼？

4 如果表「**無論何事**」、「**無論何地**」、「**無論何人**」都無所謂的時候，anything/anybody/anyone/anywhere 也可以用於**肯定句**。

With that monetary prize, you can travel anywhere you want.
有了這筆獎金，你想去哪裡旅遊都可以。

If you see anybody, please let me know.
如果你看到任何人，請通知我。

5 以 some-、any-、every-、no- 開頭的不定代名詞，都要使用**單數動詞**。

Somebody is looking for you.
有人在找你。

Everything was at the English department office.
所有的東西都在英語系辦公室。

6 這類不定代名詞的後面經常接「**加 to 的不定詞**」。

I have something to say.
我有話要說。

They've got nobody to rely on.
他們無依無靠。

7 everyone 和 every one 不同。

everyone 一定指「**人**」，只能單獨使用，後面不接 of 片語。

every one 可以指「**人**」或「**物**」，常**搭配 of 使用**。

Everyone had a good time in Shanghai.
每個人在上海都玩得很盡興。

Every one of the leather bags is handmade.
所有的皮包都是手工製的。

Practice

1

請從框內選出適當的「不定代名詞」填空，完成句子。部分提供詞彙可重複使用。

something

anybody

nobody

everybody

everything

anything

nothing

somewhere

anywhere

1. I don't want to go ＿＿＿＿＿＿＿＿ this weekend.

2. I want to go ＿＿＿＿＿＿＿＿ hot and exciting.

3. Didn't ＿＿＿＿＿＿＿＿ read the note I left on the table?

4. I called several times but ＿＿＿＿＿＿＿＿ was home.

5. I would like you to get me ＿＿＿＿＿＿＿＿ to drink.

6. I'm so hungry that I can eat ＿＿＿＿＿＿＿＿.

7. The gangster asked ＿＿＿＿＿＿＿＿ to put their hands on their head.

8. It was just an empty box with ＿＿＿＿＿＿＿＿ in it.

9. I'm sorry. There is ＿＿＿＿＿＿＿＿ I can reveal right now.

10. I've tried ＿＿＿＿＿＿＿＿ I can do to help him.

2

請依圖示，從框內選出適當的用語，以「to + V」的形式填空，完成句子。

play with

read

eat

talk to

drink

go

I'm thirsty. I'll have something ＿＿＿＿＿＿＿＿.

I'm bored. Do you have anything ＿＿＿＿＿＿＿＿?

I'm hungry. I need something ＿＿＿＿＿＿＿＿.

I feel sad. I need someone ＿＿＿＿＿＿＿＿.

I don't want to be alone. I want someone ＿＿＿＿＿＿＿＿.

I shouldn't have trusted this map. Now I have nowhere ＿＿＿＿＿＿＿＿.

Part 4 數量

38 以 **Some-**、**Any-**、**Every-**、**No-** 開頭的不定代名詞

Unit **39**

Introduction of Verb Tenses
動詞的時態介紹

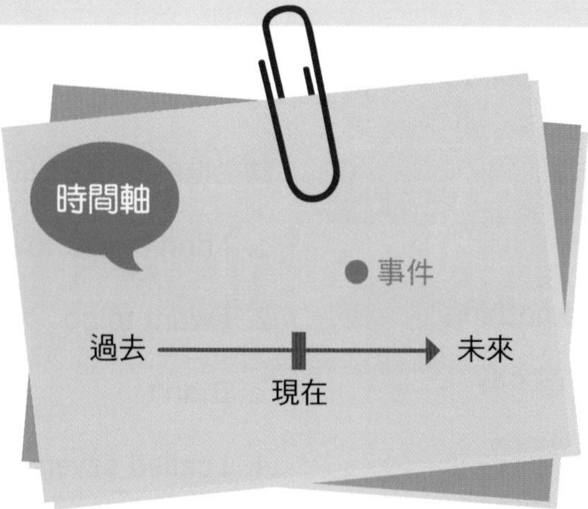

時間軸

● 事件

過去 ——————→ 未來
現在

1 **動詞**依照動作進行的時間，可分為現在式、過去式和未來式；依照動作進行的狀態，又可分為簡單式、進行式和完成式。

簡單　　　　　　　　　　　**進行**

現在

1 現在簡單式

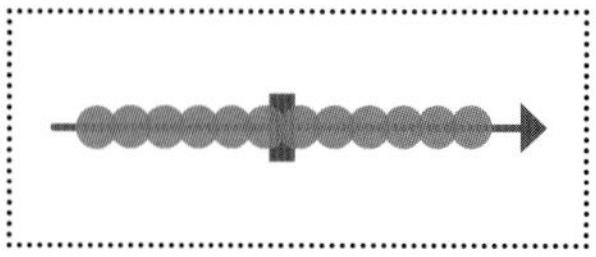

主詞 + 動詞現在式

Peter drives to work every weekday.
彼德每天開車去上班。

2 現在進行式

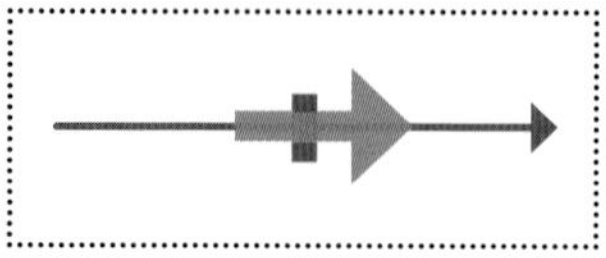

主詞 + am/is/are + 現在分詞（V-ing）

Andrew is writing a proposal to produce a series of household robots. 安德魯正在寫一份生產系列家用機器人的企畫。

過去

3 過去簡單式

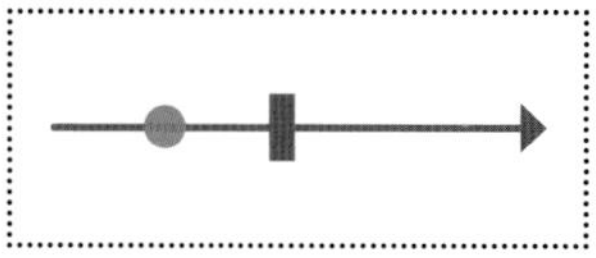

主詞 + 動詞過去式

Ann passed the exam.
安通過考試了。

4 過去進行式

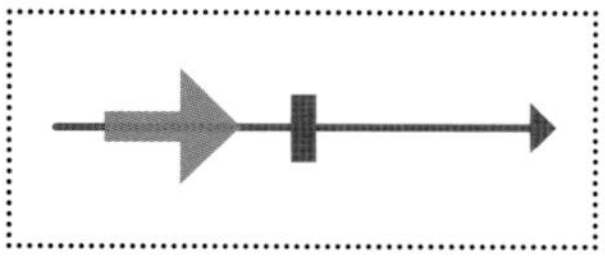

主詞 + was/were + 現在分詞（V-ing）

Vicky was cooking in the kitchen.
維琪那時正在廚房煮飯。

未來

5 未來簡單式

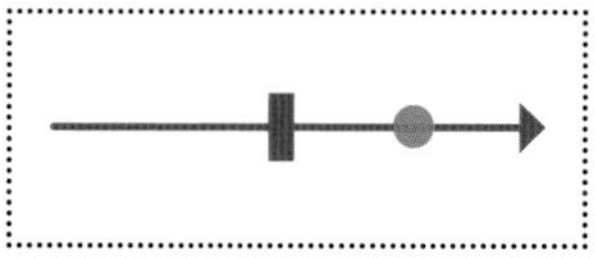

主詞 + will + 動詞原形

I will buy the tickets tomorrow.
我明天會去買票。

6 未來進行式

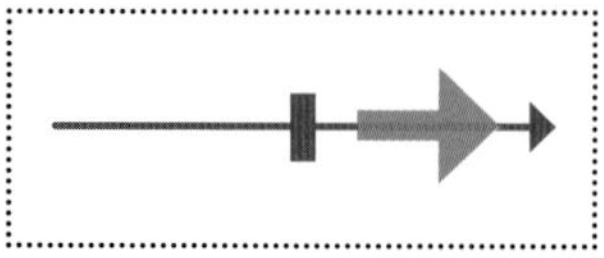

主詞 + will be + 現在分詞（V-ing）

Kevin will be watching a football game tomorrow night.
明天晚上凱文會看美式足球賽。

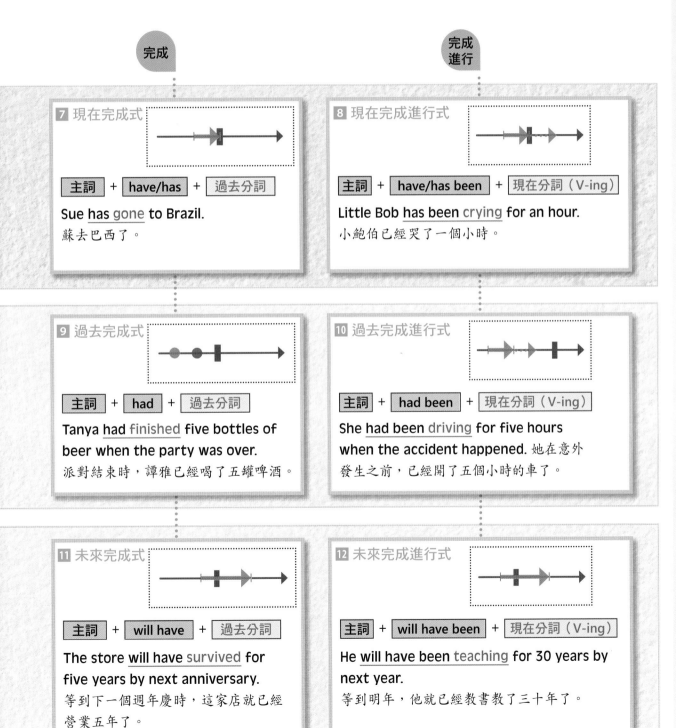

完成

完成
進行

7 現在完成式

主詞 + have/has + 過去分詞

Sue has gone to Brazil.
蘇去巴西了。

8 現在完成進行式

主詞 + have/has been + 現在分詞（V-ing）

Little Bob has been crying for an hour.
小鮑伯已經哭了一個小時。

9 過去完成式

主詞 + had + 過去分詞

Tanya had finished five bottles of
beer when the party was over.
派對結束時，譚雅已經喝了五罐啤酒。

10 過去完成進行式

主詞 + had been + 現在分詞（V-ing）

She had been driving for five hours
when the accident happened. 她在意外
發生之前，已經開了五個小時的車了。

11 未來完成式

主詞 + will have + 過去分詞

The store will have survived for
five years by next anniversary.
等到下一個週年慶時，這家店就已經
營業五年了。

12 未來完成進行式

主詞 + will have been + 現在分詞（V-ing）

He will have been teaching for 30 years by
next year.
等到明年，他就已經教書教了三十年了。

Unit 40

Present Simple Tense
現在簡單式

● 事件

過去 ●●●●●●●●●●●● → 未來
現在

Form 構句

肯定句的句型	I/you/we/they listen
	he/she/it listens

否定句的句型	I/you/we/they do not listen
	he/she/it does not listen

否定句的縮寫	I/you/we/they don't listen
	he/she/it doesn't listen

疑問句的句型	Do I/you/we/they listen?
	Does he/she/it listen?

Use 用法

1 現在簡單式可用來表示「**習慣**」和「**重複發生的行為**」。

We recycle cans and bottles once a month.
我們每月回收一次瓶罐。

He commutes downtown every weekday.
他每個工作日都要通勤往來市中心。

The news always finishes at 11:30 p.m.
新聞都在晚上 11 點 30 分播報完畢。

Do you visit relatives in the South every Chinese New Year?
你每年農曆春節都會到南部探望親戚嗎？

2 現在簡單式可以用來說明「**長期持續不變的情況**」，也就是說，過去如此、現在如此，未來也如此。

Typhoons come every year.
每年都會颳颱風。

Grandmother comes every winter.
外婆每年冬天都會來。

3 現在簡單式可以用來說明「**一件事實**」或「**正確無誤的事**」。

Julie graduates this year. 茱莉今年畢業。

Politicians fear the truth. 政客畏懼真相。

4 現在簡單式經常和一些頻率副詞搭配，形容「**規律發生的事件**」，同時指出到底「**多常發生**」。

頻率副詞
- always
- usually
- often
- sometimes
- never
- every day
- every year

My mother always cooks me breakfast.
我媽媽都會幫我準備早餐。

Jack gets up early every morning, and he is never late for school.
傑克每天早上都很早起，而且上學從不遲到。

5 現在簡單式也可以用來表示「**未來將會發生的事**」，並且是按照時刻表和計劃表「**安排好的事**」。

The client arrives at 2:00 tomorrow afternoon. 客戶將於明天下午 2 點抵達。

The train to Kyoto departs at 6 p.m.
往京都的火車於晚上 6 點發車。

What time does the earliest flight to Hong Kong leave?
飛往香港的班機最早的是幾點？

Practice

1

請將括弧內的動詞以「現在簡單式」填空，完成對話。

1. Q _____ you _____ (shave) every morning?
   A Yes, I _____ (shave) every morning after taking a shower.

2. Q _____ the café _____ (open) at 8 a.m.?
   A No, it _____ (open) at 9 a.m.

3. Q _____ whales _____ (migrate) to warm waters every winter?
   A Yes, whales _____ (migrate) to warm waters every winter.

4. Q _____ Brandon _____ (come) from England?
   A Yes, he _____ (come) from England.

5. Q How often _____ Brandon _____ (return) to England?
   A He _____ (return) once every couple of years.

6. Q _____ Jessie _____ (eat) pinto beans?
   A No, she _____ (not eat) pinto beans.

7. Q How many kilometers _____ you _____ (drive) to work?
   A I _____ (drive) 10 kilometers to my office every day.

8. Q Why _____ John _____ (feel) bad?
   A He _____ (feel) bad about yesterday's car accident.

9. Q When _____ the earliest MRT train _____ (depart)?
   A The earliest train _____ (depart) at 6 a.m.

10. Q How often _____ you _____ (check out) books from a library?
    A I _____ (check out) books from a library once a week.

2

請將括弧內的動詞以「現在簡單式」填空，完成句子。

1. Fran _____ (like) peanut butter and banana sandwiches.

2. Alice and Larry _____ (prepare) their food at home every night.

3. Aunt Sue _____ (live) in a cabin in the woods.

4. We _____ (not raise) pigs anymore.

5. _____ Emma _____ (study) hard?

6. It _____ (take) hours on high heat to roast a turkey.

7. Bernie always _____ (finish) eating before anybody else.

8. Fay always _____ (pay) her cell phone bill at the FamilyMart around the corner.

9. The sea level _____ (rise) gradually.

Unit 41

Present Continuous Tense
現在進行式

● 事件

過去 ————→ 未來
現在

Form 構句

肯定句的句型	I am studying
	you/we/they are studying
	he/she/it is studying
肯定句的縮寫	I'm studying
	you/we/they 're studying
	he/she/it 's studying
否定句的句型	I am not studying
	you/we/they are not studying
	he/she/it is not studying
否定句的縮寫	I'm not studying
	you/we/they aren't studying
	he/she/it isn't studying
疑問句的句型	Am I studying?
	Are you/we/they studying?
	Is he/she/it studying?

Use 用法

1 現在進行式用來說明「說話當時正在進行的動作」。

Mavis: What are you doing?
Steve: I am peeling potatoes.
Mavis: Are you cooking dinner?
Steve: Of course, I am cooking dinner. Why else would I be cooking potatoes?

梅菲絲：你在做什麼？
史帝夫：我在削馬鈴薯皮。
梅菲絲：你在準備晚餐嗎？
史帝夫：沒錯！我正在做晚餐。不然我何必煮馬鈴薯呢？

2 現在進行式可以用來說明「**目前這段期間在發生的事**」或「**某人目前的狀態**」，不必然是說話當下正在進行的動作。

Sam is looking for an apartment in Tokyo at this moment.
山姆現在正在找一間東京的公寓。
You're working very hard these days.
這些日子你很努力工作。

3 現在進行式可以用來說明「**正在改變或進展的事物**」。

It's getting cold at night. 晚上天氣變冷了。
Cell phones are rapidly adding new features. 手機正迅速發展出新的功能。

4 現在進行式有時用來表示「**已經安排好、未來將會發生的事**」。

I am visiting Bert and Ernie on Saturday.
我星期六將會去拜訪柏特和爾尼。
He's flying to Los Angeles on a business trip next Monday.
他下星期一要搭機前往洛杉磯出差。

5 現在進行式經常和頻率副詞 always 連用，表示「**總是、經常在做的事**」。

She's always vacationing in some exotic spots.
她總是到一些充滿異國風情的地方度假。
He's always making promises that cannot be fulfilled. 他老是在做一些無法實現的承諾。

6 有些動詞不能使用**現在進行式**（詳見 Unit 43 說明）。

✗ I am liking strawberry jam.
✓ I like strawberry jam.
我喜歡草莓果醬。
✗ I am knowing Jane Robinson.
✓ I know Jane Robinson.
我認識珍‧羅賓森。

Practice

1

請將括弧中的動詞以「現在進行式」填空，完成句子。

1. The global climate _____ (get) warmer every year.

2. I _____ (send) you the contract via email.

3. _____ you _____ (practice) your golf swing?

4. Tony _____ (apply for) a management job.

5. The government _____ (carry out) an environmental policy.

6. Pam _____ (sell) bubble milk tea at the night market.

7. Joe _____ (go) to a movie with his girlfriend on Saturday.

8. The crowd _____ (wait) for the President in the square.

9. Who _____ (bring) the pizza and soft drinks tonight?

10. Denise _____ (have) a birthday party on Sunday night.

11. I _____ (fly) to Osaka next Tuesday.

12. The kids _____ (enjoy) the sun on the beach.

13. Meg _____ (rock) the baby to sleep.

14. I _____ (write) a book about imaginary creatures.

15. My hair _____ (grow) white, but I _____ (not work) harder.

2

請依圖示，從框內選出適當的動詞，用「be + always + V-ing」的句型填空，完成句子。

mess

work

lose

jump

1

He _____ up and down on the bed.

2

He _____ at the computer.

3

He _____ up the bathroom.

4

He _____ his cell phone.

Unit 42

Comparison Between the Present Simple and the Present Continuous

「現在簡單式」與「現在進行式」的比較

比較

Are you drinking your soy milk now? ↳ 現在進行式

你正在喝豆漿嗎？

Do you drink soy milk for breakfast every morning? ↳ 現在簡單式

你每天早餐都喝豆漿嗎？

1 現在進行式用來表示「說話當時正在進行的事」。

It is snowing outside now.
現在外面正下著雪。

Are you eating your dumplings?
你正在吃水餃嗎？

現在簡單式用來表達「習慣、重複發生的行為」。

Do you cook at home every night?
你每晚都在家煮飯嗎？
He swears too much.
他滿口粗話。

2 現在進行式用來表示「目前暫時發生的情況」。

I'm wearing a tie because I have a job interview. 我現在打著領帶，是因為我要去面試應徵工作。

現在簡單式用來表達「長期維持不變的狀況」。

She always has breakfast at the same café.
她每天都在同一家咖啡店吃早餐。

3 現在進行式和現在簡單式，都可以用來表示「未來將會發生的事」。

Are we planning to visit your mother this weekend?

我們這個週末要去拜訪你媽媽嗎？

Do we plan to visit your aunt next week?

我們下星期要去拜訪你阿姨嗎？

Practice

1

請勾選正確的答案。

1. The sausages ☐ burn ☐ are burning.

2. Flowers ☐ are blooming ☐ bloom in the spring.

3. I ☐ eat ☐ am eating now because I missed breakfast.

4. I ☐ am hiding ☐ hides because the boss is looking for me.

5. ☐ Is Lonny reading ☐ Does Lonny read a newspaper now?

6. I ☐ often watch ☐ am often watching movies late at night.

7. ☐ Do you play ☐ Are you playing football every Saturday morning?

8. People ☐ are traveling ☐ travel overseas every year.

2

請將括弧內的動詞以「現在進行式」或「現在簡單式」填空，完成句子。

1. Julia _____ (weed) the garden now.
   She _____ (weed) the garden twice a week.

2. Do not go out because it _____ (rain) heavily outside.
   It _____ (rain) a lot this time of year.

3. Susan _____ (check) her emails right now.
   She _____ (receive) a lot of emails every day.

4. We _____ (take) the bus home now.
   We _____ (take) the bus home after work every day.

3

請將括弧內的動詞以「現在簡單式」或「現在進行式」填空，完成句子。並且從框內選出該用法的依據，填入句子後面的空格內。

Ⓐ 事實或正確無誤的事　　Ⓒ 說話當時正在進行的事　　Ⓔ 已經安排好、未來將會發生的事
Ⓑ 習慣或重複發生的行為　Ⓓ 目前這段時間在發生的事　Ⓕ 正在改變或進展的事物

1. The atmosphere of Mars ___consists___ (consist) of 95% carbon dioxide. → __A__

2. I _____ (take) a yoga class this month. → _____

3. I _____ (not eat) meat. I'm a vegetarian. → _____

4. Africa's climate _____ (change) dramatically due to global warming. → _____

5. I can't answer the phone right now because I _____ (play) video games. → _____

6. I _____ (attend) Professor Whelan's speech tomorrow. → _____

7. The Moon _____ (orbit) the Earth. → _____

8. My English _____ (get) better and better. → _____

9. Jessie _____ (sit) in the yard with her dog and _____ (enjoy) the sunshine every morning. → _____

10. I _____ (teach) two elementary courses and one advanced course this semester. → _____

Unit 43

Verbs Not Used in the Continuous Forms
不能用於進行式的動詞

1 有些動詞不能用於**進行式**，只能用於**簡單式**。描述「思想」的動詞，通常不能用於**進行式**。

- doubt
- see
- imagine
- believe
- recognize
- forget
- understand
- suppose
- mean
- know
- remember
- realize

✗ I am knowing the answer to the question.

✓ I know the answer to the question.
我知道這個問題的答案。

✗ Are you knowing Janet's phone number?

✓ Do you know Janet's phone number?
你知道珍娜的電話號碼嗎？

2 see 和 hear 屬於「非刻意進行的動作」，也不用於**進行式**。

When I was at Gail's apartment, I saw her new painting.
我去蓋兒的公寓時，看到了她的新畫作。

When I lay in bed at night, I heard my parents talk.
深夜我躺在床上時，聽到父母親的談話。

listen、look 和 watch 則屬於「刻意進行的動作」，可以用於**進行式**。

I am listening to the song. Wait until it's finished. 我正在聽這首歌，先等我聽完。

Are you looking at that photo album? I'd like to look at it when you're finished.
你在看那本相簿嗎？等你看完，我也想要看。

3 描述「感受」的動詞，通常不能用於**進行式**。

- like
- dislike
- love
- hate
- prefer
- want
- wish

✗ Jean is loving this song.

✓ Jean loves this song.
琴很愛這首歌。

✗ Beth is not wanting a pet.

✓ Beth does not want a pet.
貝絲不想養寵物。

感官動詞和說明「思想」的動詞，如 see、hear 和 understand，常常搭配 can 或 could 使用。

Scott can see the whole office from his desk.
史考特從他的書桌，能看到整間辦公室。

Meredith could hear her grandmother snoring.
梅麗狄絲可以聽到祖母在打呼。

Louis can remember everybody's name.
路易斯能記住每個人的名字。

4 以下動詞，通常也不使用**進行式**。

- exist
- need
- consist of
- own
- include
- sound
- belong
- cost
- seem
- owe
- constrain
- deserve

✗ Are you owning a 3-in-1 printer, scanner, fax machine?

✓ Do you own a 3-in-1 printer, scanner, fax machine?
你有影印、掃描、傳真三合一的事務機嗎？

✗ Dan is not needing any more new clothes.

✓ Dan does not need any more new clothes.
丹不需要更多新衣服了。

Practice

1

請勾選正確的答案。

1. I □ am recognizing □ recognize your face.
2. He □ is not liking □ does not like durian ice cream.
3. I □ am having □ have my own bicycle.
4. Give me a minute. I □ think □ am thinking about it.
5. □ Are you believing □ Do you believe his guarantee?
6. Emma □ heard □ was hearing her neighbors arguing.
7. Be quiet. I □ am listening □ listen to an important news report.
8. Sarah □ deserves □ is deserving a holiday after such hard work.

2

哪些動詞通常用於簡單式而不用於進行式？請從框內選出適當的動詞，用「現在簡單式」填空，完成下列描述各個圖片的句子。

| cost | prefer | belong | exist | know | weigh | own | include | forget |

1
Life _____ (not) on Saturn.

2
The jeans _____ $80.

3
Tammy always _____ her credit card password.

4
The spa set _____ essential oil, bath salt, and handmade lavender soap.

5
Johnny _____ every animal in the picture book.

6
The family _____ a black SUV.

7
Which _____ you _____, fruit or cake?

8
The peppers _____ 500 grams.

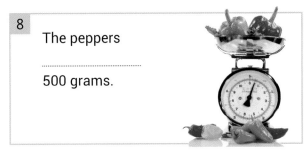

Part 5　現在式　43 不能用於進行式的動詞

95

Unit 44

Verbs Used in the Present Simple and the Present Continuous With Different Meanings

用於「現在簡單式」與「現在進行式」意義不同的動詞

---

see see 指「明白」的時候，只能用於**簡單式**；指「會見」的時候，則可以用於**進行式**。

現在簡單式	現在進行式
Do **you** see **my point of view?** 你明白我的觀點嗎？	Are **you** seeing **your doctor tomorrow?** 你明天要去看醫生嗎？

look look 指「**看起來**」時，只能用於**簡單式**；指「**尋找**」或「**看**」時，則可以用於**進行式**。

現在簡單式	現在進行式
It looks **like a good job.** 這似乎是個很好的工作。	Eric **is** looking **for a job.** 艾瑞克在找工作。

smell smell 指「**聞起來**」或「**聞到**」時，只能用於**簡單式**；指「**嗅聞**」時，則可以用於**進行式**。

現在簡單式	現在進行式
Do **you** smell **the bread in the oven?** 你聞到烤箱裡的麵包香味了嗎？	The chef **is** smelling **the beef stew on the plate.** 廚師在聞盤內的燉牛肉。

taste taste 指「**嚐起來**」時，只能用於**簡單式**；指「**品嚐**」時，則可以用於**進行式**。

現在簡單式	現在進行式
The soup tastes **better with some rosemary.** 這湯加了迷迭香之後，喝起來更美味。	The sommelier **is** tasting **the 1944 wine.** 這名品酒師正在品嚐1944年分的葡萄酒。

feel feel 指「**摸起來給人某種感覺**」或「**認為、覺得**」時，只能用於**簡單式**；指「**觸摸**」或「**感覺**」時，則可以用於**進行式**。

現在簡單式	現在進行式
This silk shirt feels **so soft.** 這件絲質襯衫摸起來好柔軟。	I'm feeling **woozy.** (= I feel woozy.) 我覺得頭暈不舒服。

be 動詞 be 通常用於**簡單式**；當動詞 be 指「**（刻意）表現**」時，則可用於**進行式**。

現在簡單式	現在進行式
He **is** cool. 他很酷。	He **is being** cool. 他表現得很酷。

have have 指「**擁有**」時，只能用於**簡單式**；指「**進行某動作**」時，則可用於**進行式**。

現在簡單式	現在進行式
She has **many antiques.** 她有很多古董。	She **is having a** sandwich. 她正在吃三明治。

weigh weigh 指「**秤起來多重**」時，只能用於**簡單式**；指「**秤某物的重量**」時，則可用於**進行式**。

現在簡單式	現在進行式
These oranges weigh **2 kilograms.** 這些柳橙秤起來有兩公斤重。	The clerk **is** weighing **the Chinese herbs.** 店員正在秤這些中藥的重量。

Practice

1

請勾選正確的答案。

1. Your idea ☐ sounds ☐ is sounding very good.

2. He ☐ cannot see ☐ is not seeing the words in the book without his glasses.

3. This apartment ☐ looks ☐ is looking old.

4. Sandpaper ☐ is feeling ☐ feels rough.

5. He ☐ is ☐ is being late for his lunch meeting.

6. He ☐ has ☐ is having a shower.

7. Raymond ☐ is looking after ☐ looks after his sick dad in the hospital now.

8. I have a stuffed nose. I ☐ can't smell ☐ am not smelling anything.

2

請依據題意，將括弧內的動詞以「現在簡單式」或「現在進行式」填空，完成句子。

1

Johnny _____ (look) at
a butterfly. The butterfly _____
(look) beautiful.

2

Mom and Ginny _____ (taste)
the soup. The soup _____ (taste)
delicious.

3

Kelly _____ (smell)
the flowers. The flowers in her hands
_____ (smell) good.

4

Sandy _____ (feel) the cotton
towels. The cotton towels _____
(feel) soft.

5

Tina _____
(weigh) herself.
David is eager to know
how much she _____
(weigh).

6

Jessica _____ (have)
some chocolate.
She _____ (have)
lots of chocolate in her
refrigerator.

Unit 45

Past Simple Tense
過去簡單式

● 事件

過去 ──●──┃──→ 未來
　　　　　　現在

Form 構句

肯定句的句型	I/you/he/she/it/we/they walked
否定句的句型	I/you/he/she/it/we/they did not walk
否定句的縮寫	I/you/he/she/it/we/they didn't walk
疑問句的句型	Did I/you/he/she/it/we/they walk?

1 規則動詞的過去式和過去分詞拼法一樣，構成也有規則可循：

1 大多數規則動詞，直接在字尾加上 ed。
- talk → talked 說話
- enjoy → enjoyed 享受

2 字尾是 e 的規則動詞，只要加 d。
- like → liked 喜歡
- phone → phoned 打電話

3 字尾是「子音 + y」的動詞，先刪除 y，再加 ied。
- study → studied 學習；研讀
- empty → emptied 清空

4 字尾是「單母音 + 單子音」的動詞，要重覆字尾，再加 ed。
- dim → dimmed 使模糊
- stop → stopped 停止

2 不規則動詞的過去式和過去分詞則要逐一牢記。詳見《Unit 46 不規則動詞表》。

- come → came → come 來
- drive → drove → driven 駕駛
- hit → hit → hit 打

Use 用法

3 過去簡單式用來形容「**過去的行為和情況**」，經常和一些表示「**過去意義**」的副詞或副詞片語連用。

- yesterday
- last month
- last night
- last year
- last week
- a year ago

He visited his aunt last weekend.
上週末他去拜訪阿姨。
They bought a house last year.
去年他們買了一棟房子。
I did not go to work last week.
我上星期沒上班。
The team did not lose the game last night.
這個隊伍昨晚並沒有輸掉比賽。
Did you drive here by yourself yesterday?
你昨天自己開車來的嗎？
Did Tina graduate from high school last month? 蒂娜上個月高中畢業了嗎？

4 過去簡單式常用來「**講故事**」。

A hundred years ago, our ancestors immigrated to this land and built up our farmstead. They started growing coffee soon after that and made their living by selling high quality coffee beans.

一百年前，我們的祖先來到這片土地，建立了我們這個莊園。
不久後，他們開始種植咖啡，靠販售高品質咖啡豆維生。

Practice

1

請將括弧內的動詞以「過去簡單式」填空，完成右列段落。

Ludwig van Beethoven ❶＿＿＿＿ (be) born in Germany on December 17th, 1770. His father ❷＿＿＿＿ (give) him piano lessons at the age of five. His father ❸＿＿＿＿ (hope) his son was a child genius like Mozart. As a teenager, Beethoven ❹＿＿＿＿ (work) as a court musician. He also ❺＿＿＿＿ (play) in theaters and churches. Beethoven ❻＿＿＿＿ (compose) his first music in his late teens. By the age of 25, he ❼＿＿＿＿ (earn) a living from performing, composing, and teaching music. Beethoven ❽＿＿＿ (lose) his hearing in 1801. He ❾＿＿＿ (write) his most important symphonies after he became deaf. Beethoven ❿＿＿＿ (die) on March 26th, 1827.

2

請將括弧內的動詞以正確的時態填空，完成對話。

Bob: I ❶＿＿＿＿ (call) you yesterday, but you were not home.

Sue: I ❷＿＿＿＿ (go) to the fashion district.

Bob: ❸＿＿＿＿ you ＿＿＿＿ (spend) a lot of money?

Sue: Well, I ❹＿＿＿ (see) some great shoes.

Bob: ❺＿＿＿ you ＿＿＿ (get) a pair?

Sue: No, I ❻＿＿＿ not ＿＿＿＿ (buy) any shoes.

Bob: ❼＿＿＿ you ＿＿＿＿ (pick up) any nylons?

Sue: No, but I ❽＿＿＿＿ (buy) four pairs of socks.

Bob: ❾＿＿＿ you ＿＿＿ (need) socks?

Sue: Yes, I ❿＿＿＿ (need) some socks.

Bob: How much ⓫＿＿＿ you ＿＿＿ (pay)?

Sue: I ⓬＿＿＿ (get) four pairs for $100.

Bob: ⓭＿＿＿ you ＿＿＿ (buy) them on sale?

Sue: No, I ⓮＿＿＿＿ (bargain) with the saleswoman.

Bob: You don't usually bargain with salespeople. You usually avoid arguing about prices.

Sue: But this time I did. I ⓯＿＿＿＿ (get) her to lower the price from $200.

Bob: Good job! Let's go see that saleswoman. I need some socks, too.

Unit 46

List of Irregular Verbs 不規則動詞表

📌 三態同形

📌 不同的意義下，有不同的過去式與過去分詞。

arise	arose	arisen	升起
awake	awoke	awoken	喚醒
be	was/were	been	be 動詞
📌 bear	bore	borne	承受；生孩子
	bore	born	誕生
beat	beat	beaten	打
become	became	become	變成
begin	began	begun	開始
behold	beheld	beheld	看見
bend	bent	bent	彎曲
📌 bet	bet	bet	打賭
📌 bid	bid	bid	出價
bind	bound	bound	綑綁
bite	bit	bitten	咬
bleed	bled	bled	流血
blow	blew	blown	吹
break	broke	broken	打破
breed	bred	bred	使繁殖
bring	brought	brought	帶來
📌 broadcast	broadcast	broadcast	廣播
build	built	built	建造
burn	burned/burnt	burned/burnt	燃燒
📌 burst	burst	burst	爆炸
📌 bust	bust/busted	bust/busted	使失敗
buy	bought	bought	買
📌 cast	cast	cast	投擲
catch	caught	caught	抓住
choose	chose	chosen	選擇
cling	clung	clung	黏著
come	came	come	來
📌 cost	cost	cost	花費
creep	crept	crept	躡手躡腳地走
📌 cut	cut	cut	切
deal	dealt	dealt	處理
dig	dug	dug	挖掘
dive	美 dived/dove	dived/dove	潛水
	英 dived	dived	
do	did	done	做
draw	drew	drawn	畫
dream	dreamed/dreamt	dreamed/dreamt	做夢
drink	drank	drunk	喝
drive	drove	driven	駕駛
dwell	dwelled/dwelt	dwelled/dwelt	居住
eat	ate	eaten	吃
fall	fell	fallen	落下
feed	fed	fed	餵養

feel	felt	felt	摸；感覺
fight	fought	fought	打架
find	found	found	找到
📌 fit	美 fitted/fit	fitted/fit*	合身
	英 fitted	fitted	
flee	fled	fled	逃
fling	flung	flung	用力丟
📌 fly	flew	flown	飛
	flied	flied	擊出高飛球
forbid	forbade	forbidden	禁止
📌 forecast	forecast/ forecasted	forecast/ forecasted	預測
foresee	foresaw	foreseen	預見
forget	forgot	forgotten	忘記
forgive	forgave	forgiven	原諒
forsake	forsook	forsaken	拋棄
freeze	froze	frozen	結冰
get	美 got	gotten	得到
	英 got	got	
give	gave	given	給
go	went	gone	去
grind	ground	ground	磨碎
grow	grew	grown	成長
📌 hang	hanged	hanged	絞死
	hung	hung	懸掛
have/has	had	had	擁有
hear	heard	heard	聽見
hide	hid	hidden	躲藏
📌 hit	hit	hit	打
hold	held	held	握著
📌 hurt	hurt	hurt	傷害
📌 input	input	input	輸入
keep	kept	kept	持有
kneel	美 kneeled/knelt	kneeled/knelt	跪下
	英 knelt	knelt	
📌 knit	knitted	knitted	編織
	knit	knit	接合
know	knew	known	知道
lay	laid	laid	放置
lead	led	led	引導
lean	美 leaned	leaned	傾身
	英 leaned/leant	leaned/leant	
leap	美 leaped	leaped	跳躍
	英 leapt	leapt	
learn	美 learned	learned	學習
	英 learned/learnt	learned/learnt	
leave	left	left	離開；遺留
lend	lent	lent	借給
📌 let	let	let	讓

原形	過去式	過去分詞	中文
lie	lay	lain	躺
light	lighted/lit	lighted/lit	點燃;照亮
lose	lost	lost	遺失
make	made	made	製造
mean	meant	meant	意指
meet	met	met	遇到
mislead	misled	misled	誤導
mistake	mistook	mistaken	弄錯
mow	mowed	mowed/mown	割草
outdo	outdid	outdone	勝過
output	output	output	輸出
overcome	overcame	overcome	克服
overeat	overate	overeaten	吃太飽
overhear	overheard	overheard	無意中聽到
oversleep	overslept	overslept	睡過頭
overthrow	overthrew	overthrown	推翻
pay	paid	paid	支付
plead	美 pleaded/pled / 英 pleaded	pleaded/pled / pleaded	懇請;辯護
proofread ['prufrid]	proofread ['prufrɛd]	proofread ['prufrɛd]	校對
prove	美 proved / 英 proved	proved/proven / proved	證明
put	put	put	放
quit	美 quit / 英 quit/quitted	quit / quit/quitted	放棄;辭職
read [rid]	read [rɛd]	read [rɛd]	閱讀
relay	relaid	relaid	轉達
repay	repaid	repaid	償還
reset	reset	reset	重置
rid	rid	rid	使免除
ride	rode	ridden	乘坐
ring	rang	rung	使成環形
rise	rose	risen	上升
run	ran	run	跑
saw	美 sawed / 英 sawed	sawn/sawed / sawn	鋸開
say	said	said	說
see	saw	seen	看見
seek	sought	sought	尋找
sell	sold	sold	賣
send	sent	sent	寄;送
set	set	set	放;豎立
sew	sewed	sewed/sewn	縫補
shake	shook	shaken	搖
shed	shed	shed	流出
shine	shone / shined	shone / shined	發光 / 擦亮
shoot	shot	shot	發射
show	showed	shown/showed	顯示;陳列
shrink	shrank/shrunk	shrunk	收縮
shut	shut	shut	關閉
sing	sang	sung	唱
sink	sank	sunk	下沉
sit	sat	sat	坐
sleep	slept	slept	睡覺
slide	slid	slid	滑動
smell	美 smelled / 英 smelt	smelled / smelt	嗅聞;聞到
sow	sowed	sowed/sown	播種
speak	spoke	spoken	說話
speed	speeded/sped	speeded/sped	迅速前進
spell	spelled/spelt	spelled/spelt	拼字
spend	spent	spent	花費
spill	美 spilled / 英 spilt	spilled / spilt	濺出;溢出
spin	spun	spun	旋轉
spit	美 spit / 英 spat	spit / spat	吐;吐痰
split	split	spilt	劈開
spoil	美 spoiled / 英 spoilt	spoiled / spoilt	搞砸;寵壞
spread	spread	spread	散布
spring	美 sprang/sprung / 英 sprang	sprung / sprung	跳
stand	stood	stood	站立
steal	stole	stolen	偷
stick	stuck	stuck	黏貼;釘住
sting	stung	stung	刺;螫;叮
stink	stank/stunk	stank/stunk	發臭
stride	strode	stridden	邁大步走
strike	struck	struck/stricken	攻擊
string	strung	strung	(用線繩)紮
swear	swore	sworn	發誓;咒罵
sweat	sweat/sweated	sweat/sweated	流汗
sweep	swept	swept	清掃
swim	swam	swum	游泳
swing	swung	swung	搖擺
take	took	taken	拿
teach	taught	taught	教
tear	tore	torn	撕裂
tell	told	told	告訴
think	thought	thought	想
throw	threw	thrown	丟
thrust	thrust	thrust	刺
tread	trod	trodden/trod	踩
understand	understood	understood	理解
undertake	undertook	undertaken	著手做
undo	undid	undone	解開;取消
upset	upset	upset	使心煩
wake	woke/waked	woken/waked	醒來
wear	wore	worn	穿著
weave	wove	woven	編織
weep	wept	wept	哭泣
win	won	won	贏
wind	wound	wound	纏繞
withdraw	withdrew	withdrawn	收回
write	wrote	written	寫

* 在被動語態中,會用 fitted。

Part 6 Past Tenses 過去式

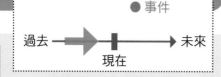

Unit **47**

Past Continuous Tense
過去進行式

● 事件

過去 ➡ ┃ ➡ 未來
　　　　　現在

Form 構句

| 肯定句的句型 | I/he/she/it was thinking |
| | you/we/they were thinking |

| 否定句的句型 | I/he/she/it was not thinking |
| | you/we/they were not thinking |

| 否定句的縮寫 | I/he/she/it wasn't thinking |
| | you/we/they weren't thinking |

| 疑問句的句型 | Was I/he/she/it thinking? |
| | Were you/we/they thinking? |

1 過去進行式的構句方式是：
was/were + V-ing

I was celebrating my 26th birthday with my friends when you called.
你打電話來的時候，我正在和朋友慶祝我的 26 歲生日。

Were you driving on the highway at that time?
當時你正行駛在高速公路上嗎？

Use 用法

2 過去進行式用來形容「**過去某一時間內正在進行的行為或狀態**」。

At 9:00 last night I was doing my homework. 昨天晚上 9 點我正在做功課。
The wind was blowing this morning when I woke up.
今天早上我起床的時候，風還蠻大的。

3 過去進行式也常用來「**說故事**」，和過去簡單式搭配使用。

此時，須用**過去進行式**來說明「**故事背景**」，用**過去簡單式**來描述「**行為或動作**」。

I was dreaming about eating vanilla ice cream with chocolate chips when I heard a knock on my door. I opened the door, and my friend Jeff handed me a vanilla ice cream cone.

當我聽到有人在敲門時，我正在幻想可以吃到灑了巧克力碎片的香草冰淇淋。我把門打開，我的朋友傑夫就拿了一個香草冰淇淋甜筒給我。

4 過去進行式經常搭配 always 使用，說明「**過去時常發生的事**」。

My girlfriend was always telling me to shave my beard and get a haircut.
我女朋友老是叫我要刮鬍子和剪頭髮。

5 不能用於**進行式**的動詞，也沒有**過去進行式**。

✗ I was believing the story.
✓ I believed the story.
　我那時相信這件事是真的。

102

Practice

1

請依圖示，用「過去進行式」回答右列各問題。

install the tiles
hang the drape
fix the pipe
put up wallpaper
inspect the bike
wash the car

1 Ⓐ What was she doing in the living room?

Ⓑ *She was hanging the drape.*

2 Ⓐ What were they doing?

Ⓑ ....

3 Ⓐ What was he doing in the kitchen?

Ⓑ ....

4 Ⓐ What was he doing in the bathroom?

Ⓑ ....

5 Ⓐ What was he doing in the garage?

Ⓑ ....

6 Ⓐ What were they doing in their new house?

Ⓑ ....

2 請將括弧內的動詞以正確的時態填空，完成對話。

1. Ⓐ Why didn't you open the door?

   Ⓑ I didn't hear the doorbell ring, because I .... (take) a shower.

2. Ⓐ Why did Keith go downstairs?

   Ⓑ Keith went downstairs to pick up the parcel for me, because I ....
   (change) the baby's diaper.

3. Ⓐ Did you see him go into that room?

   Ⓑ I didn't. I .... (study) at my desk at that time.

4. Ⓐ How did he stain the shirt?

   Ⓑ He .... (eat) some chicken nuggets and .... (squeeze) the
   ketchup. He squeezed it so hard that it splattered on his shirt.

Unit 48

Comparison Between the Past Simple and the Past Continuous

「過去簡單式」與「過去進行式」的比較

1 過去簡單式通常描述的是「**過去已經結束的動作**」；過去進行式描述的是「**過去持續、尚未完成的動作**」。

I was eating dessert. 我當時正在吃甜點。
↳ 當時還在吃

I ate dessert before dinner.
↳ 已經吃完了
我在晚飯前吃了甜點。

I heard you snoring last night.
昨晚我有聽到你的打呼聲。

You were blasting rock music.
你那時在大聲播放搖滾樂。

2 過去簡單式描述的是「**過去長期的動作或情況**」；過去進行式描述的則是「**過去暫時的情況**」。

I worked for IBM for two years.
我曾在 IBM 任職兩年。

I was looking for a job in a bank.
當時我在找銀行的工作。

3 描述「**過去某段時間內的短暫動作或事件**」要用過去簡單式。若這段時間內發生了兩個短暫動作或事件，則兩者會依照發生順序，用過去簡單式分別描述。

We caught the fish. Then we ate the fish.
我們捕到魚，後來把魚吃了。

I drank some orange juice, and I felt better. 我喝了一些柳橙汁，覺得舒服多了。

4 如果是「**過去的習慣**」或「**過去反覆發生的事**」，要用過去簡單式。

I jogged every day last year.
去年的時候，我每天都慢跑。

I called him four times, but he didn't answer. 我打了四通電話給他，他都沒接。

5 while 經常搭配過去進行式使用，來描述一個「**持續較長時間的動作或背景**」。這時候，主要的子句會用過去簡單式。

I finished watching my favorite TV program while my wife was reading a financial magazine. 我太太在看財經雜誌的時候，我看完了我最愛的電視節目。

6 when 可搭配**過去進行式**，也可搭配**過去簡單式**使用。如果 when 後面描述的是「**短暫的動作**」，就用過去簡單式；如果描述的是「**持續較長時間的動作**」，就用過去進行式。

I was walking down the street when I found some money. 我走在街上時，發現了一些錢。
When Yvonne was driving home, she saw a car accident. 伊芳開車回家時，目睹了一場車禍。
My brother and I were singing when somebody knocked at the door.
我和哥哥在唱歌時，有人敲門。
We ran into the convenience store when it began to rain.
↳ 也有可能兩個動作都屬於短暫動作，都用簡單式。
開始下雨的時候，我們跑進了便利商店。

比較

• I was making a beef pot pie when Teddy walked in with a lunch box. He sat down and began to eat his lunch.
↳ 在一個較長動作（was making）之中，發生了三個短暫動作（walked in、sat down、began）。
我正在做牛肉派時，泰迪拿著午餐便當走了進來，並且坐下來開始吃午餐。

• While I was eating the beef pot pie, Teddy went out to buy some orange juice.
↳ 在一個較長動作（was eating）之中，發生了一個短暫動作（went out）。
我在吃牛肉派時，泰迪走出去買一些柳橙汁。

Practice

1

請將括弧內的動詞以「過去進行式」或「過去簡單式」填空，完成段落。

I ❶＿＿＿＿＿＿＿＿＿ (walk) down the street. I ❷＿＿＿＿＿＿＿＿＿ (mind) my own business. I had just left the café and ❸＿＿＿＿＿＿＿＿＿ (go) to my car. I ❹＿＿＿＿＿＿＿＿＿ (pass) a strange-looking guy. He ❺＿＿＿＿＿＿＿＿＿ (lean) against a street light. Suddenly, I ❻＿＿＿＿＿＿＿＿＿ (feel) nervous.

I ❼＿＿＿＿＿＿＿＿＿ (look) over my shoulder. The guy ❽＿＿＿＿＿＿＿＿＿ (stare) right at me.

He ❾＿＿＿＿＿＿＿＿＿ (raise) his hand and ❿＿＿＿＿＿＿＿＿ (say) something. I ⓫＿＿＿＿＿＿＿＿＿ (walk) faster. He ⓬＿＿＿＿＿＿＿＿＿ (run) after me. I ⓭＿＿＿＿＿＿＿＿＿ (sprint) toward my car. I ⓮＿＿＿＿＿＿＿＿＿ (stop) in front of my car. I ⓯＿＿＿＿＿＿＿＿＿ (look) for my keys. The guy ⓰＿＿＿＿＿＿＿＿＿ (slow) down and called after me, "You dropped your keys."

2

請從 A 欄和 B 欄選出適當的片語，用 when 連結，寫出完整的句子，並將括弧裡的動詞改為正確的時態。

A

I (play) football
I (fight) with my sister
I (buy) a wedding present
I (lose) my passport
I (sleep) soundly
I (crank) the volume

I (hear) you were getting married
I (blow) out the speakers
I (sprain) my ankle
the alarm clock (ring)
I (vacation) in Italy
Mom (come) home

B

1. *I was playing football when I sprained my ankle.*
＿＿＿＿＿＿＿＿＿＿＿＿＿＿＿＿＿＿＿＿＿＿＿＿＿＿＿＿＿＿＿

2. ＿＿＿＿＿＿＿＿＿＿＿＿＿＿＿＿＿＿＿＿＿＿＿＿＿＿＿＿＿＿＿
＿＿＿＿＿＿＿＿＿＿＿＿＿＿＿＿＿＿＿＿＿＿＿＿＿＿＿＿＿＿＿

3. ＿＿＿＿＿＿＿＿＿＿＿＿＿＿＿＿＿＿＿＿＿＿＿＿＿＿＿＿＿＿＿
＿＿＿＿＿＿＿＿＿＿＿＿＿＿＿＿＿＿＿＿＿＿＿＿＿＿＿＿＿＿＿

4. ＿＿＿＿＿＿＿＿＿＿＿＿＿＿＿＿＿＿＿＿＿＿＿＿＿＿＿＿＿＿＿
＿＿＿＿＿＿＿＿＿＿＿＿＿＿＿＿＿＿＿＿＿＿＿＿＿＿＿＿＿＿＿

5. ＿＿＿＿＿＿＿＿＿＿＿＿＿＿＿＿＿＿＿＿＿＿＿＿＿＿＿＿＿＿＿
＿＿＿＿＿＿＿＿＿＿＿＿＿＿＿＿＿＿＿＿＿＿＿＿＿＿＿＿＿＿＿

6. ＿＿＿＿＿＿＿＿＿＿＿＿＿＿＿＿＿＿＿＿＿＿＿＿＿＿＿＿＿＿＿
＿＿＿＿＿＿＿＿＿＿＿＿＿＿＿＿＿＿＿＿＿＿＿＿＿＿＿＿＿＿＿

Part 6 Past Tenses 過去式

Continuous Forms With "Always" for Expressing Complaints
進行式搭配 Always 表示抱怨的用法

1 always 常和現在進行式或過去進行式搭配使用，表示「某事發生得過於頻繁，造成困擾」。

He is always tapping his fingers.
他老是在敲手指。

He was always hurrying from one place to another.
他總是來去匆匆。

簡單式	進行式
always 搭配簡單式的時候，只是表達「某事不斷發生」。	always 搭配進行式的時候，則帶有**抱怨**的意味。
現在式 Steven always drives at the speed limit. 史蒂芬開車總是開在速限邊緣。	Steven is always driving too fast. 史蒂芬老是愛開快車。
過去式 Tim always called when he was in town. 提姆每次進城都會打電話來。	Tim was always calling late at night. 提姆老是在深夜打電話來。

2 除了 always 以外，forever、continually 和 constantly 也常和現在進行式或過去進行式連用，表示「**抱怨**」。

You are forever gambling away your salary. 你永遠只會把薪水拿去輸光。
Herbert is constantly missing family holidays.
賀柏特不斷錯過和家人相聚的假期。
Francis is constantly dreaming about being rich. 法蘭西斯只想做著富貴夢。

My brothers were constantly talking about going to Antarctica on vacation.
我哥哥以前總說要去南極洲度假。

Sandy was continuously buying shoes.
珊蒂以前很愛買鞋子。

3 always 在**進行式**中，不與 **not** 連用。

✗ She is always not going to school.

✓ She is always skipping school.
她老是蹺課。

Practice

1 請將括弧內的動詞，以正確的「進行式」型態，搭配 always 填空，完成句子。

1. The faucet __was always dripping__ (drip). Fortunately, Dad repaired it.

2. My brother _____ (jump) on my teddy bear. He also kicked my purple dinosaur.

3. That computer _____ (crash) when I was doing my homework. That's why I bought a new computer.

4. Patty is grounded for a week, and she is not allowed to watch TV. However, she _____ (watch) TV when her mom is out.

5. His parents treated him better than they treated his sister. His little sister _____ (complain) about the unfair treatment.

6. Tommy _____ (play) online computer games with his friends. He plays every day after school and late into the evening every night.

7. You _____ (tell) me that your house is like a zoo, but your family is nice. You should speak more respectfully about your family.

2 請依圖示，從框內選出適當的動詞或動詞片語，搭配 always 填空，完成句子。

| pile up | drink | leave | store up | cry | scatter |

1. He _is always piling up_ his desk with books and papers.

2. My son _____ his toys all over the floor.

3. Mom _____ things where nobody can find them.

4. She _____ Coke for breakfast.

5. Little Susie _____ loudly when she is hungry.

6. I wrote a note for him because he _____ things behind.

Unit **50**

Present Perfect Simple Tense (1)
現在完成式（I）

過去 ←——————→ 未來
現在
● 事件

Form 構句

肯定句的句型	I/you/we/they have eaten
	he/she/it has eaten
肯定句的縮寫	I/you/we/they 've eaten
	he/she/it 's eaten
否定句的句型	I/you/we/they have not eaten
	he/she/it has not eaten
否定句的縮寫	I/you/we/they haven't eaten
	he/she/it hasn't eaten
疑問句的句型	Have I/you/we/they eaten?
	Has he/she/it eaten?

Use 用法

1 現在完成式用來描述一個「**從過去某個時刻開始，一直持續到現在的動作或狀態**」。

How long have you driven?
↳ 從某個時刻一直開車到現在
你已經開了多久的車？

Danny has been a student for years.
↳ 從他生命的某段時間一直到現在
丹尼當學生已經好多年了。

Have you ever held a job?
↳ 從你生命的某段時間一直到現在
你有做過什麼工作嗎？

2 當某件事已經結束，但強調「**對現在產生影響**」，也可以使用現在完成式。

The pizza has arrived.
↳ 對現在產生的影響是：披薩已經在這裡，隨時可以吃。
披薩已經送到了。

Our meeting has been canceled.
↳ 對現在產生的影響是：會議取消，無法討論。
我們的會議取消了。

I have tried bungee jumping many times. I don't want to do it anymore.
↳ 從以前到現在發生過好幾次，對現在產生的影響是：已經不想再玩了。
我已經玩過高空彈跳好幾次，都玩到不想玩了。

past

使用現在完成式的時候，事情發生的確切時間並不重要。

Practice

1

請將括弧內的動詞，
以「現在完成式」填
空，完成對話。

I have been waiting for Dr. Smith since eight this morning.
I ❶_____ (read) every magazine in the waiting room.

Two hours ago, I asked a woman, "Have you been waiting long?"
She said, "I ❷_____ (not be) here very long." I sat and
waited some more. I chatted on my cell phone with everybody I
knew. Then I called the doctor's office to ask if Dr. Smith was in. The
receptionist asked, "❸_____ you _____
(see) Dr. Smith before?"

I replied, "No, I ❹_____ (never see) Dr. Smith before."
The receptionist asked me to hold on for a second. Now I
❺_____ (be) on hold on the phone for fifteen minutes!

2

請將括弧內的動詞，
以「現在完成式」填
空，完成對話。

Ⓐ ❶_____ you ever _____ (use) Happy Hair Shampoo?

Ⓑ No, I ❷_____ not _____ (try) it.

Ⓐ ❸_____ you _____ (see) the Happy Hair Shampoo
TV commercial?

Ⓑ Yes, I ❹_____ (see) it many times.

Ⓐ What do you think of it?

Ⓑ I don't believe it. She has too much dirt in her hair.

Ⓐ Yeah, that commercial always catches my attention.

Ⓑ I ❺_____ (hear) my friends talk about it.

Ⓐ I ❻_____ never _____ (see) such dirty hair before.

Ⓑ And after she uses Happy Hair Shampoo, her hair is beautiful.

Ⓐ Yes, and she seems really happy.

Present Perfect Simple Tense (2)
現在完成式（2）

Use 用法

1 現在完成式常表示「**事情發生了多久**」，此時不能用其他現在式。

✗ He is thinking about going to the beach for a long time.

✓ He has been thinking about going to the beach for a long time.

他想著要去海灘想了好久。

✗ I expect to see you again since last year.

✓ I have expected to see you again since last year.

我從去年就期待再和你見面。

2 現在完成式常用來表示「**事情發生的次數**」。

I have tried fresh carrot juice twice.

我嘗試喝過兩次鮮榨紅蘿蔔汁。

I have been to Prague many times.

我去過布拉格很多次。

3 現在完成式也常用來「**發布消息**」。

The ball game has started.

球賽已經開始了。

The team has lost the game.

這隊輸了比賽。

4 現在完成式不能和「**已經結束的過去時間**」連用，但是可以和與「現在」、「今天」等「**尚未結束的時間**」連用。

today 今天
this afternoon 今天下午
this evening 今天晚上

yesterday 昨天
last week 上星期
in 1999 在 1999 年時

✗ They've gone to Peru yesterday.

✓ They went to Peru yesterday.
↳ 事件和說話發生在不同一天，不能用現在完成式。

他們昨天去秘魯了。

I have taken my medicine today.
↳ 發生在同一天，可以用現在完成式。

我今天吃過藥了。

5 been 是 be 動詞的過去分詞，have been 用來說明「**去過某處，現在已經回來了**」。

I have been out twice today.

我今天已經外出兩次了。

He has been to Singapore only once.
↳ 去過新加坡，但現在不在新加坡。

他只去過新加坡一次。

6 gone 是 go 的過去分詞，have gone 用來說明「**去了某處，現在還在那裡**」。

She has gone to Nova Scotia.
↳ 人離開去了某處，還沒回來。

她去了新斯科細亞。

He has gone to the movie theater without cleaning his room.
↳ 工作尚未完成就離開，人不在房間裡了。

他沒打掃房間就去電影院了。

Practice

1

請將括弧內的動詞以「現在完成式」填空，完成段落。

I ❶ _____ (plan) this party for a long time. We
❷ _____ (invite) many guests. We now have almost
everything ready. The party ❸ _____ not _____ (start).
The food ❹ _____ (arrive). The cleaning service
❺ _____ (leave). The floor ❻ _____ (dry). Let me
think. ❼ _____ I _____ (miss) anything? Yes, I ❽ _____
not _____ (throw) the garbage out. Good. Now we are ready.

2

請將右列錯誤的句子改
寫為正確的句子。

1. Lawrence is working at the Flying Tomato Pizzeria for six months.
   → _____
   _____

2. Iris stars in a soap opera since last year.
   → _____

3. Tom is owning this car since several months.
   → _____

4. How long are you working on this proposal?
   → _____

3

請依據題意，用 have/has been 或 have/has gone 填空，完成對話。

1. Ⓐ I looked for Grandpa in the house, but he's not home. Where is
   Grandpa?
   Ⓑ He _____ to work in the garden.

2. Ⓐ Grandma looks so different. What happened to her?
   Ⓑ She _____ to the hair salon.

3. Ⓐ The restaurant is closed. I wonder why it's closed.
   Ⓑ They _____ on a trip to Guam.

4. Ⓐ I have always wanted to go to Brazil. Have you ever traveled to
   South America?
   Ⓑ Yes, I _____ to Chile and Argentina.

Part 7 Perfect Tenses 完成式

Unit 52

Present Perfect Simple With Some Adverbs and Prepositions
常與「現在完成式」連用的一些副詞和介系詞

1 現在完成式常和一些表示「從某個不特定的時間一直到現在」的副詞連用，最常見的是 ever 和 never，通常放在 **have** 和主要動詞的中間。

What is the most interesting book you have ever read?
↳ 過去任何時間至今
你看過最有趣的書是哪一本？

I have never met such a big guy.
↳ 過去任何時間至今都未發生
我從沒碰過塊頭這麼大的男生。

2 already 是「已經」的意思，常和現在完成式連用，描述「事情比預期早發生」。already 通常放在 **have** 和主要動詞的中間。

He has already left for work.
他已經出門上班了。

The cake has already cooled off.
蛋糕已經涼了。

3 just 常和現在完成式連用，表示「才剛發生的事」。just 要放在 **have** 和主要動詞的中間。

The movie has just finished.
電影剛演完。

The food has just arrived at the table.
食物才剛端上桌。

4 yet 常和現在完成式連用，並且只能用於否定句和疑問句。

1 yet 在疑問句裡用來詢問「某件事發生了沒」，並且具有「期待某事發生」的意味；

2 在否定句裡表示「某件事還沒發生」。yet 在兩種句型裡都要放在句尾。

Has Thomas married Mary yet?
湯瑪士和瑪麗結婚了沒？

Hasn't Anna called yet?
安娜還沒打電話來嗎？

I haven't found my keys yet.
我還沒找到鑰匙。

5 before 也可以和現在完成式連用，表示「在之前」。before 會放在句尾。

She hasn't been married before.
她過去從未結過婚。

I haven't eaten caviar before.
我以前沒有吃過魚子醬。

CAVIAR

6 現在完成式常和 for 連用，說明「某件事持續進行了多久的時間」。for 的後面要接「時間單位／一段時間」。

Isabel has been pregnant for six months.
依莎貝兒已經懷孕六個月了。

I have been an editor for two years.
我做編輯已經兩年了。

7 現在完成式常和 since 連用，說明「某件事從何時開始」。since 的後面要接「一個時間點」。

They have lived in California since 2012.
他們從 2012 年開始，就在加州定居。

I have known Jim since he was four years old. 從吉姆四歲時我就認識他了。

Practice

1

請將括弧裡的動詞改寫為「現在完成式」，並將題目提示的副詞插入句中的正確位置。

1. We (eat) dinner. [already]
   → We have already eaten dinner.

2. We (not finish) our coffee. [yet]
   → _____

3. We (receive) her phone call. [just]
   → _____

4. The singer (get) her first single on the top ten chart. [just]
   → _____

5. Have you (throw away) your old books? [already]
   → _____

6. I (not discuss) the problem with my doctor. [yet]
   → _____

7. I (buy) anything online. [never]
   → _____

8. Have you (run) in a marathon? [ever]
   → _____

9. I (not be) to Russia. [before]
   → _____

10. This is the most splendid view I (see). [ever]
    → _____

2

請用 for 或 since 填空，完成句子。

1. Patti has studied at Marymount University _____ three years.

2. Tony has owned his current house _____ 2017.

3. Vivian has collected Warhol's soup cans _____ six months.

4. Duane has worked as a sales rep _____ he graduated from college.

5. Neal has been a city councilor _____ two terms.

6. I have been telling you to start studying harder for your final exams _____ last month, but you never listen.

113

Unit 53

Comparison Between the Present Perfect Simple and the Past Simple (1)

「現在完成式」與「過去簡單式」的比較（1）

比較

- I've been a member of the Wilderness Society for five years.
  ↳ 使用現在完成式：我現在還是會員。

  我擔任「荒野保護協會」的會員已經五年了。

- I was a member of the Wilderness Society for five years.
  ↳ 使用過去簡單式：我已經不是會員了。

  我過去有五年曾是「荒野保護協會」的會員。

	現在完成式		過去簡單式
說明「從過去發生到現在的事」，就時間上來說，是將「過去與現在連結」。	I've grown vegetables in my garden for six years. ↳ 現在我仍然在花園裡種蔬菜。 我在花園裡種蔬菜已經有六年了。 He has planted flowers in his yard for two years. ↳ 他現在還在院子裡種花。 他在院子裡種花兩年了。 How long have you been a gardener? ↳ 你現在還是園丁。 你做園丁做了多久？	說明「過去開始並已於過去結束的事」，沒有持續到現在，與現在無關，「純粹描述一個過去事件」。	Eve collected butterflies for one summer. ↳ 她現在已經不再採集蝴蝶了。 有一年夏天伊芙曾採集蝴蝶。 Larry tried chocolate-covered ants only once. ↳ 從那次起他就沒再吃過了。 賴瑞只吃過一次巧克力螞蟻。 How long were you a snake owner? ↳ 你現在沒有養蛇。 你以前養蛇養了多久？
強調「發生於過去的行為或事件，對現在仍產生影響」。	I have invested some money in a biotechnology company. ↳ 使用現在完成式，表示投資仍在進行，現在錢還在股票市場裡。 我投資了一些錢在一家生技公司。	描述「已經結束的事件，對現在沒有影響」。	I invested my money in a biotechnology company, but I sold the stock. ↳ 使用過去簡單式，表示投資已成為過去，錢已經不在股票市場裡，已換成現金。 我投資了一些錢在一家生技公司，不過我把股票賣了。
用來「發布消息」，或在對話時「提供初步資訊」。	My investment has doubled. 我的投資增值了兩倍。	提供更多關於此事件的「細節」。	I bought the stock at $25 per share. The stock jumped to $55 per share. I sold it at $50. I cleaned up on that stock deal. 我在每股 25 元的時候買下股票，後來升到 55 元，我在 50 元時把股票賣掉，這回股票出手我大賺了一筆。

Have you ever seen a real whale?

你有沒有看過真正的鯨魚？

No, I haven't seen a real whale, but I saw some white dolphins for the first time last year.

我沒看過真正的鯨魚，但是去年我第一次看到白海豚。

Practice

1

請將括弧內的動詞以正確的時態填空，完成句子。

1. The police _____ (search) the mountain for the suspect for three days. Now they claim that the suspect _____ (leave) the area.

2. I _____ (find) your watch under the bed.

3. The global climate _____ (change) dramatically in the last ten years.

4. A huge tornado _____ (hit) the village yesterday and _____ (cause) a great damage.

2

請用「現在完成式」搭配「過去簡單式」，來描述事件及其細節。

I ❶ _____ (adopt) a golden retriever from an animal shelter. He ❷ _____ (be abandoned) by the previous family and ❸ _____ (wander) the streets looking for food. One day, he ❹ _____ (be brought) into the shelter. He had stayed in the shelter for two weeks before we took him home. He ❺ _____ (be) so slim and dirty at that time. Now, he ❻ _____ (become) a happy, healthy, and smiley dog.

3

請依照範例，利用圖片的資訊，分別用三種句型造句。

1

went to bed
wake up now

→ Gilbert _went to bed at 1:00._
(go to bed / at)

→ Gilbert _has slept since 1:00._
(sleep / since)

→ Gilbert _has slept for four hours._
(sleep / for)

- -

2

JULY

moved in here
still here today

→ We _____
(move in here / on)

→ We _____
(live here / since)

→ We _____
(live here / for)

Unit 54

Comparison Between the Present Perfect Simple and the Past Simple (2)

「現在完成式」與「過去簡單式」的比較（2）

現在完成式 Present Perfect Simple

現在

未來

2010 — 2030

過去簡單式 Past Simple

現在完成式		過去簡單式	
句中出現了意味著「**從過去某時一直延續到現在**」之副詞或副詞片語時使用。	**Sheena** has begun **coloring her hair** recently. ↳ 句中出現 recently，是一個不確切的時間副詞，常用現在完成式。 席娜最近開始染髮。	句中出現了指明「**過去確切時間**」之副詞或副詞片語時使用。	**Shirley** began **highlighting her hair** last month. ↳ 句中出現 last month，是一個確切的過去時間，須用過去簡單式。 雪莉上個月開始挑染頭髮。
	I've started **writing a book about economic recessions** recently. 我最近著手寫一本關於經濟衰退的書。		✗ I have read **about a hot mutual fund** yesterday. ✓ I read **about a hot mutual fund** yesterday. 昨天我讀到一支熱門的共同基金的消息。
• recently • ever • never	**Have you** ever bought **any books on the Internet?** 你在網路上買過書嗎？		**Did you** buy **camping gear on the Internet** last week? 你上星期在網路上買了露營用具嗎？
I have never eaten a kiwi.		• yesterday • last week • two months ago • in the 20th Century	**I** swallowed **a mosquito while bicycling** yesterday. 我昨天騎腳踏車時吞下了一隻蚊子。
句中出現與「**今天**」有關的副詞或副詞片語，但這個動作「**尚未結束**」。	**Ginny** has driven **halfway to Detroit** this afternoon. ↳ 現在時間依然是今天下午，她還得繼續開車。 吉妮今天下午前往底特律的路程只開到了一半。	句中出現與「**今天**」有關的副詞或副詞片語，但這個動作「**已經結束**」。	**Ginny** drove **all the way to Detroit** this afternoon. ↳ 現在時間可能還是今天下午，或者已晚上，她已經開完整段路程。 吉妮今天下午一路開車到達底特律。
• today • this morning • this afternoon • this evening • tonight		詢問某件事「**發生的時間**」只能用過去簡單式。	**When did you** finish **painting the house** this week? 你這星期是何時完成房子的粉刷的？

Practice

1

請將括弧內的動詞以正確時態填空，完成對話。

Dialog 1

Ⓐ When ❶_____ you _____ (arrive) in Taiwan?

Ⓑ I ❷_____ (arrive) today.

Ⓐ ❸_____ you _____ (be) here before?

Ⓑ Yes, I ❹_____ (be) here twice before.

Dialog 2

Ⓐ When ❺_____ you _____ (buy) this bicycle?

Ⓑ Someone ❻_____ (give) me the bicycle last week.

Ⓐ ❼_____ you _____ (start) riding your bicycle?

Ⓑ Yes, I ❽_____ (start) riding my bicycle to work.

2

請勾選正確的答案。

Ⓐ How long have you played baseball?

Ⓑ I ❶ ☐ have played ☐ played baseball for two decades.

Ⓐ ❷ ☐ Have you ever been injured ☐ Did you injure on the field?

Ⓑ I ❸ ☐ had ☐ have had several injuries during the past fifteen years, but I'm OK now.

Ⓐ What was the longest period of time ❹ ☐ you have played ☐ you played with an injury?

Ⓑ The longest period of time I ❺ ☐ played ☐ have played with an injury was about four months.

Ⓐ When ❻ ☐ have you hurt ☐ did you hurt your arm this year?

Ⓑ I ❼ ☐ hurt ☐ have hurt my arm in April right before the season opener, but now I have full use of my arm.

Ⓐ ❽ ☐ Have you ever played ☐ Did you ever play other sports?

Ⓑ Yeah, I ❾ ☐ played ☐ have played soccer in college.

Ⓐ ❿ ☐ Have you liked ☐ Did you like to play soccer in college?

Ⓑ I ⓫ ☐ loved ☐ have loved to play soccer when I was in college.

Ⓐ ⓬ ☐ Have you ever been recruited ☐ Were you ever recruited by other teams?

Ⓑ My agent ⓭ ☐ received ☐ has received a few calls.

Ⓐ People ⓮ ☐ said ☐ have said you are a natural-born athlete. I'll see you on the baseball diamond next week. Keep on hitting those homers.

Unit 55

Present Perfect Continuous Tense
現在完成進行式

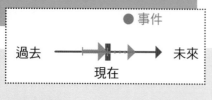

I have been writing a novel about secret agent dogs.

我一直在寫一本關於特務狗的小說。

Form 構句

肯定句的句型	I/you/we/they have been listening
	he/she/it has been listening
肯定句的縮寫	I/you/we/they 've been listening
	he/she/it 's been listening
否定句的句型	I/you/we/they have not been listening
	he/she/it has not been listening
否定句的縮寫	I/you/we/they haven't been listening
	he/she/it hasn't been listening
疑問句的句型	Have I/you/we/they been listening?
	Has he/she/it been listening?

Use 用法

1 現在完成進行式也是用來「**連接過去與現在**」的時態，描述「**從過去一直持續到現在仍然在進行的動作**」，或者「**從過去一直持續到現在，才剛結束，並對現在產生影響的動作**」。

He has been waiting an hour for the pizza. ↳ 到現在還一直在等

他等披薩送來已經等了一個小時。

It has been raining. 雨一直下個不停。
↳ 說明街上為何是濕的

She has been swimming in the pool at the gym. ↳ 說明某人身上為何濕答答的

她一直都在健身房的游泳池游泳。

Have you been exercising?
↳ 詢問他人為何覺得熱且流汗

你一直在運動嗎？

2 現在完成進行式可用來說明「**近期不斷重複的行為或狀態**」、「**度過時間的方式**」。

I has been jogging every weekend over the last month.
↳ 一段時間內重複的活動

上個月我每週末都在慢跑。

How long have you been using the tennis courts at the park?
↳ 詢問近期內的狀況

你在公園的網球場打球多久了？

Have you been lifting weights?
↳ 詢問近期內的狀況

你一直都有在練舉重嗎？

Practice

1

請以「現在完成進行式」改寫句子。

1. It is raining.
   → _It has been raining._

2. We are drinking.
   → ....

3. Those people are chatting.
   → ....

4. Camille is wearing high heels.
   → ....

5. People are boarding the plane.
   → ....

6. Have you practiced your Spanish?
   → ....

7. Did you redecorate your house?
   → ....

2

請從框內選出適當的動詞，以「現在完成進行式」填空，完成句子。

argue

rain

wash

reel

1. They're still mad. They ....
   .... for two hours.

2. It's damp in here. It ....
   .... for two days.

3. There are so many dishes.
   I .... for more than an
   hour.

4. The test is so hard. My head
   .... for hours.

Unit 56

Comparison Between the Present Perfect
Continuous and the Present Perfect
Simple (1)

「現在完成進行式」與「現在完成式」
的比較（1）

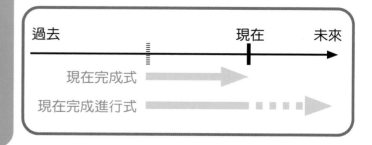

	現在完成式		現在完成進行式
動作已經結束。	Tom has eaten his dinner. 湯姆吃完晚餐了。 Sheila has celebrated her promotion to Director. ↳ 已經慶祝完，現在要回去工作 席拉慶祝了自己升上董事。	動作可能已經結束，也可能仍在進行中。	Tom has been eating his dinner. 湯姆一直在吃晚餐。 Sheila has been celebrating her promotion to Director. ↳ 還在慶祝或已經慶祝完 席拉一直在慶祝她升上董事。
強調事件在某一段時間已被完成。	Mary has practiced her violin for eight hours today. 瑪麗今天花了八小時練習小提琴。 How many pieces of music have you composed? 你已經寫完多少曲子了？	強調事件持續了多久。	Mary has been practicing her violin all day. 瑪麗一整天都在練習拉小提琴。 How long have you been composing music? 你寫曲子寫了多久？
說明「固定的情況」（持續較長時間）。	Mick has played that song in concert for many years. 米克在音樂會上演奏那首歌好多年了。 Sara has cooked healthy food all her life. 莎拉這輩子煮的都是健康食物。	說明「暫時的情況」（持續較短時間）。	Mick has been playing that song in concert for a couple of weeks. 米克已經好幾個星期都在音樂會上演奏那首歌。 Sara has been cooking healthy food recently. 最近莎拉煮的都是健康食物。
詢問事件發生的頻率要用現在完成式。	I have tried fried mushrooms five times. 我吃過五次炸蘑菇。		
		說明「度日、打發時間」的方式要用現在完成進行式。	He has been working on the project since last night. 他從昨天晚上就一直在處理這個案子。
不能用於進行式的動詞，即使動作還沒結束，也要用現在完成式。	How long has Trisha known Tom? 翠莎認識湯姆多久了？		

1

請用「現在完成式」或「現在完成進行式」填空，完成句子。並從框內找出作答的依據，填入題後的空格內。

Ⓐ 完成的動作或情況

Ⓑ 尚未完成的動作或情況

Ⓒ 強調事件或情況持續了多久

Ⓓ 強調事件或情況在某一段時間已被完成

Ⓔ 暫時的情況

Ⓕ 固定的情況

Ⓖ 不能用於進行式的動詞

1. How many cherries _have you eaten_ (you / eat) today? → __D__

2. Anton _____ (sit) in the café for the whole afternoon. → _____

3. Bernie _____ (clean) the staircase voluntarily for many years. → _____

4. Since when _____ (you / realize) that fact? → _____

5. You _____ (chat) with your friends all night. Turn off the computer and go to bed now. → _____

6. Ron _____ (send) strange messages since yesterday. Does his computer have a virus? → _____

7. I _____ (work) day and night recently. I need a vacation. → _____

8. I _____ (finish) five cases in the past four months. → _____

9. I _____ (imagine) life on Mars since I was little. → _____

10. Pete _____ (travel) around Europe for two months. Now he will go back to work. → _____

Unit 57

Comparison Between the Present Perfect Continuous and the Present Perfect Simple (2)
「現在完成進行式」與「現在完成式」的比較（2）

1 現在完成式和現在完成進行式都不能與**表示已經結束的時間副詞或片語**連用，這時要使用過去簡單式。

- yesterday
- at six
- until 10 p.m.

yesterday

I ate six slices of cherry pie yesterday. 我昨天吃了六片櫻桃派。

today

I have eaten six slices of cherry pie today.

我今天已經吃了六片櫻桃派。

I have been eating cherry pie today.

我今天一直在吃櫻桃派。

✗ Cynthia has called at 5 p.m.

✗ Cynthia has been calling at 5 p.m.

✓ Cynthia called at 5 p.m.

　辛西亞傍晚 5 點的時候來過電話。

✗ Sunny hasn't gone to bed until 11:30.

✗ Sunny hasn't been going to bed until 11:30.

✓ Sunny didn't go to bed until 11:30.

　桑尼 11 點半才睡。

2 有時候，使用現在完成式或現在完成進行式的差別並不大。

Paul has been dating Virginia for a year.
= Paul has dated Virginia for a year.

保羅和維吉妮亞已經交往一年了。

How long has Virginia been dreaming of marriage?
= How long has Virginia dreamed of marriage?

維吉妮亞想結婚想了多久？

3 現在完成式和現在完成進行式都常與 for 連用，說明該動作的「**持續時間**」。

Lonny has painted the room for three hours.

朗尼已經粉刷房間三個小時了。

Hans has been repairing the roof for four hours.

漢斯修屋頂已經修四個小時了。

4 現在完成式和現在完成進行式都常與 since 連用，說明該動作的「**起始時間**」。

Daniel has studied chemistry since high school. 丹尼爾從高中就開始唸化學。

Stan has been playing hockey since he was twelve.

史丹從 12 歲就開始打曲棍球。

Practice

1

請將右列錯誤的句子改寫為正確的句子。

1. I have been out for dinner last night.

   → ....

2. Roy has held a party yesterday afternoon.

   → ....

3. Sandra wrote her essay since this morning.

   → ....

4. Larry hasn't gone home until his boss left the office.

   → ....

2

請依圖示，從框內選出適當的用語，以「現在完成式」填空，再以「現在完成進行式」改寫句子。

make trips with a hot air balloon

stand by the window

take photos

decorate the Christmas tree

1 Jessica and her kids ....
.... for three hours.

= ....
....
....

2 Emma ....
for *National Geographic*.

= ....
....
....

3 Daniel ....
across America since 2019.

= ....
....
....

4 Nicky ....
since 2 p.m.

= ....
....
....

Unit 58

Past Perfect Simple Tense
過去完成式

Form 構句

● 事件
過去 ————●——●—▌————→ 未來
現在

肯定句的句型	I/you/we/they/he/she/it	had moved
肯定句的縮寫	I/you/we/they/he/she/it	'd moved
否定句的句型	I/you/we/they/he/she/it	had not moved
否定句的縮寫	I/you/we/they/he/she/it	hadn't moved
疑問句的句型	Had	I/you/we/they/he/she/it moved?

Use 用法

1 過去完成式用來描述「**兩個過去事件中，較早發生的那一個**」，強調事件的先後。

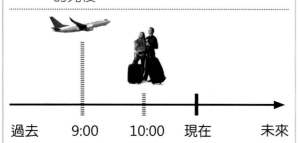

過去　　9:00　　10:00　　現在　　未來

We arrived at the airport at 10:00, but our plane had left at 9:00.

我們 10 點抵達機場，不過我們要搭的班機 9 點就起飛了。

2 過去完成式表達的是「**過去的過去**」，當說話的當下已經是過去式，要描述在那之前所發生的事，就要用過去完成式。

While I was canoeing in the Amazon, I realized I had forgotten my mosquito repellant.

在亞馬遜河划獨木舟時，我才發現自己忘了塗防蚊液了。

I said I hadn't seen anyone in that cabin, but nobody believed me.

↳ 說話（said）的當下已經是過去式，說的內容是更早發生的事，要使用過去完成式。而 believe 的動作和 said 同時發生，因此也用過去式。

我說我在那棟小屋裡沒看到任何人，卻沒人相信我。

	過去簡單式		過去完成式
只提及一個過去事件。	**I smoked my last cigarette two weeks ago.** 兩星期前我抽了最後一根菸。	提及兩個過去事件或動作，並且強調其先後順序。	**When a stranger handed me a carton of cigarettes, I realized I had quit smoking and wasn't even tempted.** ↳ 兩個過去動作：realized 和 had quit。 當一位陌生人遞了一包菸給我，我才發現自己真的戒菸成功了，我甚至連一點抽菸的欲望都沒有。
純粹描述兩個接續的過去事件，並不強調其先後順序。	**I smoked my last cigarette two weeks ago, so I didn't smoke any cigarette yesterday.** 兩星期前我抽了最後一根菸，所以昨天我一根菸也沒抽。		

	現在完成式		過去完成式
說明「**當下**」，描述的一個動作用**現在式**，在這之前一直持續到說話當下的動作要用**現在完成式**。	**I haven't smoked a cigarette for two weeks, so I am dying for a smoke.** 我兩星期沒抽菸了，現在我真想哈一根。	用於「**回想**」，描述的一個動作用**過去式**，在這之前發生的動作要用**過去完成式**。	**I hadn't smoked a cigarette for two weeks, so I was having a nicotine fit when I smelled tobacco smoke.** ↳ 提及兩件事：「戒菸兩星期」和「聞到菸味」。 我兩星期沒抽菸了，所以當我聞到菸味時，我的菸癮又來了。

Practice

1

請勾選正確的答案。

1. At about 9 p.m. we ☐ called ☐ had called to get directions to the party at Kenny Wheeler's house, but the party ☐ ended ☐ had ended at 8:30 p.m.

2. Before the guest of honor ☐ had arrived ☐ arrived, the bachelor party ☐ started ☐ had already started.

3. Terry, the guest of honor, ☐ had proposed ☐ proposed to his girlfriend over a year ago, and finally the bachelor party ☐ was ☐ had been here.

4. We ☐ had wanted ☐ wanted to go to a bar, but Terry ☐ had told ☐ told his fiancée he would go home early.

5. We ☐ accepted ☐ had accepted his request and ☐ took ☐ had taken him home around 1:00 in the morning.

2

請將括弧內的動詞以「過去完成式」或「過去簡單式」填空，完成句子。

1. When I _____ (talk) to the musician, I realized I _____ (see) his picture in the newspaper.

2. I _____ (not practice) my juggling enough, and so I often _____ (drop) balls and pins.

3. I _____ (look at) the milk container and noticed that the milk _____ (already pass) its expiration date.

4. We _____ (leave) the club after the last act _____ (be finished).

5. I knew that Philip _____ (give) many speeches about the global pandemic.

6. It _____ (not dawn) on me that I _____ (need) a full-time job until after my high school graduation.

7. After I _____ (open) the envelope from the graduate school, the rejection letter _____ (dash) my hope about staying in school.

8. I told Grandma that Frank _____ (take) all her jewelry, but she wouldn't believe.

9. They said that the ancient Egyptians _____ (build) the great pyramids by the help of aliens.

Unit **59**

Past Perfect Continuous Tense
過去完成進行式

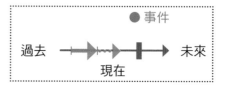

● 事件

過去 ➡➡➡ 未來
現在

Form 構句

肯定句的句型	I/you/we/they/he/she/it had been sleeping
肯定句的縮寫	I/you/we/they/he/she/it 'd been sleeping
否定句的句型	I/you/we/they/he/she/it had not been sleeping
否定句的縮寫	I/you/we/they/he/she/it hadn't been sleeping
疑問句的句型	Had I/you/we/they/he/she/it been sleeping?

Use 用法

1 過去完成進行式表示「發生於過去某個動作之前的另一個動作,且該動作一直持續到某過去動作發生之時」。

I'd been avoiding the stage at the karaoke bar for 30 minutes when Tom pushed me toward the front.

在湯姆把我推到台前時,我已經逃避了 30 分鐘不想站上卡拉 OK 的舞台。

Julia had been sitting in the restaurant for 10 minutes when she saw her ex-boyfriend arrive.

茱麗亞見到前男友到來之前,已經在餐廳裡坐了 10 分鐘。

He had been hiding in the woods when the police finally caught him.

他一直在藏匿在樹林裡,終究還是落網。

2 過去完成進行式可用來說明「過去某個動作發生時,另一個動作正在持續進行」。

I had been ironing my shirt when the doorbell rang.

我在燙襯衫的時候,門鈴響了。

I had been cooking lamb stew when Pete came home with two lunch boxes.

我一直在燉羊肉,結果彼特買了兩個午餐便當回來。

比較

比較現在完成進行式與過去完成進行式:

• I've been practicing my song all week, so I'm ready now.
↳ 從過去一直到說話的當下,持續進行的事。
我已經練唱了一整個星期,所以現在我已經準備好了。

• I'd been practicing my song all week, so I was ready last night.
↳ 從更早的過去一直到回憶的過去時間,持續進行的事。
我之前練唱了一整個星期,所以昨晚我是準備好的。

Practice

1

請將括弧內的動詞以「過去完成進行式」填空,完成句子。

1. Fran _____ (play) the lottery for two months when she won $1,000.

2. Irene _____ (not try) out for parts too long when she was cast in a small role.

3. How many years _____ (Charlie / crack) online games when he was busted by the police?

4. I _____ (eat) lunch at that restaurant for months before the waitress caught my eye.

5. Bobby _____ (smile) and nodding so long that everybody was shocked when they found out he was deaf.

6. Carla _____ (trade) so long in the stock market without collateral. She was surprised when she finally got a margin call.

7. Sally _____ (not live) on the 22nd floor too long before she decided she was afraid of heights.

8. I wanted to know how long _____ (Louise / plan) to become an airline pilot.

2

請從框內選出適當的動詞,以「過去完成進行式」填空,完成句子。

prepare
talk
wash
eat

Tom _____ fried chicken when Dad came home.

Jack _____ the car before it rained.

Susan _____ on the phone when the water boiled over.

Gary _____ the document for the meeting before he realized the next day was a holiday.

Unit 60

Simple Future "Will"
未來簡單式 Will

● 事件

過去 ————■————●——→ 未來
　　　　現在

Form 構句

肯定句的句型	I/you/we/they/he/she/it	will sing
肯定句的縮寫	I/you/we/they/he/she/it	'll + sing
否定句的句型	I/you/we/they/he/she/it	will not sing
否定句的縮寫	I/you/we/they/he/she/it	won't + sing
疑問句的句型	Will I/you/we/they/he/she/it	sing?

1 平常對話時，通常會以縮寫「'll」取代正式的 will。

I'll drop by if I have a little extra time.
如果我有一點多的時間，我就會去找你。

2 當主詞是 I 或 we 時，助動詞也常用 shall，否定句型為 shall not，但這種用法現在已經很少見了。

We shall overcome poverty.
我們會戰勝貧窮的。
I shall veto the legislation.
我會反對那項法律。
We shall appeal the verdict.
我們將對判決提出上訴。

Use 用法

3 當我們純粹要說明一個「未來事件」時，就可以用未來簡單式 will。

I will be in my office next week.
下星期我會在辦公室。
Ernie will pitch the new program in June.
爾尼 6 月會開始進行新專案。
We won't leave the country until August.
我們一直要到 8 月才會出國。

4 will 可以用來「預測未來事件」，此時經常和某些動詞連用。

I will think about the new design.
我會考慮新的設計。
The boss will expect us to decide on the packaging by Friday.
老闆會期待我們在星期五前決定好包裝方式。
He will believe the projected costs if we show him the estimates.
如果我們告訴他評估的結果，他就會相信預估的成本了。
I will hope for the best, but you never know with our boss.
我會往最好的方面想，不過老闆會怎麼想就不得而知了。

- think
- expect
- believe
- hope

5 will 可用來表達「說話當時所做的決定」。

I think I will take a cup of lobster bisque, a Caesar salad, and the roast chicken, and I'll have a glass of chardonnay with that.
我要點一份龍蝦濃湯、一份凱薩沙拉、一份烤雞，還要搭配一杯夏多內紅酒。
I will go with this one.
Yeah, I will go for it.
No, I changed my mind.
That one will go better.
我要選這一個，沒錯，我選這個；等一下，我改變主意了，那個看起來好像更好。

6 will 經常用來詢問「意願」或「可能性」；won't 除了表示「未來不會做某事」，還常用來表示「拒絕」。

Will you be able to come over tomorrow?
你明天能夠過來一趟嗎？
She said, "I won't see you again."
她說：「我不想再看到你了。」

Practice

1

請將括弧內的動詞以「未來簡單式」填空，完成句子。

1. Someday people _____ (recognize) his genius.
2. My wife _____ (not be) at the gallery opening until after 4 p.m.
3. The gallery owner says she _____ (sell) one or two pieces.
4. A drunk customer wants to know if we _____ (serve) her some more wine.
5. Your kids _____ (have) to play in my backyard, not in the house.
6. The reporter from *The Times* _____ (arrive) soon.
7. The museum director _____ (not be) able to attend the meeting because she is leaving early for her trip.
8. What _____ you _____ (do) while we are getting ready for the opening?
9. I _____ (be) in the bathroom throwing up since I am so nervous about directing my first show.

2

請從框內選出適當的動詞，搭配 will 或 won't 填空，完成句子。

finish

buy

go

eat

hear

find

1

I bet I _____ a parking space around here.

2
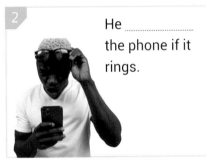
He _____ the phone if it rings.

3

_____ you _____ the magazine so I can look at it?

4

Daddy _____ to the office because he is going out of town.

5

Mommy _____ me some new clothes later today.

6

We _____ three pieces of pizza and drink one soda.

Unit **61**

"Be Going To" for the Future
Be Going To 表示未來意義的用法

Form 構句

肯定句的句型	am/are/is going to work
肯定句的縮寫	I'm going to work
	you/we/they 're going to work
	he/she/it 's going to work
否定句的句型	am/are/is not going to work
否定句的縮寫	I'm not going to work
	you/we/they aren't going to work
	he/she/it isn't going to work
疑問句的句型	Am I going to work?
	Are you/we/they going to work?
	Is he/she/it going to work?

Use 用法

1 be going to 常用來描述「**未來事件**」，具有「**連結現在與未來**」的意味。

I have decided that I am not going to buy a house. I am going to rent an apartment. I am going to call your aunt about her available apartment sometime next week.

我決定不要買房子，而是租間公寓。我下星期會找個時間打電話給你阿姨，問問她有沒有多的公寓。

2 be going to 常用來表示「**由當前的一些跡象判斷，預測未來會發生的事**」。

The snow and ice on the runway has delayed our departure. We are going to take off late. We may miss our connecting flight.

機場跑道上的冰雪導致我們無法準時起飛，飛機稍晚才會起飛，我們可能會錯過轉機。

3 be going to 常用來描述「**事先做好的決定**」或「**意圖**」。

I am going to buy a big work bench and put it in the garage.

我要去買個大型工作台放在車庫裡。

I am going to build a deck on the side of the house, but first I am going to buy a book about carpentry.

我要在房子旁邊蓋個平台，不過首先我要去買本木工的書。

I am all hot and sweaty from mowing the grass. I am going to take a shower before lunch. After lunch, I am going to watch TV for a while.

除完草後我熱得要命，全身都是汗。我要在吃午飯前先沖個澡，吃過午飯後再看一下電視。

4 如果在過去時間，要描述「**過去的未來**」，則使用「was/were + going to」的句型。使用這種句型通常表示「**該事件並未發生**」。

I was going to buy a $10,000,000 house, but I realized I couldn't afford it.

我本來打算買一間一千萬的房子，不過後來發現我根本買不起。

We were going to take a month off, but the plan was canceled.

我們本來要休假一個月，但後來取消計畫了。

He was going to sell his house, but he changed his mind.

他本來要把房子賣掉，不過後來他改變主意。

Practice

1

請從框內選出適當的動詞，以「be going to」的句型填空，完成句子。其中一字會出現兩次。

smash

work

lend

win

quit

rewrite

have

buy

get

1

This résumé doesn't look good.
I _____ it.

2

I've got hired! I _____
_____ hard from now on.

3

You're a crazy driver. One of
these days, you _____
_____ a bad accident.

4

Now that you have smashed up
your car, how _____ you
_____ to your office?

5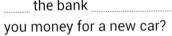

_____ the bank _____
you money for a new car?

6

I _____
a fast little car.

7

You are driving recklessly. You
_____ your
new car.

8

OK. I _____
driving my car on the sidewalk.

9

What type of bicycle _____
you _____ ?

10

You _____ the
race and get to work on time.

131

Unit 62

Comparison Between the Simple Future "Will" and "Be Going To"

未來簡單式 Will 與 Be Going To 的比較

will		be going to	
「認為」未來可能會發生的事	I love my girlfriend. I will marry her someday. 我很愛我女朋友，將來有一天我會娶她。	由當前狀況可以「預見」的未來事件	Slow down! You're going to bump into that tree. 快減速！你要撞上那棵樹了。 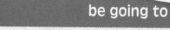
說話當下突然決定的事	I caught some squid in the bay this morning. I will cook them for lunch. 我今天早上在海灣抓到一些烏賊，我要把牠們煮了當午餐。		He bought a diamond ring. He is going to ask his girlfriend to marry him tonight. 他買了一顆鑽戒，打算今晚向女友求婚。
		事先就做好的決定	This afternoon I went to the fish market to get some squid for our dinner party. I am going to cook your favorite squid dish, calamari spaghetti. 我到魚市場去買晚宴派對要用的烏賊，我打算做你最喜歡的一道烏賊料理：花枝義大利麵。

比較

- I'll grill a chicken leg.
  ↳ 臨時起意

  我來烤隻雞腿吧。

- I'm going to grill a chicken leg.
  ↳ 原本就打算好

  我要烤雞腿。

Practice

1

請勾選正確的答案，
有些句子可能兩個答
案皆適用。

1. I think I □ **will leave** □ **am going to leave** now instead of later as I planned yesterday.

2. I □ **am going to take** □ **will take** the GEPT test tomorrow.

3. I □ **will start** □ **am going to start** my annual vacation next week.

4. □ **I'll have** □ **I'll going to have** a ham on rye bread with a sour dill pickle.

5. I □ **will do** □ **am going to do** it anytime you ask me to do it.

6. I forgot about the party. I □ **will come** □ **am going to come** immediately.

7. Jimmy □ **will begin** □ **is going to begin** his new job on Monday.

8. Kelly has just decided to drive, and I □ **will grab** □ **am going to grab** a ride with her.

2

請參考題目提示的情
境，將括弧裡的動詞
改寫為「未來簡單式
will」或「be going
to」，完成句子。

1. Edmond _____ (apply) for a new job. (Simple future)
   → *Edmond will apply for a new job.*

2. He _____ (apply) for a job at a cookie factory. (Previous decision)
   → ....

3. He said, "I _____ (be) the best cookie tester in the world!"
   (Simple future)
   → ....

4. He said, "I _____ (pass) the exam with flying colors."
   (Intention; previous decision)
   → ....

5. He said, "First, I _____ (practice) testing some cookies."
   (Simple future)
   → ....

6. Lou asked, "_____ you _____ (bake) cookies as well?"
   (Previous decision)
   → ....

7. Lou claimed, "You _____ (burn) those cookies." (Probable future)
   → ....

8. Edmond retorted, "I _____ (bake) some cookies right away!"
   (Sudden decision)
   → ....

Part 8 Future Tenses 未來式

Unit 63

Present Continuous for the Future and the Comparison With "Be Going To"

「現在進行式」表示未來意義的用法，以及與 Be Going To 的比較

1 現在進行式也常用來表示**未來事件**，此時指的是「**計畫好的未來事件**」。

Where are you meeting the buyers from Japan?

你和日本的採購員約在哪裡見面？

I'm meeting them in the Yokosuka sales office. 我會和他們在橫須賀的業務辦公室見面。

Joanna is moving to the international sales office.

喬安娜要轉到國際業務辦公室。

2 現在進行式表示「**未來事件**」時，經常會在句中指出「**確切的時間**」。

- Friday afternoon
- Saturday
- this morning
- next month

What are you doing for your grandmother's birthday?

你祖母生日的那天你會有什麼表示？

We are taking her to dinner and the opera next Saturday night.

下星期六晚上，我們要帶她去吃晚餐、看歌劇。

Ruth is starting her new job on May 1st.

露絲 5 月 1 日起開始新工作。

	be going to		現在進行式
強調「意圖」	I am going to work extremely hard and buy my first house before the age of thirty. 我要非常努力，在三十歲之前買到我人生中的第一間房子。	強調「事先做好的安排」	I am signing the contract with Union Studio next Monday. Is there anything else I should know? 我將於下星期一和聯合工作室簽約，有什麼其他我該知道的事項嗎？

不過，使用 be going to 或現在進行式來描述未來事件時，兩者的差別並不大，上面所述其實只是極細微的差別，實際使用上，尤其是美式英語，兩者的意義相當。

- I am leaving for my trip tomorrow at 6 a.m.
  = I am going to leave for my trip tomorrow at 6 a.m.

  我明天早上 6 點出發旅行。

be going to 和現在進行式都不能用來說明「**預測的未來事件**」，此時只能用未來簡單式 will。

✗ Cynthia is crying for joy when she sees this present.

✗ Cynthia is going to cry for joy when she sees this present.

✓ Cynthia will cry for joy when she sees this present.

辛西亞看到這份禮物的時候，一定會喜極而泣。

Practice

1

plan

cut

perform

close

transfer

inspect

請從框內選出適當的動詞，以「現在進行式」填空，完成句子。

1. Bella Conchita, the famous soprano, _____ at the Lyric Opera next weekend.

2. The mayor _____ the ribbon at the groundbreaking ceremony on Monday, August 15th.

3. Ellen _____ to the European sales office next month.

4. The textiles division _____ its Vietnamese factory in the next couple of months.

5. Director Van Stolten _____ the city's fire department sub-stations for compliance with the new EMT regulations all next week.

6. The IMF _____ a major review of all loan portfolios for undeveloped nations in the coming six months.

2

請將括弧內的動詞以「現在進行式」或「**be going to**」的句型填空，完成句子。有些句子可能兩種句型皆適用。

1. Ron *is going to leave / is leaving* (leave) on his trip to Geneva tomorrow.

2. The stock market _____ (tank) tomorrow.

3. The plumber _____ (fix) the pipes next week.

4. The gas tank _____ (run out) on Monday.

5. Bobby _____ (pay) the electricity bill on Tuesday afternoon.

6. Mary _____ (graduate) this June.

7. After the earthquake, Japan _____ (have) many economic problems.

8. The owner's son _____ (bankrupt) the company.

Part 8 Future Tenses 未來式

Unit 64

Present Simple for the Future
「現在簡單式」表示未來意義的用法

1 現在簡單式有時也會用來表示「固定、安排好的未來事件」，經常用於「時刻表」等。

What time does the family swimming time start on Sunday?

星期日家庭游泳池開放的時間是幾點？

On Sunday afternoons, the family swimming time begins at 2 p.m. and finishes at 5 p.m.

星期日下午，開放給家庭成員游泳的時間是從下午 2 點到 5 點。

The swimming pool also opens from 6 p.m. to 8 p.m. on Sunday evenings.

游泳池星期日晚上也從 6 點開放至 8 點。

OPEN

Sunday

2 p.m. – 5 p.m.
family members only

6 p.m. – 8 p.m.
all members

2 現在簡單式常用來「請求指示」，此時也具有「未來」含意。

How do I get to the National Palace Museum?

故宮博物院要怎麼去？

Where do I buy the tickets?

票要在哪裡買？

3 在「時間或條件子句」裡，當主要子句使用了 will 的未來式時，時間或條件子句要以現在簡單式來代替未來式。

- when 當……
- while 當……時
- as soon as 一……就
- after 在……之後
- before 在……之前
- until 直到
- if 如果
- unless 除非
- as long as 只要
- so long as 只要
- provided that 假若
- providing that 假若

I will get you a hot Americano when I go to buy lunch.

我去買午餐時，會幫你買一杯熱美式。

I will also choose a piece of cake for myself while I am in the café.

我在咖啡廳時，也會幫我自己選一片蛋糕。

I will rent the movie you want as soon as it arrives.

等你想看的那部電影一上架，我就去租。

We won't watch the video before we eat lunch.

我們吃完午餐才會開始看影片。

比較

若「時間和條件子句」後接的是現在完成式，則等到該子句中的行為完成後，主要子句所描述的情況才會發生。

- I will vacuum the carpet after you have picked up your clothes.

  等你把地上的衣服都撿起來後，我要吸地毯。

136

Practice

1

請將括弧內的動詞以「現在簡單式」填空。

1. Jackson _____ (make) breakfast at home every morning at 6:15 a.m.

2. Jackson's wife _____ (wash) the dishes every morning after Jackson _____ (leave) home to catch the 7:20 train.

3. Every night Jackson's wife _____ (pick up) Jackson at the train station at 6:30.

4. When _____ (do) the aquarium _____ (open) on Sunday?

5. The aquarium _____ (open) after the fish have breakfast.

6. The cafeteria _____ (serve) fried chicken every Friday.

7. The city libraries _____ (be closed) on Mondays.

8. The band at the pub _____ (start) at 9:00 in the evening.

2

請將括弧內的動詞以「簡單未來式 will」或「現在簡單式」填空，完成句子。

1. I _____ (go) to the movies when my mom _____ (go) out.

2. I _____ (sneak out) while my family _____ (be) asleep.

3. My brother _____ (enlist) in the military as soon as he _____ (graduate) from high school.

4. I _____ (tour) the South Pole before I _____ (visit) the North Pole.

5. I _____ (stay up) late every night before I _____ (turn in) my assignment.

6. I _____ (stay) right here in this tree until you _____ (bring) a ladder.

7. The crocodile _____ (appear) in the circus act if it _____ (perform) well.

8. It _____ (be) difficult to travel to Mars unless the space shuttle's computer _____ (accept) my VISA credit card.

9. Tammy _____ (sing) as long as the music _____ (play).

10. I _____ (eat) my peas provided that you _____ (put) honey on them.

Part 8 未來式 64 「現在簡單式」表示未來意義的用法

Unit 65

Future Continuous Tense
未來進行式

Form 構句

過去 ——————→ 未來
現在
● 事件

| 肯定句的句型 | I/you/we/they/he/she/it | will be giving |
| 肯定句的縮寫 | I/you/we/they/he/she/it | 'll be giving |

| 否定句的句型 | I/you/we/they/he/she/it | will not be giving |
| 否定句的縮寫 | I/you/we/they/he/she/it | won't be giving |

| 疑問句的句型 | Will | I/you/we/they/he/she/it | be giving? |

Use 用法

1 未來進行式用來描述「未來某特定時刻正在進行的事件」。

We **will be watching** TV when Mom arrives home.

當媽媽到家時，我們將會在看電視。

I **will be driving** at 7:30 tomorrow. It usually takes me an hour to drive to work. I often leave my house at 7 a.m. and get to my office at 8 a.m. Tomorrow at 10 a.m., I **will be drinking** coffee. I **won't be working** at that time. I **will be sitting** in the coffee shop next door to my office. Will you join me for a cup of coffee tomorrow morning?

明天早上7點半我會在開車，
開車上班通常要花一小時，
所以我常常早上7點出門，
8點抵達辦公室。
明天早上10點我會喝咖啡，
這時候我沒有在工作，我會
坐在辦公室旁邊的咖啡店。
明天早上你要和我一起喝杯
咖啡嗎？

2 未來進行式可指「確定的未來計畫」，此時並沒有「進行」的意味。

Dad will be going to the library at 7:00 tonight. Do you want him to return the library books?

爸爸今天晚上7點要去圖書館，你要請他幫你還書嗎？

Mom will be taking a yoga class every Wednesday night from 7:00 to 9:00.

媽媽以後每個星期三晚上7點到9點要上瑜伽課。

3 未來進行式可以表示「依照正常的發展，應該會發生的事」，此時該事件並非人為安排或意圖，而是「自然而然會發生的」。

Dad won't be coming back home soon. **He is still working** in his office.

↳ 因為爸爸現在仍然在辦公室，照理無法馬上回家。

爸爸不會馬上回家，他現在人還在他的辦公室裡工作。

4 **請別人幫忙做事時**，可以先用「Will you be + V-ing」詢問對方的計畫、行程，再提出要求。

使用這種句型表示你並不希望因為自己的要求，而改變對方原本的計畫。

Will you be walking home past the mini-mart? Could you please pick up some soy milk on your way home?

你走路回家時會經過便利商店嗎？那你回家時可以順便幫我買點豆漿嗎？

Will you be attending the opening of the Monet show at the art museum? I was wondering if my son could have your stamped admission ticket if you are not planning to save it.

你會去參加美術館舉辦的莫內展覽開幕式嗎？如果你不想保留入場券的話，可以送給我兒子嗎？

Practice

1

右表是 Dr. Edwards 明天的行程，請用「未來進行式」寫出他在各時間正在進行的事。

8:00-10:00	Meet the committee members
10:00-12:00	Watch the demonstration of sterilization equipment
12:00-14:00	Eat lunch
14:00-16:00	Listen to a panel discussion about childhood disease
16:00-18:00	Present a paper about disease treatment plans
18:00-24:00	Tour the city

1. → *Dr. Edwards will be meeting the committee members at 9:00.*

2. →

3. →

4. →

5. →

6. →

2

請將括弧內的動詞以「未來進行式」填空，完成句子，再從框內選出適當的問句接在句子後面。

選項：
- Are you planning to watch it again?
- Can I come to listen to you play?
- Can I walk with you on the Nature Trail?
- Can you buy us a pizza?
- Could I get a ride from you?
- Would you like to use my computer this afternoon?

1. My mom _____won't be cooking_____ (not cook) tonight. *Can you buy us a pizza?*

2. Dad _____ (not drive) tomorrow.

3. I _____ (leave) the office around noon.

4. I _____ (return) the video later tonight.

5. When _____ you _____ (walk) the Nature Trail?

6. _____ you _____ (play) the cello at the music school?

Part 8 Future Tenses 未來式

Unit 66

Future Perfect Tense and Future Perfect Continuous Tense
「未來完成式」與「未來完成進行式」

未來完成式的形式

肯定句的句型	will have watched
否定句的句型	will not have watched
否定句的縮寫	won't have watched
疑問句的句型	Will . . . have watched?

未來完成進行式的形式

肯定句的句型	will have been drinking
否定句的句型	will not have been drinking
否定句的縮寫	won't have been drinking
疑問句的句型	Will . . . have been drinking?

未來完成式的用法

1 未來完成式表示「現在尚未完成，但在未來某特定時刻將會完成的動作」。這裡的 have 代表事情的完成，不可省略。

He will have finished his novel by the end of July. 他會在 7 月底前寫完小說。
He will have written the editorial by 2:00 this afternoon.
今天下午 2 點以前他會把社論寫好。

2 未來完成式可以表示「期待在未來某特定時刻完成的動作」，此時句中通常會有一個表示「直到未來某時刻」的時間副詞或片語。

I will have reinstalled my operating system before bedtime tonight.
↳ 此句表示期待能完成安裝
我會在今晚睡覺前把作業系統重新灌好。

- before next Monday
- by tomorrow
- by next Christmas
- by noon

By tomorrow, I will have debugged my operating system.
↳ 表示期待到時能解決作業系統問題
到明天時，我會把作業系統的問題都解決。

未來完成進行式的用法

3 未來完成進行式表示「在未來某特定時刻之前持續進行的動作」。

I will have been riding my bicycle for four hours when I arrive at the top of the mountain.
我抵達山頂時，將已經騎了四個小時的自行車。

4 未來完成式和未來完成進行式所描述的動作，都可能開始於「過去」。

Sue will have worked for the FBI for 35 years by the time she retires.
= Sue will have been working for the FBI for 35 years by the time she retires.
等到蘇退休時，她就已經在聯邦調查局工作 35 年了。

Practice

1　請將括弧內的動詞以「未來完成式」填空，完成句子。

1. I ＿＿＿＿＿＿＿＿＿＿ (move) into my new apartment by next week.

2. By next month, I ＿＿＿＿＿＿＿＿＿＿ (settle) in my new house.

3. I ＿＿＿＿＿＿＿＿＿＿ (climb) to the top of the mountain via the north trail by lunch.

4. I ＿＿＿＿＿＿＿＿＿＿ (start) down the mountain via the east trail by 2 p.m.

5. Jerry ＿＿＿＿＿＿＿＿＿＿ (finish) his research project by early July.

6. Jerry ＿＿＿＿＿＿＿＿＿＿ (begin) his new job by early August.

2　請將各題提供的用語，以 **How long** 搭配「未來完成進行式」的句型，寫出問句；再依圖示回答問題。

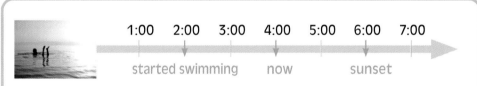

1. How long / he / swim in the ocean / by sunset?

Ⓠ _How long will he have been swimming in the ocean by sunset?_

Ⓐ _He will have been swimming in the ocean for four hours by sunset._

2. How long / he / travel / by the time he get to Buenos Aires?

Ⓠ ＿＿＿＿＿＿＿＿＿＿＿＿＿＿＿＿＿＿

Ⓐ ＿＿＿＿＿＿＿＿＿＿＿＿＿＿＿＿＿＿

Unit **67**

"Have" and "Have Got"
Have 與 Have Got 的用法

Form 構句

在英式英語裡，經常將 have 當作助動詞一般地變化，此時**否定句**會用 have not 或 has not，**疑問句**會用「Have/Has . . .?」。

have

肯定句的句型	have/has money
否定句的句型	do not / does not have money
否定句的縮寫	don't/doesn't have money
疑問句的句型	Do/Does . . . have money?

have got

肯定句的句型	have got / has got money
肯定句的縮寫	've got / 's got money
否定句的句型	have not got / has not got money
否定句的縮寫	haven't got / hasn't got money
疑問句的句型	Have/Has . . . got money?

1 have 和 have got 都可以指「**擁有**」，此時兩者的意義完全相同。

I have got a new cell phone. = I have a new cell phone. 我有一支新手機。

He hasn't got a scooter. = He doesn't have a scooter. 他沒有摩托車。

Have you got a date? = Do you have a date?
你有約會嗎？

對於何時該使用 have 和 have got 有很多不同的說法，其中一種是認為**美式英語多用 have**，英式英語則多用 **have got**。
另一種說法是認為 **have got** 是用在非正式的**對話裡**，**have** 則多用於正式場合或寫作中。

2 have 常用來說明「**重複發生的事件**」；have got 則多用於說明「**單一事件**」。

That clothing store often has sales.
那家服飾店常打折。

That clothing store has got a sale right now. 那間服飾店現在有折扣。

3 have 和 have got 當作「**擁有**」解釋時，沒有**進行式**，也不能用於**被動語態**。

✗ Shelly is having got a new suit.
　　↳ 不能用進行式

✗ The new suit is had by Shelly.
　　↳ 不能用被動語態

✓ Shelly has a new suit.

✓ Shelly has got a new suit.
　　↳ 要使用簡單式及主動語態

雪莉有一件新衣服。

4 have got 只能用於**現在式**，沒有過去式。如果要表示「**過去擁有**」，要使用 have 的過去式 had；**否定句**和**疑問句**也要用過去式助動詞 did 來構成。

Sally had a cute collie for about 13 years, but he died of old age last week.

莎莉有一隻養了 13 年的牧羊犬，不過狗狗上星期過世了。

"Did you have a big house while working in Detroit two years ago?"
「你兩年前在底特律工作時，就有了大房子了嗎？」

"No, I had a small apartment."
「沒有，我那時只有一間小公寓。」

5 have got 也不能用於**未來式**，如果要表示「**未來擁有**」，要使用 will have。

✗ I will have got a new sports car.

✓ I will have a new sports car.
我將會擁有一輛新的跑車。

6 have got 的問句，簡答要使用 have 來回答，不能加 got。

A: Have **you** got **a toothpick?** 請問你有牙籤嗎？
B: **Yes,** I have. 是的，我有。
B: **No,** I haven't. 不，我沒有。

Practice

1

請勾選正確的答案。

1. ☐ **Have you got** ☐ **Have you** your bowling ball?

2. I ☐ **have got** ☐ **have not** three children.

3. She ☐ **has not** ☐ **does not have** any time to take a break.

4. It ☐ **does not have got** ☐ **does not have** a battery.

5. ☐ **Does she have** ☐ **Does she have got** any idea about this blog?

2

請以 have、have got 或「助動詞」填空，完成句子。如果 have、have got 兩個用語都可以，請兩個都填。

1 I _____ a happy family.

2 Everyone will _____ a pay raise next month.

3 Have you got a pencil sharpener?
Yes, I _____.

4 Do you have any hand cream?
No, I _____.

Unit 68

"Have" for Action
Have 當作行為動詞的用法

1 have 經常用來描述「**動作**」，此時不可用 **have got** 代替。

表示「喝飲料」

have a soft drink 喝飲料
have a cup of tea 喝杯茶
have a cup of coffee 喝杯咖啡
have a Coke 喝可樂

表示「吃東西」

have a bite 吃一口
have breakfast 吃早餐
have lunch 吃午餐
have dinner 吃晚餐

表示「休假、遊樂」

have a day off 放一天假
have a holiday 放假
have a party 舉辦派對
have a good time 玩得開心

表示「說話」

have a conversation 對話
have a talk 交談
have a chat 聊天
have a meeting 開會

表示「疾病」

have a headache 頭痛
have a sore throat 喉嚨痛
have diarrhea 拉肚子
have a runny nose 流鼻水

表示「爭論」

have a disagreement 意見不合
have a fight 吵架
have a quarrel 爭吵
have an argument 爭論

表示「沐浴梳洗」

have a shower 淋浴
have a bath 洗澡
have a shave 刮鬍子

其他用語

have a try 試試看
have a baby 生小孩
have a look 看看

2 have 作「**行為動詞**」時，可以使用進行式。

Alfred is having dinner at this time.
阿爾發此刻正在吃晚餐。
Are you still having dinner?
你們還在吃晚餐嗎？
We're not having dinner.
We're having dessert.
我們沒有在吃晚餐，我們在吃甜點。

3 have 作「**行為動詞**」時，不能用 **have got** 代替。

✗ I always have got a cup of coffee during my break.

✓ I always have a cup of coffee during my break.
休息時我都會來上一杯咖啡。

4 have 作「**行為動詞**」時，否定句和**疑問句**要使用助動詞 do/does 或 did 來構成。

I don't usually have lunch before 1 p.m.
我通常下午一點之後才吃午餐。
Where do you have lunch?
你都在哪裡吃午餐？
Did you have lunch at the new restaurant?
你去那家新開的餐廳吃午餐了嗎？

5 have 作「**行為動詞**」時，不能縮寫為「**'ve**」，has 不能縮寫為「**'s**」，had 不能縮寫為「**'d**」。

✗ I've a meeting in a few minutes.

✓ I have a meeting in a few minutes.
幾分鐘後我有個會要開。

Practice

1　請從圖中選出適當的片語並以正確的形式填空，完成句子。

have a look

have a glass of orange juice

have a fight

have a baby

have a bubble bath

have a bowl of soup

1. I _____ with my neighbor last night.

2. Laura is pregnant. She is _____ in June.

3. Let's buy some orange juice. I want to _____ while I'm watching TV.

4. Irma usually _____ for dinner.

5. I love to _____ in our bathtub on winter nights.

6. Did you _____ at the newspaper this morning?

2

請選出正確的答案。

_____ 1. Dad and Mom usually _____ after dinner every night.
Ⓐ have a nice day　Ⓑ have a nightmare　Ⓒ have a walk

_____ 2. Have you _____ already? There is so much left.
Ⓐ had a piece of apple pie　　Ⓑ have your shoes washed
Ⓒ have a nap

_____ 3. We _____ in Taitung. We will definitely visit it again.
Ⓐ had everything ready　　Ⓑ had a good time
Ⓒ had nothing to do

_____ 4. I _____ yesterday afternoon, so I went home, leaving all the work undone.
Ⓐ had a headache　Ⓑ had a picnic　Ⓒ had a dream

_____ 5. I am _____ tomorrow. Shall we go to a movie?
Ⓐ having a day off　Ⓑ having a feeling　Ⓒ having some wine

Unit 69

Be Being
Be Being 的用法

1 「be + 形容詞」可表達一種「狀態」。

Susan is aggressive.
蘇珊的個性很衝。

Bobby is impatient.
巴比很沒耐性。

2 be being 可以視為 be 動詞的進行式，being 就是 be 的現在分詞。此時後面雖然也接形容詞，但其實描述的是一種「**動作**」而非「**狀態**」，而且是「**暫時的動作**」。

What's wrong with you? You are being very rude today.
↳ 其實是 You are acting rude today.
怎麼了你？今天怎麼會這麼失禮。

3 be being 表示：個性並非如此，但今天卻表現的不一樣。

She is being naughty today.
↳ 她個性並不調皮，但今天表現得比較調皮
她今天表現得比較調皮。
Yesterday Mrs. Wang was being very hospitable.
↳ 暗示她平時並不是一個好客的人
王太太昨天表現得很好客。

4 並非所有形容詞都適合接在 be being 的後面。

可以用於 be being 句型的形容詞			不適用於 be being 句型的形容詞	
bad	impolite	pleasant	beautiful	old
careful	kind	polite	handsome	short
careless	lazy	quiet	happy	sick
foolish	naughty	reasonable	healthy	tall
funny	nice	rude	hungry	thirsty
generous	noisy	serious	lucky	well
impatient	patient	unreasonable	nervous	young

比較
✗ Sam is being tall.
✓ Sam is tall.
↳ tall 並不是一個暫時的動作，不適用 be being 的句型。
山姆很高。

比較
✗ Larry was being happy to help.
✓ Larry was happy to help.
↳ happy 只適合用於描述狀態，不適合描述動作。
賴瑞很樂意幫忙。

1

請勾選出正確的答案。如果在語意和文法上兩個答案都可以，可都勾選。

1. Judy □ is □ is being healthy.

2. I don't think he was sincere. He □ was just □ was just being polite.

3. Today Lily □ was □ was being naughty in scattering the dog cookies all over the floor.

4. Joe □ was □ was being very rude to talk like that.

5. Nancy □ was □ was being lucky to win the lottery.

6. Sam □ is □ is being sick. He has been lying in bed for several days.

7. Normally Stanley is a careful person, but yesterday he □ was □ was being careless when looking after his brother in the hospital.

8. Heather's little girl □ is □ is being very cute.

9. I □ was □ was being foolish to give him with all my savings.

10. Selina □ was □ was being generous to help me when I was unemployed.

11. I □ was □ was being very nervous on my first day of work.

12. Alice □ was □ was being quiet in the meeting.

13. I □ am □ am being hungry. When will lunch be ready?

Unit 70

Linking Verbs 連綴動詞

---

1 連綴動詞是用來「**描述主詞狀態**」的動詞，與一般描述動作的動詞不同。
連綴動詞後面要接**主詞補語**，也就是**名詞、代名詞**或**形容詞**，通常不能接副詞。
最常見的連綴動詞就是 be 動詞。

Wade is the product manager of our firm.
> ↳ be 動詞後面接名詞 product manager，補充說明主詞 Wade 的身分狀態。

韋德是我們公司的產品經理。

It was he who opened the jewel box.
> ↳ be 動詞後面接代名詞 he。這是一個強調句型：It is/was . . . who/that . . .

就是他打開珠寶盒的。

Danny is smart but lazy.
> ↳ be 動詞後面接形容詞 smart 和 lazy，補充說明主詞 Danny 的狀態。

丹尼很聰明，但是很懶惰。

---

2 感官動詞也屬於連綴動詞，後面可以直接加**形容詞**或「**like + 名詞**」。

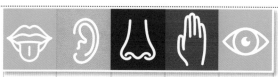

taste	sound	smell	feel	look
嚐起來	聽起來	聞起來	感覺	看起來

The stinky tofu smells like some used socks that haven't been washed for a week, but it tastes wonderful.

臭豆腐聞起來像是一星期沒洗的臭襪子，但是好吃極了。

The Milan Cathedral looks solemn.

米蘭大教堂的外觀莊嚴肅穆。

A caterpillar feels soft and hairy.

毛毛蟲摸起來軟綿綿、毛茸茸的。

He sounds depressed. What happened?

他的口氣聽起來很沮喪，發生什麼事了？

---

3 連綴動詞還包含一些表示「**狀態**」或「**狀態的改變情況**」的動詞。

- **appear** 似乎
- **become** 變成
- **get** 變得
- **go** 變得
- **grow** 變得
- **prove** 證明是
- **remain** 維持
- **seem** 似乎
- **turn** 變得

The man seems lost. Shall we go over and give him a hand?

那個人看起來迷路了，我們要不要過去幫他一下？

Everything went wrong.

每件事都不順利。

When I grow old, I'll move to a nursing home and chat with other elderly people all day.

等我年紀大了，我要搬去老人院，整天和其他老人聊天。

---

4 上述連綴動詞，同時也是**一般動詞**。

Taste the soup before you serve it.

把湯端上桌之前，記得嚐一下味道。

What are you looking at?

你在看什麼？

Can you get a jar of marmalade for me?

幫我買一罐橘子果醬好嗎？

I think I can feel the rain. Let's move fast.

好像有雨滴在我身上，我們走快一點。

Gary turned his head and saw a man in black following him.

蓋瑞回過頭，發現他遭到一名黑衣男子尾隨。

You don't want to smell my shoes.

你不會想聞我的鞋子的。

Practice

1

請勾選正確的答案。

smell

1. The coffee beans smell □ fruit □ fruity.

2. The coffee beans smell □ raspberry □ like raspberry.

3. We can smell □ the aroma □ aromatic of their home-made coffee from outside the house.

look

4. Do I look □ a graceful woman □ graceful in this silk dress?

5. In that dress, you look like □ the most beautiful lady □ the most beautiful in the world.

6. How did you know? You didn't even look □ me □ at me.

taste

7. Would you like to taste □ my Mapo tofu □ like my Mapo tofu?

8. Hmm, it tastes □ like spicy □ spicy.

9. It tastes □ like a dish □ a dish Dad would love.

feel

10. Yesterday, I saw an unusual plant on the path to our wooden hut in the valley. I reached out my hand to touch it. It felt □ cool and hairy □ like cool and hairy.

11. Soon after I touched it, I realized that it was poisonous, because I couldn't feel □ like my finger □ my finger.

others

12. My finger began to swell and turned □ like red □ red.

13. I put on some ointment, but my finger didn't seem to get □ better □ well.

14. The swelling grew □ a bigger one □ bigger.

15. At last I had to see a doctor. He said my finger had gotten □ more badly □ worse.

16. I could have lost my finger if I had turned □ him □ to him any later.

17. He gave me a prescription and told me to get □ the medicine □ medicinal at the pharmacy next to the clinic.

18. My finger appears □ normal □ normality today.

Unit 71

Causative Verbs: Make, Have, Get
使役動詞 Make、Have、Get 的用法

---

1 使役動詞是用來「**使另一個動作發生**」的動詞。

- make it happen 使之發生
- have her call back 請她回電
- get it done 把它做完

---

2 make 可以當作使役動詞，句型為：

| make | + | 人／物 | + | 原形動詞 |

表示「**讓某人或某物去做某個動作**」。

No one can make him change his mind.
沒人可以改變他的心意。

He tried using magic to make that glass move, but it stayed on the table.
他試著施展魔法移動那個杯子，但杯子還是停在桌子上。

---

3 have 可以當作使役動詞，句型為：

❶ | have | + | 人／物 | + | 原形動詞 |
❷ | have | + | 物 | + | 過去分詞 |

表示「**叫某人或某物去做某個動作**」或「**讓某物接受某個動作**」。

I'll have Jason rewrite the proposal.
我會請傑森重寫企畫案。

Please have the proposal rewritten. It's awful.
這份企畫書寫得不好，請重寫一份。

---

4 get 可以當作使役動詞，句型為：

❶ | get | + | 人 | + | 加 to 的不定詞 |

表示「**叫某人去做某個動作**」。

❷ | get | + | 物 | + | 過去分詞 |

表示「**讓某物接受某個動作**」。

No one can get me to do the things that I don't want to do.
沒人能叫我做我不願意做的事。

Did you get the air conditioner fixed?
你找人修好冷氣了沒？

---

5 這三個字當中，make 的語氣最強烈，get 次之，have 的語氣最和緩。

Norman can't make his son eat vegetables.
諾曼無法逼他兒子吃青菜。

He can't get his son to do dishes either.
他也叫不動他兒子去洗碗。

At least, he had his son take ping-pong lessons.
至少，他讓兒子上桌球課了。

---

6 這三個字除了作為使役動詞之外，都可以當作**一般動詞**使用，分別有它們的意義在。

Jeffery is making a wooden chair at his yard.　↳ 製造
傑弗瑞正在院子裡做木頭椅子。

Jennifer had lunch with her teammates at　↳ 吃
a Chinese restaurant yesterday.
昨天，珍妮佛和她的隊友在一家中式餐館吃了午餐。

Patti got a new cell phone from her　↳ 獲得
boyfriend last week.
上星期，佩蒂的男友送了她一支新手機。

1

請選出正確的答案。

.... 1. Kelly saw a giant spider in her room, but she couldn't get it _____ out of the window.

    Ⓐ move   Ⓑ to move   Ⓒ moving   Ⓓ moved

.... 2. If I don't have Isabella _____ for her bad manner, how do I teach other kids to behave?

    Ⓐ punish   Ⓑ to punish   Ⓒ punishing   Ⓓ punished

.... 3. What makes you _____ he'll win the race? He is falling behind other runners now.

    Ⓐ to believe   Ⓑ believed   Ⓒ believing   Ⓓ believe

.... 4. Jimmy is not in now. I'll have him _____ you back when he returns.

    Ⓐ call   Ⓑ to call   Ⓒ calling   Ⓓ called

.... 5. The air conditioner is not working! I must get it _____ as soon as possible. I can't stand the heat this summer.

    Ⓐ repair   Ⓑ to repair   Ⓒ repairing   Ⓓ repaired

.... 6. You can't get things _____. I suggest you let it go.

    Ⓐ undo   Ⓑ to undo   Ⓒ undoing   Ⓓ undone

2

請勾選屬於「使役動詞」的用法。

- ☐ make a fire
- ☐ make her go away
- ☐ make the baby cry
- ☐ make a birthday card for Lisa
- ☐ get him a glass of water
- ☐ get him to move over a little
- ☐ get the coffee cup washed
- ☐ get me a coffee cup
- ☐ have her write an article
- ☐ have a writer's block
- ☐ have a terrible dream
- ☐ have the pillowcase changed

Unit **72**

Causative Verb: Let
Let 當作使役動詞的用法

1 let 是使役動詞，句型為：

$$\boxed{\text{let}} + \boxed{\text{人／物}} + \boxed{\text{原形動詞}}$$

表示「**讓某人或某物去做某個動作**」。

Joe let me drive his car to school.
喬讓我開他的車上學。

Susan let the dog rest before the next race started.

下一場比賽開始前，蘇珊讓狗狗休息了一下。

2 let's 常用來「**提議**」，會接「**不加 to 的不定詞**」，形成祈使句。let's 句型被視為「**第一人稱複數**」的祈使句。

Let's get away from it all.
我們全都離它遠一點吧！

Let's go now before they realize we're not busy.

趁他們還不知道我們很閒的時候快走吧！

3 let me、let us 和 let's 有所區別。

Let me explain in detail.
↳ 說話者一個人解釋

讓我詳細解釋給你聽。

Let's get / Let us get started right now.
↳ 建議聽者和說話者一起行動

我們立刻行動吧。

We can't be of any help here. Why don't you let us go?
↳ 要走的人不包含聽者

我們在這裡也沒用，你何不讓我們走？

4 $\boxed{\text{let's}} + \boxed{\text{not}} + \boxed{\text{不加 to 的不定詞}}$
可以形成否定祈使句。

Let's not stay at this boring meeting.
我們別待在這麼無趣的會議吧。

Let's not get caught leaving early.

別被人家抓到我們提早離開。

let's 和 don't 放在一起的用法很少見，有些人認為這是老式的用法，不過大多數人都認為這是錯誤的文法。

✗ Don't let's finish this food.
✓ Let's not finish this food.
　 我們別把這些食物吃光。
✗ Let's don't take the 295 bus.
✓ Let's not take the 295 bus.
　 我們不要搭 295 號公車。

5 在 let's 句子的句尾加上附加問句「shall we?」，也可以**加強語氣**。

Let's order another round of soft drinks, shall we? 我們再點一次飲料，好嗎？

Let's go on the roller coaster one more time, shall we?

我們再玩一次雲霄飛車，好不好？

let me 只包含「**說話者**」。

let us 包含「**包括說話者的群體**」，但不包括「**聽者**」，這種情況不用 **let's**。

let's 包含「**說話者一方和聽者**」，這種情況也可以用 let us（= let's）。

Practice

1 請將句中錯誤的用語劃上底線，並寫出正確的用語（不須寫出完整的句子）。

1. One of the employees said to the boss, "Please don't fire us. <u>Let's</u> stay and keep working here. We promise not to make such a serious mistake again."
   → *Let us*

2. Let's not <u>to</u> have dinner in the same restaurant every day. I want to try something different.
   → ....

3. Sarah lets her daughter to go to a bilingual school. However, I doubt if it's a good idea.
   → ....

4. Let's build another sand castle, don't we?
   → ....

5. Let's don't cry. We'll have another chance someday.
   → ....

6. Let's hang up your coat on the rack over there.
   → ....

7. Father won't let's come near the stove in the kitchen, but I want to help Mom with the cooking.
   → ....

8. Let's do make a cake for Trent. It's his birthday.
   → ....

9. Let us race to the bridge, do we?
   → ....

10. Let's not entering that house. It looks spooky.
    → ....

11. Let me to have a talk with him. Maybe he'll listen to me.
    → ....

12. Don't let's go to that beach. The undertow is dangerous this time of year.
    → ....

Unit 73

Infinitives and -ing Forms
不定詞與動名詞

1 動詞可分為**不定詞**與**動名詞**。動名詞就是 V-ing 的形式，具有**動詞**的性質，也有**名詞**的性質。

Picking strawberries at a local farm is fun. ↳ picking 是動名詞，而非進行式中的動詞。

到地方農場採草莓很有趣。

2 **不定詞**主要指「加 to 的不定詞」。大部分動詞後面，都可以接「加 to 的不定詞」。

We want to join the June Mediterranean tour group.

我們想參加 6 月的地中海旅行團。

3 「不加 to 的不定詞」則用於 make、let、have 等使役動詞後面，或是助動詞後面。

That movie made my sister cry. Let's go to a movie tonight.

那部電影我妹看得都哭了，我們今晚也去看吧。

Mary must go to the hospital to get a copy of her birth certificate.

瑪麗得去醫院拿一份出生證明。

4 動名詞和「加 to 的不定詞」都可以當作**主詞**，但是「加 to 的不定詞」當作主詞是比較老式的用法。

Painting is the easiest of the building trades. 粉刷是建築工程業最簡單的一種。

Moving a house is not easy.

移動房子不是一件容易的事。

Selling houses is a tough job with long hours. 賣房子是得花長時間的難差事。

5 以 it 為虛主詞的句子，後面會以「加 to 的不定詞」作為真正的**主詞**。

It is a good idea to keep your job skills current.

↳ 真正的主詞是 to keep your job skills current。

讓工作技巧不斷符合現狀的需求是最好的。

Is it practical to cross train for all the jobs in your department?

↳ 真正的主詞是 to cross train for all the jobs in your department。

在你的部門內就所有工作做交叉訓練，可行嗎？

6 動名詞和「加 to 的不定詞」都可當作**受詞**，但何時該用何種形式，請見後面單元說明。

I can't stand playing volleyball in the hot

↳ 動名詞片語，是動詞 stand 的受詞。

sun. Why don't we find an indoor court?

我受不了在豔陽下打排球，能不能找一個室內球場？

I love to jog for an hour at night.

↳ 不定詞片語，是動詞 love 的受詞。

我喜歡晚上慢跑一小時。

Practice

1

請選出正確的答案。

.... 1. Lawrence can .... 100 words per minute on his computer.
Ⓐ type   Ⓑ to type   Ⓒ typing

.... 2. I ran .... the bus.
Ⓐ catch   Ⓑ to catch   Ⓒ catching

.... 3. My mom let me .... at my friend's home last night.
Ⓐ sleep over   Ⓑ to sleep over   Ⓒ sleeping over

.... 4. .... the right decision may not be easy.
Ⓐ Make   Ⓑ To make   Ⓒ Making

.... 5. The kids enjoy .... in the puddle.
Ⓐ play   Ⓑ to play   Ⓒ playing

2

請從框內選出適當的動詞，以「動名詞」或「加 to 的不定詞」填空，完成句子。

stretch

drive

enjoy

roast

compete

1 .... go-carts is fun for teenagers.

2 It is a tricky business .... almonds at home.

3 It is not easy .... in a triathlon race.

4 .... before exercise is important.

5 .... the cool water at the beach sounds like a good idea on a hot day.

Part 10 Infinitives and -ing Forms
不定詞與動名詞

Unit 74

Verbs Followed by Infinitives
要接不定詞的動詞

1 大多數的動詞後面如果要接另一個動詞，都要接「加 to 的不定詞」。

- afford
- agree
- appear
- arrange
- ask
- attempt
- care
- decide
- expect
- fail
- hope
- learn (how)
- manage
- mean
- offer
- plan
- prepare
- pretend
- promise
- refuse
- seem
- threaten
- want
- wish

We can't afford to buy new living room furniture. 客廳要買新家具，我們負擔不起。
We agreed to save 25% of our combined income every month. 我們同意要把每個月合計薪資的 25% 存起來。
Buying new furniture for our house appears to cost too much for our meager budget. 要為我們房子購買新家具，顯然超出我們微薄的預算太多。
Don't attempt to persuade me to get rid of my favorite armchair. 別試圖說服我丟掉我最愛的那張扶手椅。
We already decided to save more money, not spend it on new furniture.
我們已經決定要多存一點錢，不花錢買新家具了。

2 上述動詞後面如果要接否定意義的不定詞，句型是「動詞 + not to . . .」。

You promised not to hit your little brother again. 你答應過不會再打你弟弟的。
You can pretend not to be guilty of hitting him, but I saw you punch him twice. 你可以裝作沒有打過他，不過我親眼看到你揍他兩次了。

3 口語中，「加 to 的不定詞」可以省略動詞部分，來避免重複。

Mom, I want to go with you. I want to. I want to.
↳ = I want to go with you.
媽咪，我要跟妳一起去。我要去！我要去！

4 有些動詞要先接疑問詞，再接「加 to 的不定詞」。

- explain
- know
- teach
- show
- tell

Do you know how to make a cup of cappuccino?
你知道如何泡出一杯卡布奇諾嗎？

Alison can explain what to do with an espresso machine.
愛莉森會說明濃縮咖啡機要怎麼用。
Edna doesn't know how to explain the method for making a cheesecake.
艾德娜不知怎麼解釋要如何做起司蛋糕。
Nick had taught me how to play backgammon, but I forgot the rules.
↳ teach 要先接受詞，再接疑問詞和「加 to 的不定詞」。
尼克教過我怎麼玩西洋雙陸棋，不過我忘記規則了。
Can you show my son where to put his shoes and change into his swimming suit?
↳ show 要先接受詞，再接疑問詞和「加 to 的不定詞」。
你可以告訴我兒子要把鞋子放在哪裡，還有要去哪裡換泳衣嗎？

156

Practice

1

請從框內選出適當的動詞，以「加 to 的不定詞」形式填空，完成句子。

attend

use

tell

find

be able

play

I hoped ＿＿＿＿＿＿ my cousin's wedding in Hawaii.

I need ＿＿＿＿＿＿ a smaller size to try on.

I promise not ＿＿＿＿＿＿ anybody until you announce your engagement.

Totomi pretended not ＿＿＿＿＿＿ to speak English while traveling in France.

I offered ＿＿＿＿＿＿ his camera and take a picture of him and his son.

Randy learned how ＿＿＿＿＿＿ the piano when he was very young.

2

請從框內選出適當的「疑問詞 + 動詞」組合，以正確的形式填空，完成句子。

how / contact

what / watch

what / wear

when / arrive

where / find

1. Can you please tell me ＿＿*how to contact*＿＿ Mr. Greenwood?

2. Can you tell me ＿＿＿＿＿＿ the X-ray department?

3. Could you advise me ＿＿＿＿＿＿ for my TV appearance?

4. Could you inform me ＿＿＿＿＿＿ at the ceremony?

5. Could you describe ＿＿＿＿＿＿ for at the airport security gate?

157

Part 10 Infinitives and -ing Forms
不定詞與動名詞

Unit 75

Verbs Followed by Objects and Infinitives
要接受詞再接不定詞的動詞

1 有些動詞在接「加 to 的不定詞」之前，要先接一個受詞，其句型為：

動詞 + 受詞 + 加 to 的不定詞

- advise
- allow
- cause
- compel
- convince
- encourage
- forbid
- force
- instruct
- invite
- order
- permit
- persuade
- recommend
- remind
- request
- require
- teach
- tell
- train
- urge
- warn
- would like

The boss forced Allan to work during the weekend. 老闆強迫艾倫週末也要上班。
The salesman persuaded Virginia to apply for the credit card.
這位業務員說服維吉妮亞申辦了信用卡。
My uncle Ian invited us to visit him in the summer.

我叔叔伊恩邀請我們這個夏天去拜訪他。

2 這種句型可以改寫為被動式，此時不定詞前面就不需要受詞。

The soldier was ordered to holster his weapon. 這名軍人奉命把槍收進皮套裡。
I was persuaded to buy this set of books.
我被說服買了這套書。

- advise
- allow
- encourage
- permit
- recommend

3 有些動詞可以接受詞再接「加 to 的不定詞」，也可以不用受詞。

- ask
- beg
- choose
- expect
- get
- mean
- help
- want
- promise

Cathy wants Roland to help with the recycling project on Sunday.
凱西要羅蘭幫忙做星期日的資源回收。
Isaac wants to put woofers in the trunk of his car to improve the sound quality.
艾薩克想在後車廂放重低音喇叭，改進音響的聲音品質。
Gladys expected Rupert to call, but he never did. 葛蕾蒂絲很期待魯伯特打電話給她，但是他卻一直沒打。
Sarah expected to leave by noon.
莎拉希望中午前能出發。
Margie helped Sidney (to) wash his new car. 瑪琪幫席尼洗他的新車。
Ted helped (to) install a new navigation system in his dad's car.

泰德幫老爸在車上裝了新的導航系統。

> help 後面可接「加 to 的不定詞」，也可接「不加 to 的不定詞」，意義相同。

4 上述有些動詞除了接「受詞 + 加 to 的不定詞」之外，也可以接動名詞。

❶ I wouldn't advise traveling in some parts of Africa.
我不建議去非洲某些地區旅遊。
I wouldn't advise you to travel to some parts of Africa.
我不建議你去非洲某些地區旅遊。

❷ This bank doesn't allow depositing or withdrawing money on Saturday and Sunday. 這家銀行在星期六、日不能存提款。
This bank doesn't allow you to deposit or withdraw money on Saturday and Sunday. 這家銀行在星期六、日不能讓你存提款。

Practice

1

請勾選正確的用語。

1. Bobby invited Traci ☐ **to have** ☐ **have** dinner with him.

2. Sam asked Nancy ☐ **to help** ☐ **helping** with the dinner dishes.

3. Barbara wouldn't recommend ☐ **going** ☐ **to go** to that restaurant.

4. Jane was invited ☐ **joining** ☐ **to join** the beach party.

5. Amy's dad doesn't want her ☐ **go** ☐ **to go** to the cast party.

6. The boss ☐ **ordered Melvin to attend** ☐ **ordered to attend** the meeting at the client's office.

7. Kirk doesn't want you ☐ **to calibrate** ☐ **calibrating** the weighing scales for him.

2

請將括弧內提供的詞語以「to V」或「受詞 + to V」的形式填空，完成句子。

1. Grandma taught _____ (Colleen / knit) on the weekends.

2. Clarissa persuaded _____ (Dolly / accept) the job offer.

3. Daniel warned _____ (me / not exceed) the speed limit.

4. Trent promised _____ (drop by) this afternoon.

5. The storm caused _____ (the airport / close) for six hours.

6. The manager reminded _____ (us / finish) the work before 6 p.m.

3

請將下列各「主動句」改寫為「被動句」。

1. They instructed us how to key in the code to open the gate.
   → _____
   _____

2. Mr. White encouraged Simon to take part in the speech contest.
   → _____
   _____

3. They advised Hal to wear a suit for the press conference.
   → _____
   _____

Part 10 Infinitives and -ing Forms
不定詞與動名詞

Unit 76

Verbs Followed by -ing Forms
要接動名詞的動詞

1 許多動詞要接動名詞。

• admit	• feel like	• miss
• avoid	• finish	• postpone
• consider	• give up	• practice
• delay	• can't help	• put off
• deny	• imagine	• risk
• dislike	• involve	• stand
• enjoy	• keep on	• suggest
• fancy	• mind	• understand

Amy admitted being in love with Tom.
愛咪承認自己愛上了湯姆。
Faith avoided doing exercise whenever possible. 菲絲盡可能逃避做運動。
Beryl considered getting to her office on time a top priority.
貝瑞兒將準時上班視為最重要的事。

2 這些動詞後面如果要接**否定意義的動名詞**，句型是：

動詞 + not + 動名詞

Mike imagined not having children.
麥可幻想自己沒有孩子。

Hanna enjoyed not following the traditional path.
漢娜樂於不遵循傳統行事。

3 前述有些動詞在接動名詞之前，可先接受詞，句型為：

動詞 + **受詞** + 動名詞

Daniel heard me asking where to find the department office.
丹尼爾聽到我問系辦公室在哪裡。
Can you imagine Tina jogging with a Labrador? 你能想像蒂娜和一隻拉不拉多一起慢跑的畫面嗎？
I dislike you wearing tights and flip-flops.
我不喜歡你穿緊身褲配夾腳拖。

4 do 經常搭配動名詞，來表示「**工作**」。句型是：

do + the/some + 動名詞

I do the driving when we go on a long trip. 我們出門長途旅行時都是我開車。
Rosie does the ordering for the department.
部門採購的工作都是蘿西在做。

5 go 經常搭配動名詞，來表示「**運動**」或「**休閒活動**」。句型是：

go + 動名詞

Roger likes to go roller-skating on campus. 羅傑喜歡在校園裡溜冰。
Ray goes bicycling in the evenings.
雷都在傍晚騎腳踏車。

6 mind 後面如果接「**受格代名詞 + 動名詞**」，是較為不正式的用法；正式用法應該接「**所有格 + 動名詞**」。

Would you mind me sending you a sample of our new product?
= Would you mind my sending you a sample of our new product?
你介意我寄我們新產品的樣品給你嗎？

Practice

1

eat
smoke
shop
vacuum
offend
invite
read
cook

請從框內選出適當的動詞，以「動名詞」的格式填空，完成句子。

1. Fran admitted _____ a box of candy before dinner.

2. Howard finished _____ dinner for his girlfriend.

3. Let's go _____ in the morning so we can have an early lunch.

4. Rosemary risked _____ her guests when she cut loose with a loud burp.

5. Melanie postponed _____ her mother-in-law for afternoon tea.

6. I will do the _____ when we clean the house next week.

7. Sam missed _____ the newspaper during lunch.

8. Would you mind not _____ your cigar inside the house?

2

use
have
watch
deliver
listen

請從框內選出適當的動詞，以「not + 動名詞」的句型填空，完成句子。

1. Florence admitted _____ the package to Mrs. Poe yesterday.

2. I suggest _____ the talk show tonight.

3. I can't imagine _____ a cell phone for three days of my life.

4. Would you mind _____ to that loud music for half an hour?

5. Belinda enjoys _____ to rush to the office every day.

3

請將括弧內的動名詞搭配 do 或 go 填空，完成句子。

1. Arthur loves to _____ (fishing) when he is on vacation.

2. Conrad always _____ (some reading) before he sleeps.

3. Would you like to _____ (the painting) of the outer wall?

4. Sandra always _____ (swimming) on Friday nights.

5. Who's _____ (the washing) today?

Part 10 Infinitives and -ing Forms
不定詞與動名詞

Verbs Followed by -ing Forms or Infinitives With the Same Meaning
接動名詞或不定詞意義相同的動詞

1 有些動詞後面可以接動名詞，也可以接「加 to 的不定詞」，並且意義相同。

- begin
- love
- hate
- continue
- start
- like
- prefer
- can't bear

Lauren began to juggle when she was sixteen years old.
= Lauren began juggling when she was sixteen years old.

蘿倫從十六歲起開始練習雜耍。

Margaret continued to practice magic during senior high school.
= Margaret continued practicing magic during senior high school.

瑪格莉特高中的時候繼續練習變魔術。

Lynn loved to perform on the stage.
= Lynn loved performing on the stage.

琳恩喜愛在舞台上表演。

2 但有時，這些動詞接動名詞或不定詞仍有極細微的差異。

1「like + 動名詞」表某人很愛做某事。
2「like + 加 to 的不定詞」強調「習慣」。

Carl likes volunteering at the history museum. ↳ 某人很愛當義工。

卡爾喜歡在歷史博物館當義工。

Joy likes to put lots of sugar in her tea.
↳ 強調習慣。

喬伊喝茶喜歡加很多糖。

3 begin、start 和 continue 若已使用進行式，後面就不要用動名詞，避免重複。

Frank is beginning to grow herbs.

法蘭克正開始種植藥草。

4 begin、start 和 continue 後面，如果接的是 **know**、**realize** 或 **understand** 這類的動詞，要用不定詞的格式。

✗ Sally began realizing her limitations as a gardener.

✓ Sally began to realize her limitations as a gardener.

莎莉開始明白她身為園藝家的限制。

5 這四種句型都是用來「泛指」，指「比較喜歡；寧可」：

❶ prefer to do *something*
❷ prefer doing *something*
❸ prefer to do *something* rather than do *something* else〔美式〕
❹ prefer doing *something* to doing *something* else〔英式〕

但是 would prefer 用來特指一個決定，則會用：

| would prefer | + | 加 to 的不定詞 | + | rather than | + | 不加 to 的不定詞 |

Ginny prefers to grow vegetables rather than raise chickens. 吉妮喜歡種菜更勝養雞。
It's cold today. I would prefer to stay at home rather than go to the park.

今天天氣冷，我不去公園，寧願待在家裡。

6 上述動詞如果搭配 would，變成 would like、would love、would hate、would prefer，那麼通常會接「加 to 的不定詞」。

Willa would like to teach a class in house restoration techniques.

薇拉想要開一堂建築修復技巧的課。

Janet would hate to see the restoration plan being postponed.

珍妮不希望見到重建計畫被拖延。

比較
would like 是「**想要**」，like 是「**喜歡**」兩者意義不同。

- Would you like to rebuild this old temple?

你想要重建這間老寺廟嗎？

- Do you like restoring old buildings?

你喜歡整修老舊建築嗎？

Practice

1

請將括號裡的單字以正確的「動名詞」或「不定詞」格式填空，某些題目中可以同時使用兩種格式。

1. Bill loves _barbequing / to barbeque_ (barbeque) on the deck.

2. Phil started _____ (heat) the grill.

3. Calvin likes _____ (fast) for a couple of days each month.

4. Would you like _____ (join) me for a workout at the gym?

5. Do you like _____ (exercise)?

6. I prefer to watch sports rather than _____ (participate) in them.

7. I would prefer _____ (read) a book today rather than _____ (play) basketball.

8. Sandy is beginning _____ (feel) faint.

9. I began _____ (realize) that there was something wrong with the medication.

10. I started _____ (feel) bad for Quentin.

2

請從框內選出適當的動詞，以「不定詞」的形式填空，完成句子。

reduce   spend   buy   help

1. Whitney would love _____ you with this report.

2. Verna would like _____ the new Coach perfume.

3. Luther would hate _____ money on interior decoration.

4. The editor would prefer _____ the budget for the illustrations in the book.

3

請從圖片中選出適當的用語，以「動名詞」或「不定詞（加 to 或不加 to）」的形式填空，完成句子。

1. Would you prefer to go snorkeling rather than _____?

2. Do you prefer swimming in the ocean or _____?

3. I prefer _____ rather than climb a mountain on my vacation.

relax on a tropical island

ride a banana boat

climb a mountain

Unit **78**

Verbs Followed by -ing Forms or
Infinitives With Different Meanings (1)
接動名詞與不定詞意義不同的動詞（Ⅰ）

> 有些動詞後面可以接動名詞，
> 也可以接「加 to 的不定詞」，
> 但是**意義不同**。
> · remember　· stop　· regret
> · forget　· go on
> · try　· mean

1 remember 和 forget 如果接動名詞
（V-ing），表示這事是「**已經做過的**」。

Joanne remembered writing
her resignation letter.
瓊安記得她已經寫好辭呈了。

Tiffany forgot mailing a gift
to her grandmother.
蒂芬妮忘記她已經把禮物寄給
祖母了。

2 remember 和 forget 如果接「加 to 的
不定詞」，表示這件事是「**還沒做的**」。

Joanne remembered to write her
resignation letter.
瓊安記得要寫辭呈。

Tiffany forgot to mail a gift to her
grandmother.
蒂芬妮忘記要把禮物寄給祖母了。

3 try 後面接動名詞（V-ing），表示「**實驗性
地做某事**」、「**試試看結果會如何**」。

Did you try smiling at the security guard to see
if you could get into the building? 你有試著對警
衛微笑，看看他願不願意讓你進大樓嗎？

Have you tried negotiating with your mom to
keep the cat?
你有嘗試和媽媽溝通要把貓留下來養的事嗎？

4 try 如果接「加 to 的不定詞」，
表示「**非常盡力做某事**」。

Yesterday I tried to climb to the
top of the mountain, but I failed.
我昨天想攻頂，但是沒有成功。

I tried to negotiate with my mom
to keep the cat. 我有試著和媽媽溝
通把貓留下來養的事。

5 stop 如果接動名詞（V-ing），
表示「**停止做某件事**」。

Timmy stopped smoking cigarettes three
years ago after his daughter was born.
提米三年前女兒出生後，就不再抽菸了。

The weather had been sweltering,
so I stopped buying hot coffee.
天氣熱得不得了，
所以我不再買熱咖啡了。

6 stop 如果接「加 to 的不定詞」，表示
「**停止手邊的事，去做另一件事**」，
常用來說明「**停止做某事的原因**」。

Timmy stopped to smoke a cigarette
outside because his wife doesn't let him
smoke in the house.
提米停了下來，要到屋外抽菸，因為他太太
不讓他在屋裡抽菸。

The weather was sweltering, so I stopped
to buy an ice cream cone.
天氣熱得不得了，所以我停下來買個冰淇淋
甜筒。

Practice

1

請勾選正確的答案。

1. I forgot ☐ **to bring** ☐ **bring** my lunch box to school. Now I'm so hungry.

2. Here are your books. Have you forgotten ☐ **to lend** ☐ **lending** them to me?

3. The jar won't open. Have you tried ☐ **running** ☐ **to run** the cap under hot water?

4. I tried ☐ **sending** ☐ **to send** my résumé to as many companies as possible, but none of them has ever contacted me.

5. I lost my running shoes, so I stopped ☐ **to jog** ☐ **jogging**.

6. Since my shoe came untied, I stopped ☐ **to rest** ☐ **resting**.

2

請將括弧內的動詞以正確的「動名詞」或「不定詞」填空，完成句子。

1. Brian forgot _____ (put) the leftovers into the refrigerator, and now the food has gone bad.

2. Chuck forgot _____ (finish) the last piece of apple pie. He had rummaged in his refrigerator for five minutes, but he couldn't find any sweets.

3. I remember _____ (take) this garbage bag outside. Who brought it back in?

4. I'll remember _____ (pay) the telephone bill on time, so they won't have the service cut next month.

5. I tried _____ (talk) to him, but he wouldn't listen.

6. I tried _____ (stay) calm, but what he said was really infuriating.

7. I stopped _____ (hang) out with my friends every day after I got married.

8. Momo had been barking near the door for ten minutes. He stopped _____ (drink) some water and then went back to the door and bark some more.

Part 10 Infinitives and -ing Forms
不定詞與動名詞

Unit 79

Verbs Followed by -ing Forms or Infinitives With Different Meanings (2)
接動名詞或不定詞意義不同的動詞（2）

1 go on 接動名詞，表「**繼續做某事**」。

She goes on swimming lap after lap without stopping.
她持續游泳，游了一趟又一趟不停止。

John went on eating all afternoon at the free buffet. 約翰整個下午都在免費的自助餐廳吃個不停。

2 go on 接「加 to 的不定詞」，表示「**繼續做事，但改做不同的事**」。

She went on to run on the track after swimming in the lap pool.
她在直線泳區游完後，接著又去跑道跑步。

John ate his jumbo burger, and then he went on to finish my French fries.
約翰吃完他的超大漢堡後，接著又把我的薯條吃完了。

3 mean 接動名詞，表示「**意味著**」。

If Tony signs the contract, it will mean playing baseball in this city for three years.
如果湯尼簽了約，就表示他將在此城市打棒球打三年。

4 mean 接「加 to 的不定詞」，表示「**打算、意圖**」。

I'm sorry. I didn't mean to tell her the sad truth. 很抱歉，我不是故意要告訴她這個令人傷心的真相的。

Did you mean to break into the house of a police officer? 你的意思是說，要闖入警察的家？

5 regret 接動名詞，表示「**對已發生的事感到悔恨**」。

Miranda regrets accepting Jonathan's marriage proposal.
米蘭達懊悔接受強納森的求婚。

I regret giving up chocolate.
我很後悔沒吃巧克力。

6 regret 接「加 to 的不定詞」，表示「**對於不得不做的決定表達遺憾**」。

Miranda regrets to say that she is unable to accept Jonathan's marriage proposal. 米蘭達很遺憾的說，她無法接受強納森的求婚。

I regret to say that I gave up chocolate.
我很遺憾地說我不吃巧克力了。

regret to say 是一種正式的用語。

Please inform the Minister of the Interior that the Deputy Secretary regrets to say he is unable to attend the council meeting this afternoon in Senate Conference Room 10. 請轉告內政部長，祕書長很抱歉無法參加今天下午在參議院 10 號議事廳舉辦的議會。

Practice

1

請勾選正確的答案。

1. Kevin went on ☐ playing ☐ to play ☐ play the same song over and over.

2. She has been doing very well in college. She may go on ☐ becoming ☐ to become a lawyer.

3. Ted regrets ☐ withdrawing ☐ to withdraw his name from the speech contest.

4. I regret ☐ to cancel ☐ cancel ☐ canceling the trip to India.

2

請將括弧內的動詞以正確的「動名詞」或「不定詞」填空，完成句子。

1. Now that we've come to a conclusion on this issue, shall we go on _____ (discuss) the next one?

2. The HR manager got a phone call in the middle of the meeting. Now that he has hung up the phone, we can go on _____ (discuss) a new topic.

3. When you bring a stray dog home, it will mean _____ (take) care of him for the rest of his life. You should think it through.

4. I understand. You mean _____ (feed) him, _____ (play) with him, _____ (love) him, and never _____ (abandon) him.

5. When you say going mountain climbing, do you mean _____ (walk) up hundreds of steps to the small park on the top?

6. I didn't mean _____ (lie) to you. We just wanted to give you a surprise.

7. Do you regret _____ (move) to the city and living on your own?

8. I regret _____ (tell) you that your proposal has been rejected.

9. I regret _____ (not join) their picnic at the beach as they had so much fun.

10. Jenny regrets _____ (recommend) the dinner in this restaurant.

Part 10 Infinitives and -ing Forms
不定詞與動名詞

Unit 80

Infinitives Used as Complements and Infinitives of Purpose
不定詞當作補語與表示「目的」的用法

1 「加 to 的不定詞」經常放在名詞或代名詞的後面當作補語。

Holly bought a newspaper to look in the classified ads for a used car.
荷莉買了一份報紙，要看分類廣告的二手車資訊。
Would you like something to drink?
你想要喝點東西嗎？
Do you want him to meet you at the café?
你想要他到咖啡廳跟你碰面嗎？
The decision to quit my current job and to enter a new field is very hard to make.
要我離開目前的工作，投入另一個新的領域，是個困難的決定。

2 「加 to 的不定詞」也可以放在形容詞後面，當作補充說明。

The university is honored to announce a hundred million dollar gift from the family of Dr. Chambers. 大學很榮幸地宣布獲得來自錢伯斯博士一家人捐贈的一億元。
I am pleased to explain that the terms of the gift from Dr. Hogan include an endowed chair and a new science center.
我很開心能說明霍根博士捐贈的項目，包括一個基金教授職位，和一座新的科學中心。

3 「It is/was + 形容詞 + of somebody」的後面，會用「加 to 的不定詞」當作補充說明。

It is very kind of *Dr. Lampert* to contribute to the endowment funds of our university.
藍伯特博士真是非常的好心，他對這次的大學捐獻基金也做了捐贈。
It was so generous of *the Winthrop family* to donate a new building.
溫索柏家族非常慷慨地捐贈了一棟新大樓。

4 「It is/was + 形容詞 + for somebody」後面，也會用「加 to 的不定詞」當作補充說明。

It's not easy for *Barbara* to get airline tickets over the holiday.
芭芭拉很難在假期間買到機票。
It is important for *Michelle* to visit her family members in her hometown.
對蜜雪兒來說，回家鄉去探望家人是很重要的。

5 「加 to 的不定詞」，也常用於說明「某人從事某活動的目的」。

Mary is planning to save money for a house. 瑪莉計畫要存錢買房子。
Eddie went to the store to buy some milk. 艾迪去商店買了些牛奶。

6 表示「目的」時，用 in order to 或 so as to，是比單用 **to** 更正式的方法。
否定句型是 in order not to 和 so as not to。

Kathryn proposed the reform in order to help those orphans.
為了幫助那些孤兒，凱瑟琳提出改革方案。
Joseph retired early so as to spend more time with his family.
喬瑟夫為了有多點時間與家人相處，所以提早退休。
Pam takes the bus in order not to pay for parking.
為了不要付停車費，潘選擇搭公車。
Randy picks up his children at school every day so as not to miss their formative years.
藍迪每天放學都去學校接孩子，就是為了不要錯過他們的人格發展期。

Practice

1

請勾選正確的答案。

1. Would you like something ☐ **to drink** ☐ **drinking**?

2. I need somebody ☐ **to help** ☐ **helping** me paint the house.

3. ☐ **We are happy to hear** ☐ **It is happy for us to hear** from you.

4. It is considered ill-mannered ☐ **to ask** ☐ **for asking** a woman her age.

5. It is ☐ **you clever to open** ☐ **clever of you to open** the car door without a key.

6. It is ☐ **polite of you to knock on** ☐ **polite for you to knock on** the door before entering a room.

7. It won't be necessary ☐ **to mail** ☐ **for mailing** the certificate.

8. It is a mistake for children in an unsafe neighborhood ☐ **to play** ☐ **playing** in the park after dark.

2

請從框內選出適當的動詞,以正確的「不定詞」形式填空,完成句子。

buy	see	celebrate	help	update	check

1. Sarah went to the phone store ___to buy___ a new battery.

2. June bought some aspirin _____ reduce the pain in her back.

3. Emma made a cake _____ her son's birthday.

4. Felix called the kindergarten _____ on his daughter.

5. Avery went to the zoo _____ the baby koala.

6. Barry sent an email to his boss _____ her on the project.

3

請從圖中選出適當的用語填空,完成句子。

1. Lisa left the office early so as to _____ in the hospital.

2. Brenda goes to the gym every weekend to _____.

3. Amanda brought her own coffee cup to the office in order to _____ and help save the planet.

4. Ethan took his dog to a vet to _____.

visit her daughter

reduce paper waste

keep fit

cure his eye disease

Unit 81

Prepositions With -ing Forms
介系詞接動名詞

1 介系詞at、of等，可用來說明「**關係**」或「**連結**」，介系詞後要接名詞，因此如果要接動詞，就要使用動名詞。

Are you interested in sending this letter by certified mail?　↳ 用動名詞

你想以掛號郵件寄出這封信嗎？

I am thinking of sending it by express mail. 我在考慮用快遞寄送。

Richard is looking forward to getting the product samples.

李察很期待收到貨物樣品。

Jack is planning on placing an order in the next day or two.

傑克計畫一兩天後下單訂購。

2 不要混淆不定詞中的to和介系詞to。以**to開頭的介系詞片語**，並不是動詞的一部分。

不定詞的 to　If you want to send this parcel overnight,　↳ to 是代表不定詞，不是介系詞。then you need to use a package delivery service.

如果你想要今晚連夜送達包裹，那你得選包裹快遞服務。

不定詞的 to　Do you want to insure your package?　↳ 不定詞

你的包裹要加保險嗎？

介系詞 to　Take your attempted delivery notice to window number 12.
↳ 以 to 開頭的介系詞片語，to 是介系詞。

請你拿取件通知單到 12 號窗口辦理。

介系詞 to　Couriers can't deliver parcels to post office boxes.　↳ to post office boxes 是介系詞片語。

快遞員不能把包裹送到郵政信箱裡。

3 be used to是慣用語，表示「**習慣於**」。這裡的to是介系詞，因此要接名詞或動名詞。

Jordan is used to wearing sandals with socks. 喬登已經習慣了穿著襪子穿涼鞋。

Sofia isn't used to long price negotiations with street vendors.

蘇菲亞不習慣在街上和小販討價還價。

get used to 意指「**逐漸習慣某事**」，也要接動名詞。

• Heather is getting used to buying vegetables in the street markets near her apartment.

海瑟漸漸習慣在公寓附近的市場買菜。

比較 但是沒有 be 動詞的 used to 後面則是接不定詞。

Jordan used to wear sandals without socks all year round.

喬登以前整年都只穿涼鞋不穿襪子。

Practice

1

請從框內選出適當的介系詞，搭配括弧中的動詞，以正確的形式填空，完成句子。

on

at

about

before

of

in

for

to

1. Jean is planning _on paying_ (pay) her electricity bill at the convenience store.

2. Gary is thinking _____ (get) some money at the ATM machine.

3. This area with the white lines is _____ (park) motorcycles.

4. Check the map _____ (drive) to the meeting.

5. Aren't you tired _____ (listen) to talk radio?

6. Chuck is good _____ (find) lost packages in the warehouse.

7. Curtis isn't interested _____ (collect) Pokémon figures.

8. Are you looking forward _____ (travel) around China next week?

2

請將括弧內的動詞以「to + 動名詞」或「to + 不定詞」的形式填空，完成句子。

1. I am getting used _to hopping_ (hop) on my scooter when I need to go somewhere.

2. When I was a teenager, I used _____ (ride) a dirt bike on the hills behind my parent's house.

3. My family used _____ (own) several ATVs that we rode all over the farm.

4. I am not used _____ (fight) the intense traffic in the city.

5. It won't take long to get used _____ (navigate) a scooter in the city.

6. I am getting used _____ (move) other scooters out of the way when I need a parking place.

Unit **82**

"Need" and "See" With -ing Forms or Infinitives

Need 與 See 接動名詞與不定詞的用法

need 接動名詞與不定詞

1 need 當作**一般動詞**用時，後面經常接「加 to 的不定詞」。

Danielle needs to read more books and watch less TV.

丹尼爾得多讀點書，少看點電視。

Earl doesn't need to buy any more books. He needs to donate his old books to a library. 厄爾不需要再買書了，他應該把他的舊書捐給圖書館。

2 need 當作**一般動詞**用時，也可以接動名詞，此時句子具有「**被動意義**」，這是英式英語的用法，美式用「to be + 過去分詞」。

The library needs expanding because there isn't enough room for the new children's collection.

圖書館得擴建了，因為原有的空間不夠放新的兒童藏書。

Small independent bookstores need protecting or they will all disappear.

獨立的小書店需要被保留下來，否則將會完全消失不見。

3 need 當作一般動詞用時，也可以接「to be + 過去分詞」，此時句子也是「**被動意義**」，和使用動名詞是一樣的。

The bookstore needs to be renovated and redesigned. 這間書店得重新設計翻修。

In this age of multimedia, book readers need to be supported. 在這個多媒體的時代，傳統書籍的讀者應該受到鼓勵。

see 接動名詞與不定詞

4 see 和 hear 後面要先接受詞，再接動名詞或「不加 to 的不定詞」，且兩者的意義不同。

see 和 hear 接動名詞的時候，強調看到聽到的是「連續動作的其中一部分」。

Yesterday I saw Sue talking to her dog.

↳ 只看到動作「說話」的部分。

昨天我看到蘇在對她的狗說話。

Jessica heard Tom arguing with someone in the hallway.

↳ 只聽到動作「爭吵」的一部分。

潔西卡聽到湯姆和人在走廊上爭吵。

As I walked by the store, I saw Danny raising the shutters. 我經過商店的時候，看到丹尼正在把百葉窗拉起來。

5 see 和 hear 若接「不加 to 的不定詞」，則表看到聽到的是「從頭到尾的動作」。

Carol saw Dr. Shaw arrive at his office.

↳ 目睹整個抵達的經過。

卡蘿看見蕭博士抵達他的辦公室。

Jessica heard Sherman unlock the door.

↳ 聽到整個開鎖的過程。

潔西卡聽到雪曼打開門鎖。

As I sat in the park across from the store, I saw Danny raise the shutters.

當我坐在商店對面的公園，看見丹尼窗簾拉起了百葉窗。

6 要注意的是，如果 see、hear 後面本來接「不加 to 的不定詞」，則 see、hear 的**被動式**須接「加 to 的不定詞」。後面本來如果接動名詞則不影響。

Someone saw Sam leave the building at approximately 5:00.

→ Sam was seen to leave the building at approximately 5:00.

有人看到山姆約於 5 點時離開這棟大樓。

Practice

1

請從框內選出適當的動詞，搭配 **need**，以正確的形式填空，完成句子。

set

fix

buy

pick up

clean

wash

1. Can you move your stuff off the dining room table? I *need to set* the table for dinner.

2. The refrigerator is full. We don't ＿＿＿＿＿＿＿＿＿＿ any more food.

3. The faucet on the sink in the bathroom is dripping. The faucet ＿＿＿＿＿＿＿＿＿＿ or we will waste water and run up the water bill.

4. There is a mound of laundry in the twins' room. Their clothes ＿＿＿＿＿＿＿＿＿＿ or they won't have anything to wear.

5. There is some toothpaste on the mirror in the bathroom. The mirror ＿＿＿＿＿＿＿＿＿＿ before your parents come.

6. There are toys all over the living room floor. The toys ＿＿＿＿＿＿＿＿＿＿ and putting away before you go to bed tonight.

2

請將括弧內的動詞，以「動名詞」、「不加 to 的不定詞」或「加 to 的不定詞」填空，完成句子。

1. As I walked into the building, I saw the security guard ＿＿＿＿＿＿＿＿＿＿ (watch) a movie on TV.

2. While we were waiting at the airport, we heard a man ＿＿＿＿＿＿＿＿＿＿ (announce) our names over the public address system.

3. I saw him ＿＿＿＿＿＿＿＿＿＿ (leave) this package at the front desk.

4. As I walked to the store, I saw a man ＿＿＿＿＿＿＿＿＿＿ (walk) his pet cat on a leash.

5. I looked up for a moment and saw a man ＿＿＿＿＿＿＿＿＿＿ (float) down to earth in a parachute.

6. Jerry was heard ＿＿＿＿＿＿＿＿＿＿ (rush) downstairs.

7. The man was seen ＿＿＿＿＿＿＿＿＿＿ (run) across the street with a package in his hand.

Part 10 Infinitives and -ing Forms
不定詞與動名詞

Unit 83

Participle Phrases and Participle Clauses
分詞片語與分詞子句

1 動詞又可分為現在分詞和過去分詞，現在分詞的形式也是 V-ing。像是**進行式**就要使用現在分詞。

Mike is selling sausages at the lotus flower farm. 麥克正在蓮花園賣香腸。

2 現在分詞也可以當作**形容詞**使用。

Zelda thinks furniture design is interesting. 薩爾達覺得設計家具很有趣。
Lillian says furniture shopping in Milan, Italy, is exciting. 莉莉安說，在義大利米蘭買家具很讓人興奮。
Eco-tourism is a thriving business.
↳ 動詞 thrive 的現在分詞 thriving，用來修飾名詞 business。
生態旅遊是個熱門的生意。

3 現在分詞可以作為一個**片語的開頭**，這種片語稱為分詞片語。

Marvin is the guy standing by the office doorway.
馬爾文就是站在辦公室門口的那個傢伙。

4 分詞片語可以當作**形容詞**使用，對名詞或名詞片語「**提供更多資訊**」。

The tall man shouting at the office workers is our boss. 我們老闆就是對著辦公室員工大吼大叫的那位高大男人。
The man waving at you is the inspector general from the city government.
那個正在對你揮手的人是市政府的監察長。

5 現在分詞可以作為一個子句的開頭，這種子句稱為分詞子句。分詞子句可以當作**副詞**使用，提供關於「**時間**」的訊息。

當一個短暫行為發生在一個較長行為中間時，較長行為可以用分詞片語。
While staying at the hospital with her father, Lindsay had a premonition.
↳ 「產生預感」是發生於「在醫院陪爸爸的時候」。
琳賽在醫院陪爸爸的時候，有了不安的預感。

Fearing for the worst, Lindsay pushed the nurse call button.
↳ 先「擔心最糟的情況會發生」，再「按下呼叫鈴」。
琳賽擔心最糟的情況會發生，於是按了護士呼叫鈴。

Opening his eyes, Lindsay's father looked around the hospital room.
↳ 先「張開雙眼」，再「環顧四周」。
琳賽的父親張開雙眼後，四面環顧著醫院病房。

一前一後發生的動作，也可用現在分詞的完成式來說明「**第一個動作**」。
• Having called for a nurse, Lara stared at her father.
呼叫護士之後，拉蘿緊盯著父親。

6 分詞子句可以用來說明「**事情發生的原因**」。

Wanting to know why his son Lester was sitting here, Papa asked him what he was doing. 爸爸想知道兒子萊斯特為何坐在這裡，便問他在做什麼。
Trying to explain that Papa had hit his head, Linda showed how he had been knocked unconscious.
為了解釋爸爸撞到頭的事，琳達演示了他是如何撞到失去意識的。

Practice

1

請將括弧內的詞語以「分詞片語」或「分詞子句」的形式填空，完成句子。

1. Angela is the woman _brushing her hair_ (brush her hair).

2. The man _____ (look at himself in the mirror) is Victor.

3. While _____ (shop at the department store), Rose bought a two-piece suit.

4. _____ (think about buying a pair of new shoes), Ann got on the elevator.

5. _____ (have purchased a three-piece suit), Greg decided to buy a matching belt.

6. _____ (have bought a new dress), Maggie looked for a matching purse.

7. _____ (know she had to look sharp for her presentation), Rachel bought a whole new outfit.

8. _____ (have an attractive new hair style), Flora began to improve her use of makeup.

2

請以「分詞片語」或「分詞子句」改寫句子。

1. Howard bit his tongue while he was eating the glazed strawberries on a stick.
   → _While eating the glazed strawberries on a stick, Howard bit his tongue._

2. Irene lay on the bed and thought about the next day's presentation.
   → _____

3. Who is that woman? The woman is talking on a cell phone.
   → _____

4. After she took some medicine, Mary started to feel better.
   → _____

5. John had the ambition to win the championship, so he practiced extremely hard.
   → _____
   _____

6. Because Trudy wanted to have a bubble bath after work, she bought a cedar bathtub last week.
   → _____
   _____

Unit 84

Phrasal Verbs: Two Words, Transitive, and Separable
片語動詞：兩個字、及物、可分

片語動詞是一組具有特定意義的動詞片語，由動詞搭配副詞或介系詞所構成。

片語動詞的類型眾多，第一種由「**動詞 + 副詞**」搭配受詞組成，屬於「**可分的**」片語動詞，受詞可放在**副詞後**，也可放在**動詞**和**副詞中間**。

❶ 動詞 + 副詞 + 受詞
   → 受詞放在副詞後

❷ 動詞 + 受詞 + 副詞
   → 受詞放副詞前，但當受詞是**代名詞**時，只能放動詞和副詞中間。

Jake took off the shoes when he entered the room.
Jake took the shoes off when he entered the room.
Jake took them off when he entered the room.
傑克進入房間的時候，脫了鞋子。

bring back 帶回

Can you bring back some coffee for me?

你可以幫我買一些咖啡回來嗎？

bring in 拿進來

Lisa, please bring in those files.

莉莎，請把那些檔案拿進來。

call off 取消

The host called off the game because of the rain.

主辦單位因雨取消了賽事。

fill up 加油

Do I need to fill it up before I return the car?

還車之前需要加滿油嗎？

bring up 養育

Kenny brought up two children by himself.

肯尼獨力扶養兩個小孩。

carry out 實行；實現

She finally carried out her dream to sail around the world.

她終於實現了「帆」遊世界的夢想。

figure out 理解

I can't figure the whole thing out. It's too weird.

這整件事太奇怪了，我無法理解。

find out 發現

He couldn't believe it when he found out the truth.

當他發現真相時，他無法置信。

bring up 提出

Sophie brought up a wonderful proposal yesterday.

蘇菲昨天提出了一個絕佳方案。

fill out 填寫

Please fill out the registration form.

請填寫這張登記表。

hand in 繳交

We need to hand in the paper tomorrow.

我們明天要交報告。

hand out 分發

Santa hands out gifts on Christmas.

聖誕節時，聖誕老人都會發禮物。

hang up 懸掛

He took off his coat and hung it up. 他脫下大衣，並且把它掛起來。

look over 檢查

You should look over your test paper before handing it in.

繳交考卷之前，應該檢查一遍。

look up 查閱

Sam looked up this topic in an encyclopedia.

山姆翻閱百科全書查過這個主題。

make up 編造

He made up the whole story.

整個故事都是他捏造出來的。

pick up 接

Shall I pick you up at eight?

我 8 點去接你好嗎？

point out 指出

Mr. Sanchez pointed out the key to efficient management.

桑切斯先生指出了有效管理的關鍵。

put away 收好

Put away your pens and books after finishing your homework.

做完功課，要把筆和書本收好。

put off 拖延

The manager put off the meeting until tomorrow.

經理將會議延至明天。

put on 穿

I'll put on the new dress and go to the party.

我要穿新洋裝，然後去參加舞會。

put out 撲滅

The fire fighter arrived in five minutes and put out the fire.

消防人員在五分鐘內抵達，並且撲滅了火勢。

set off 使爆炸

People aren't allowed to set off fireworks in many countries.

許多國家禁止人民施放煙火。

shut off 關掉

Shut off the gas and electricity before you leave the house.

外出之前，記得關閉瓦斯及電源。

take out 拿出去

Luisa, please have Johnny take out the garbage.

露薏莎，麻煩叫強尼把垃圾拿出去。

talk over 討論

Jason, I think we need to talk over the merger. 傑森，我認為我們應該要就合併案進行討論。

tear down 拆除

The government decided to tear down the old bazaar building.

政府決定拆除老舊的商場大樓。

think over 考慮

I'll think it over and let you know.

我會考慮看看，再告知你。

throw away 丟棄

Don't throw away the plastic bottles. They're recyclable.

塑膠瓶可以回收，不要丟棄。

try on 試穿

Would you like to try on the high-heels?

你要不要試穿這雙高跟鞋？

turn down 將（音量）調小

Will you turn down the radio? I'm doing my research.

我在做研究，你把收音機關小聲點好嗎？

turn down 拒絕

You shouldn't have turned down such a good offer. 你實在不該拒絕這麼好的工作機會。

turn up 將（音量）調大

Please turn up the TV. I want to listen to the news.

電視開大聲一點，我要聽新聞。

turn off 關掉

Lily turned off the computer and left for work.

莉莉關了電腦去上班。

turn on 打開

It's cold in here. I'll turn on the heat.

這裡好冷，我要打開暖氣。

write down 寫下

Write down five titles of your favorite movies.

寫下你最愛的五部電影名稱。

這些片語動詞因為是「及物」的，因此也可以使用被動語態。

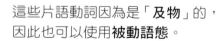

The party was called off last night.

昨晚，派對被宣布取消了。

The green building issue was talked over at the international conference on the environment.

綠建築的議題在這次的國際環保會議中被提出討論。

Practice

1

請將左欄的句子與右欄相對應的「片語動詞」連接。

1. You should _____ the TV when you are on the phone.

2. Children should always _____ their toys after playing.

3. You had better _____ the shoes before you buy them.

4. You'd better _____ the timetable before you go to the station.

5. You should _____ that offer carefully before you accept or refuse it.

6. You need to _____ if you want to reach an agreement.

- put away
- try on
- think over
- turn off
- talk it over
- look up

2

請從框內選出正確的「片語動詞」，並以「代名詞」為受詞填空，完成對話。

write down

hang up

call off

pick up

bring in

make up

turn down

figure out

1. Ⓐ How does Helen go to the office?
   Ⓑ I _____*pick her up*_____ on my way to the office.

2. Ⓐ I thought you're having a meeting now.
   Ⓑ The manager _____, so I have some free time.

3. Ⓐ The explanation is beyond my understanding.
   Ⓑ I can't _____, either.

4. Ⓐ It is starting to rain.
   Ⓑ The laundry is still outside. We have to _____ quickly.

5. Ⓐ Let me give you my phone number so that you can reach me.
   Ⓑ I'll get a pen and paper to _____.

6. Ⓐ Where are the keys?
   Ⓑ I _____ on the nail by the front door.

7. Ⓐ Do you think I should accept the invitation?
   Ⓑ I think it's a good chance to meet some local politicians. You shouldn't _____.

8. Ⓐ Do you believe the story on the front page?
   Ⓑ No, I don't. I think the reporter _____.

Unit **85**

Phrasal Verbs: Two Words, Transitive, and Nonseparable (1)
片語動詞：兩個字、及物、不可分（1）

第二種是由「**動詞 + 介系詞**」搭配受詞組成，但屬「**不可分的**」片語動詞，也就是受詞只能放在**介系詞後面**，不能放在動詞和介系詞中間。

動詞 + 介系詞 + 受詞

call on 拜訪
We will call on an important customer next Monday.
我們下週一將拜訪一位重要客戶。

(be) made from
由……製成（原料本質改變）
Paper is made from wood.
紙張是木漿製的。

(be) made of
由……製成（原料本質不變）
The dress is made of silk.
這件洋裝是絲做的。

apply for 申請
We'll apply for a permission to hold the demonstration.
我們會提出示威遊行的申請。

arrive in 抵達
Mr. and Mrs. Harper arrived in London yesterday morning.
哈波夫婦於昨天早上抵達倫敦。

belong to 屬於
The diamond ring belongs to Ms. Sophia.
這只鑽戒為蘇菲雅小姐所有。

come across 偶遇
We came across a vagrant on our way to school.
我們上學途中遇到一個流浪漢。

depend on 倚靠；端賴
Whether we can win the trip to France depends on this test. 我們有沒有機會去法國玩，就看這次考試了。

get over 克服
She cannot get over her fear of heights.
她無法克服自己的懼高症。

keep off 遠離
The sign says, "Please keep off the newly seeded grass."
牌子上寫道：「請勿踐踏新種植的草皮。」

look after 照顧
Samuel looked after his grandfather for three years.
山謬照顧他的祖父三年了。

look for / search for 尋找
Tony is looking for his necktie.
湯尼在找他的領帶。

look into 調查
The detective will look into the murder case personally.
警探將親自調查這件謀殺案。

pull for 為……喝采
The crowd are pulling for the host team.
群眾為地主國加油。

run into / run across 偶遇
I ran into Mr. Jefferson at the post office this afternoon.
我今天下午在郵局遇到傑佛遜先生。

take after 像
He takes after his father. They are real artists.
他和他父親很像，都是十足的藝術家。

wait on 為……送餐
We'll wait on the president.
我們將負責為總統送餐點和飲料。

Practice

1

請從下面框內選出適當的「片語動詞」，搭配圖中的受詞填空，完成句子。

take after

come across

look after

apply for

wait on

keep off

a scholarship   Table 2   Puffy   the grass   a stray dog   her twin sister

1. Susan cannot come to the English club today, because she has to ___*look after Puffy*___ . He has been sick for two days.

2. Let's walk on the path and _____.
   There might be snakes in it.

3. I'm _____, Table 4, and Table 6 today.

4. Lucy _____. I can hardly tell them apart.

5. We _____ on our way to school. It was so cute and friendly, but our teacher said we couldn't keep it as our school dog.

6. I've _____. If everything goes well, I'll be able to study abroad next year.

2

請從框內選出正確的「片語動詞」填空，完成句子。

be made of

be made from

get over

pull for

1

I've been studying in Frankfurt for three years, but I still can't _____ my homesickness.

2

The fans came all the way from their own countries to _____ their teams.

3

Caramel pudding _____ eggs, sugar, and cream milk.

4

The columns _____ marble stones.

Unit 86

Phrasal Verbs: Two Words, Transitive, and Nonseparable (2)

片語動詞：兩個字、及物、不可分（2）

believe in 相信

Martin believes in the importance of giving his children stability and a regular schedule.

馬丁相信讓孩子們生活穩定、作息規律，是很重要的。

bump into 巧遇

I bumped into Andy's tutor this morning. 我今天早上遇到安迪的家教老師。

care about 在意

Amanda cares about feeding her family healthy food. 亞曼達很在意家人要吃健康的食物。

care for 想要（某物）

Would you care for some tea or coffee?

你想要喝點茶或咖啡嗎？

concentrate on 專心於

Sidney needs to concentrate on his career a little more and spend less time hanging out with his friends.

席尼得更專注於他的事業，少花點時間和朋友混在一起才行。

crash into / drive into 撞上

Ellen nearly crashed into her ex-boyfriend's car.

愛倫差點撞上她前男友的車子。

die of 死於

Lorraine thought she was going to die of embarrassment.

羅蘭覺得自己快糗死了。

dream about / dream of 夢見

Last night I dreamed about/of my dear departed grandmother.

昨晚我夢到已逝的親愛祖母。

dream of 夢想；考慮

Richard has been dreaming of taking a break from his high-stress job. 李察一直夢想能從他壓力很大的工作中喘口氣休息一下。

Richard needs a break, but he wouldn't dream of quitting his job. 李察需要休息一下，但他不會考慮辭職。

hear about 聽說

Have you heard about the cold front that is coming in tomorrow?

你有聽說明天有冷鋒面會來嗎？

hear from 收到（某人的）來信；接到（某人的）電話

Have you heard from your friend Herman since he got married?

你朋友賀曼結婚後，你還有聽過他的消息嗎？

hear of 聽說

Have you heard of a dark chocolate that is 99 percent or more pure cocoa?

你知道有純可可含量 99% 或 99% 以上的黑巧克力嗎？

laugh at 嘲笑

Are you laughing at me or with me? 你是在嘲笑我，還是在和我一起笑？

shout at 對……吼叫

Stop shouting at me.

別對著我大吼大叫。

suffer from 受苦

I'm not sleeping. I am suffering from a case of extreme boredom.

我沒有在睡覺，我正為一個超無聊的案子在受苦。

think about 想著

I think about you all the time. 我一直想著你。

think of 認為

What do you think of the strategic plan written by Sue?

你對蘇撰寫的策略計畫有什麼想法？

Practice

1

請用正確的「介系詞」填空，完成句子（包含 Units 85-86 所介紹的片語動詞）。

1. Dominique applied _____ a job as an assistant manager.

2. He believes _____ her innocence.

3. That minivan belongs _____ the Sanders family.

4. Adam doesn't care _____ eating healthy food.

5. It's not easy to start a business. You will have to get _____ many difficulties.

6. Call me immediately as soon as you arrive _____ Taipei.

7. We want to sell our house, but the deal depends _____ the buyer getting a bank loan.

8. There is no use getting angry and shouting _____ me.

9. Gladys suffers _____ an inflated opinion of her self-importance.

10. Uncle Gerald died _____ old age just before his 95th birthday.

11. Byron was thinking _____ starting his own company.

12. Have you ever heard _____ an allergy turning into an infection?

13. Ed is looking _____ an excuse to invite Mary to lunch.

14. Della dreams _____ marrying Wallace, but the two have never spoken to each other.

15. We are depending _____ you to get us to the ballpark before the first inning.

16. Tom ran _____ a deer on the road, but nobody was hurt except the deer.

17. Why is that guy laughing _____ you and pointing at your hair?

18. When Jerry was a university student, he dreamed _____ traveling around the world.

Unit **87**

Phrasal Verbs: Two Words and Intransitive
片語動詞：兩個字、不及物

第三種是由「**動詞 + 副詞**」所組成的片語動詞，但是這類的動詞屬於「**不及物動詞**」，可以**單獨存在**，不需要加受詞。

動詞 + 副詞

My truck broke down on the highway.
我的卡車在高速公路上拋錨了。

---

break out 爆發

The Persian Gulf War broke out in 1990 and ended the next year. 波斯灣戰爭於 1990 年爆發，隔年結束。

fall down 跌倒

He tripped over a bucket and fell down.
他絆到一個水桶而跌倒。

go off 響起

The alarm went off in the morning.
鬧鐘早上響起。

speak up 大聲地說

Could you speak up, please? It's noisy here. I can't hear you. 你可以大聲一點嗎？這裡很吵，我聽不見。

start over 從頭來過

I spoiled it again. Let's start over.
我又搞砸了，再來一次吧。

come out 出來；出現

Who's there? Please come out.
誰在那裡？請快出來。

grow up 成長

Vincent grew up in the country and moved to the city when he was sixteen. 文森在鄉下長大，16 歲時才搬到城市裡。

dine out 外出吃晚餐

We're out of food. Let's dine out tonight.
家裡沒東西吃了，我們今晚去外面吃吧。

stay up 熬夜

Jane stayed up last night to finish the report.
珍昨晚熬夜趕完報告。

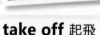

show up 出現

The magician showed up from behind the curtain and began the show. 魔術師從布幕後現身，表演便開始了。

take off 起飛

Our flight is going to take off in thirty minutes. 我們的班機將在三十分鐘後起飛。

dress up 裝扮

I need five more minutes to dress up. Why don't you sit down? 我還要五分鐘才能裝扮好，你先坐一下好嗎？

shut up 閉嘴

Please shut up, will you?
拜託你閉嘴好嗎？

throw up 嘔吐

I feel like throwing up. Can you bring me an airsickness bag? 我有點想吐，可以給我一個嘔吐袋嗎？

Practice

1

找出與劃線字同義的「片語動詞」，改寫句子。

start over

come out

dress up

stay up

break out

throw up

1. The wolf <u>showed himself</u> from behind the tree and blocked the path of Little Red Riding Hood.

   → *The wolf came out from behind the tree and blocked the path of Little Red Riding Hood.*

2. Gin is <u>burning the midnight oil</u> to watch *Emily in Paris*.

   → ....

3. I feel like <u>vomiting</u>. I'll go to the bathroom.

   → ....

4. The fire <u>started</u> in the middle of the night and spread very quickly.

   → ....

   ....

5. I've come up with an idea. Let's <u>do it again</u>.

   → ....

6. My sister is <u>putting on her clothes</u> for the masquerade.

   → ....

2

圖中發生了什麼事？請將各事件依正確的順序排列，並從下框內選出適當的「片語動詞」完成句子。

The smoke alarm ....

The police shouted, " .... of the building."

throw up	go off
break out	come out
fall down	show up

I .... while running out.

The fire .... at 2 a.m.

After I got out, I started to shake and then ....

The fire department ....

1. *The fire broke out at 2 a.m.*

2. ....
   ....

3. ....
   ....

4. ....
   ....

5. ....
   ....

6. ....
   ....

Phrasal Verbs: Three Words
片語動詞：三個字

第四種片語動詞由三個字組成，
一般來說是「**動詞 + 副詞 + 介系詞**」的組合，
通常**不可分**，而且要加**受詞**。

| 動詞 | + | 副詞 | + | 介系詞 | + | 受詞 |

I'm fed up with his temper.
我受夠了他的脾氣。

---

come up with 想出

He hasn't come up with a solution yet.

他還沒想出解決方案。

keep away from 遠離

We should keep away from the fire area.

我們應該遠離火災事故現場。

keep up with 跟上

You have to study extra hard to keep up with your classmates.

你要格外用功，才能跟得上同學。

take care of 照顧

Phyllis is taking care of her elderly parents.

菲莉絲正在照顧她年邁的雙親。

stand up for 捍衛

You must stand up for yourself.

你一定要站出來為自己說話。

look forward to 期待

We look forward to serving you again.

期待下次再為您服務。

move away from 搬離

They want to move away from the city and start a new life.

他們想要搬離都市，展開全新的生活。

put up with 忍受

I can't put up with the noise of the railway.

我受不了鐵路的噪音。

其中有些三個字的片語動詞，其實是由**兩個字**的「不及物」片語動詞衍生而來，為了接**受詞**，要加上一個**介系詞**，使之成為「及物」的片語動詞。

Elaine and George broke up last night.
↳ break up 作為「不及物」的片語動詞，可以單獨存在，不需要受詞。
Elaine broke up with George last night.
↳ 當句子需要一個受詞的時候，則使用 break up with。
伊蓮昨晚和喬治分手了。

catch up (with) 趕上

I missed two classes last week. It'll be difficult to catch up. 我上星期缺了兩堂課，進度很難趕上。

The other team has a very high score. It's not easy for us to catch up with them.

另外一隊的分數很高，我們很難追上。

move in (to) 住進（某處）

When are you moving in? 你什麼時候要搬進去？
We're planning to move in to our new apartment next week.
我們下星期要搬進新公寓去。

get through (with) 辦完

We have so much work to get through.
我們有好多工作要做。
We need to get through (with) the work by tomorrow.
我們得在明天以前把事情辦完。

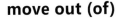

come along (with) 一起來

We're going to Palm Beach next week. Do you want to come along?

我們下星期要去棕櫚灘，你要一起來嗎？

Jerry came along with Kevin to the party.
傑瑞和凱文一起來參加派對。

move out (of) 搬出（某處）

My roommate is moving out tomorrow.
我的室友明天就要搬走了。
My grandparents moved out of their old house and into a new apartment.
我的祖父母搬離他們的老家，住進一棟新的公寓。

come over (to) 順道來訪

Pan came over to my office and hand this to me.
潘順道來了我的辦公室，把這個東西交給我。

go on (with) 繼續下去

You can't go on like this. You need a job.
你不能一直這樣下去，你需要一份工作。

Grandpa took a sip of the tea and went on with the story.
爺爺小啜了一口茶，繼續講述這則故事。

I'm free this afternoon. Would you like to come over for some tea?
我今天下午沒事，你要不要過來喝杯茶？

hang on (to)
握住（某物）不放

Ken, hang on! We're coming for you.

肯，抓好啊，我們就來救你了。

Ken hung on to a branch until the rescue team arrived.

肯緊握住一根樹枝，直到救難大隊抵達現場。

set out (for)
出發（前往某處）

We'll set out at dawn.

我們預定清晨出發。

Jerry and Annie set out for Hokkaido yesterday.

傑瑞和安妮昨天出發前往北海道了。

get along (with) 相處

Jim and Lynn can't get along.

吉姆和琳恩處不來。

Jack couldn't get along with his colleagues, so he quit.

傑克和同事處不來，就辭職了。

drop in (on) 順道拜訪

Please do drop in someday.

哪天一定要來坐坐。

I dropped in on Grandma on my way to the office.

我去上班之前，先去了奶奶家一趟。

sign up (for) 登記

I want to join the cruise tour. When shall I sign up?

我想參加郵輪之旅，什麼時候應該報名？

He just signed up for the psychology experiment at Northern Michigan University.

他剛報名做北密西根大學的一項心理學實驗。

hang out (with)
（和某人）一起出去

We should hang out some time. 有空我們應該聚聚。

Janet usually hangs out with Lisa on the weekends.

週末時，珍娜通常和莉莎在一起。

drop out (of) 退出

I dropped out when I realized the offer wasn't fair.

當我得知他們給的酬勞很不公平時，我就退出了。

He dropped out of school to wait on tables for a while.

有一段時間，他輟學跑去當服務生。

run out (of)
被用完；用完某物

The tank had a hole, and the water ran out. 水槽破了一個洞，水都流光光了。

The car has run out of gas. I'm going to buy a gas can and some gas. 車子沒油了，我要去買一個汽油桶和一些汽油。

watch out (for) 小心

Watch out! There's a car coming. 小心！有車來了。

We should watch out for falling rocks around this area.

我們要小心這一區的落石。

Practice

1 請從框內選出適當的「片語動詞」填空，完成句子。

1. I am _____ her constant complaints.

2. _____ the stove. It's very hot.

3. Debby and I are both excited about the vacation.
   We're _____ our trip to New Zealand.

4. You don't have to submit to such humiliation. You should
   _____ yourself.

5. Our production line is not fast enough. Our production cannot
   _____ the market demand.

6. Have you _____ any solutions yet?

come up with

keep away from

look forward to

fed up with

stand up for

keep up with

2

請從圖中選出適當的
受詞加入句子中，並
加上適當的「介系
詞」。

banana peel    tissue paper    buoy    the team

the bus tour

1. Watch out!
   → Watch out for the banana peel!

2. We will set off on Friday.
   → _____

my office

3. Why are you moving out?
   → _____

4. Have you signed up yet?
   → _____

Venice

5. The tissue paper is running out.
   → We _____

6. Hang on! I'll pull you up.
   → _____

7. Please come over to sign the contract.
   → _____
   _____

the apartment

8. I don't want you to drop out. We really need you.
   → _____
   _____

189

Phrasal Verbs: Usages With Slight Variations in Meaning
片語動詞：不同用法細微的意義差異

有些片語動詞，可能因為**主詞的不同**，而在用法上有所差異。這些狀況，通常在意義上也有差異，但差異不大。

---

blow out

使熄滅 → 及物、可分

Joe made a wish and blew out the candles.

喬許了個願之後，吹熄蠟燭。

吹離 → 不及物

A lot of dust blew out the first time I turned on the air conditioner this summer.

我今年夏天第一次開冷氣的時候，吹出來了一堆灰塵。

---

blow up

炸毀 → 及物、可分

They blew up a bridge to cut off the supply line of the enemy. 他們摧毀一座橋，以截斷敵方的補給路線。

爆炸 → 不及物

The missile blew up in the air.

導彈在空中爆炸。

---

calm down

使鎮靜 → 及物、可分

We tried to calm the old man down.

我們試圖使這位老人家冷靜下來。

鎮靜下來 → 不及物

The old man finally calmed down.

這位老人終於冷靜下來了。

---

cheer up

使高興起來 → 及物、可分

Jimmy cheered me up by telling a joke.

吉米說了一個笑話逗我開心。

高興起來 → 不及物

Cheer up! Nothing is impossible.
開心一點嘛！沒有什麼不可能的事。

---

wake up

喚醒 → 及物、可分

Sam, please wake me up tomorrow morning at 6:00. I've got an important meeting.

山姆，明天早上6點叫我起來，我有一個重要的會議要開。

醒來；起床 → 不及物

Hey, wake up! It's eight already!

嘿，快起床，已經8點了。

---

work out

解決 → 及物、可分

We're trying to work out the problem.

我們正設法解決這個問題。

有好結果 → 不及物

Our plan has worked out.

我們的計畫成功了。

Practice

1

calm down

blow out

work out

wake up

cheer up

blow up

請從框內選出正確的「片語動詞」填空，完成句子。

1. Susan was outraged by the policy. However, she _____ in a few minutes.

2. The explosive device _____ the train car.

3. The lunar rocket _____ 32 seconds after the launch.

4. Last night I had a nightmare and _____ with tears on my face.

5. _____! At least, the worst is past.

6. This good news will definitely _____ her _____. Let's go and tell her.

7. A strong wind _____ our campfire.

8. Lonny was disappointed after the contest, but he _____ when he heard that he had won the award.

9. The nurse gave that woman some medicine to _____ her _____.

10. _____, will you? You'll frighten the child by screaming like that.

11. The team is _____ a proposal to improve the product.

12. However, the method didn't _____. They'll have to find another solution.

13. Make three wishes before you _____ the candles _____.

14. A loud noise _____ me _____ in the middle of the night.

15. I _____ my husband and asked him to find out what was going on.

16. He lit a match, but it _____ instantly, so he lit up another one.

Let's See Grammar

Intermediate 1

彩圖初級英文文法 三版

作　　者	Alex Rath Ph.D.
審　　訂	Dennis Le Boeuf / Liming Jing
譯　　者	羅竹君／丁宥榆
校　　對	梁立芳／樊志虹／吳佳芬
編　　輯	張盛傑／丁宥榆
主　　編	丁宥暄
內文設計	洪伊珊／林書玉
內文排版	洪伊珊／蔡怡柔
封面設計	林書玉
圖片協力	周演音
製程管理	洪巧玲
出 版 者	寂天文化事業股份有限公司
發 行 人	周均亮
電　　話	+886-(0)2-2365-9739
傳　　真	+886-(0)2-2365-9835
網　　址	www.icosmos.com.tw
讀者服務	onlineservice@icosmos.com.tw
出版日期	2021 年 5 月 三版一刷

郵撥帳號 1998620-0 寂天文化事業股份有限公司
劃撥金額 600 元（含）以上者，郵資免費。
訂購金額 600 元以下者，請外加郵資 65 元。
〔若有破損，請寄回更換，謝謝。〕

國家圖書館出版品預行編目 (CIP) 資料

Let's See Grammar：彩圖中級英文文法 intermediate 1 / Alex Rath 著 . -- 三版 . -- [臺北市] : 寂天文化事業股份有限公司 , 2021.05
面；　公分
ISBN 978-626-300-011-7　(第 1 冊 : 菊 8K 平裝)
ISBN 978-626-300-012-4　(第 2 冊 : 菊 8K 平裝)
1. 英語　2. 語法
805.16　　110006245

Let's
See
Grammar

彩圖中級英文文法　三版

Answers to Practice Questions

Unit 1   p. 9

1 1. frogs 2. dishes 3. heroes 4. factories
5. knives 6. galleys 7. safes
8. loaves, cartons 9. spies 10. plays
2 1. churches 2. wives 3. toothbrushes
4. matches 5. stomachs 6. babies, months
7. keys 8. boxes
3 1. **-es:** heroes, potatoes, tomatoes
-s: memos, kilos, solos
-s/-es: mangos/mangoes, zeros/zeroes, cargos/cargoes
2. **-ves:** knives, halves, calves
-s: puffs, briefs, roofs, gulfs, chiefs, tariffs

Unit 2   p. 11

1 1. teeth 2. children 3. species 4. sheep
5. reindeer 6. lice 7. Bison
8. fungus（此處當作形容詞修飾 family〔科〕，以單數形態呈現）
9. phenomena 10. series 11. crisis
2 1. Salmon 2. Cod 3. carp 4. shellfish

Unit 3   p. 13

1 1. soda, (U/C)（soda 原本是不可數名詞，但如果在餐館裡點餐，指「一杯汽水」時，可以當可數名詞使用）
2. sugar, (U) 3. cherry, (C) 4. typhoon, (C)
5. soup, (U) 6. block, (C) 7. anger, (U)
8. lamp, (C)
2 1. Sandy went to ~~store~~ a store to buy . . .
2. Sandy bought ~~sofa~~ a sofa, four dining ~~chair~~ chairs, and a ~~nightstands~~ nightstand for . . .
3. Trent isn't satisfied with the sofa. The sofa ~~are~~ is too dark.
4. There ~~is~~ are not enough . . .
5. The nightstand ~~do~~ does not fit their bedroom . . .
6. They had ~~argument~~ an argument over the newly bought ~~furnitures~~ furniture.
7. Trent thought Sandy should take ~~an advice or two~~ some advice from him.
8. But Sandy doesn't like any of Trent's ~~opinion~~ opinions.
9. Now, Trent has convinced himself that the dark sofa ~~are~~ is easy to maintain.

Unit 4   p. 15

1 1. wheat 2. cheese 3. jewelry 4. mud
5. hail 6. perfume 7. copper 8. pepper
2 1. Chinese, French 2. water, oxygen
3. intelligence 4. bacon, toast, chocolate
5. biology, chemistry 6. gas, smoke
7. confidence 8. copper

Unit 5   p. 17

1 1. is, is 2. sunglasses, They are 3. a pair of
4. is 5. indicate
6. is（billiards〔撞球〕為複數形態，但意義為「單數」，搭配單數動詞使用）
7. are（earnings〔薪水〕為固定複數形態，沒有單數形態 *earning）
8. thanks（thanks〔謝意〕為固定複數形態，thank 則為動詞）
2 1. ruins 2. shears 3. gymnastics
4. pajamas 5. shoes 6. tights

Unit 6   p. 19

1 1. a jar of mustard 2. three slices of cheese
3. two pieces of luggage 4. a slice of melon
5. two pieces of toast 6. a can of mussels
7. two bars of soap 8. a glass of liquor
9. a bowl of bath salt 10. a jar of cookies
11. a pot of tea 12. four jars of spices
13. a bottle of shower gel
14. a tube of peach lotion

Unit 7   p. 21

1 1. is 2. is 3. need 4. are 5. Beijing
6. was 7. a large audience 8. was 9. is
10. has 11. they were
2 1. My <u>class</u> (C) elected <u>Mark</u> (P) to be the class leader.
2. An <u>army</u> (C) of five thousand men assembled at the border of <u>India</u> (P).
3. The criminal ran into the <u>crowd</u> (C) in <u>Federation Square</u> (P).
4. *La Traviata* (P) attracted an <u>audience</u> (C) of thousands to the <u>City Theater</u> (P).
5. Half of the <u>staff</u> (C) of <u>KPMG International Limited</u> (P) got a pay raise.
6. The <u>mob</u> (C) occupied hospitals and airports, causing chaos and wreaking havoc.

3

7. Football <u>teams</u> (C) from 32 countries gathered in <u>Russia</u> (P) to compete for the <u>2018 World Cup</u> (P).
8. The <u>government</u> (C) has come up with several solutions to prevent the unemployment level from getting worse.

Unit 8 p. 23

1 1. fax machine   2. cotton field
3. coffee grinder   4. screwdriver
5. drug abuse   6. starfruit / star fruit
7. campfire
2 1. tissue paper   2. animal rights
3. rock music   4. football   5. brothers-in-law
6. passers-by   7. tool boxes   8. coffee milk

Unit 9 p. 25

1 1. deer's antlers   2. dog's paw
3. parrots' cage   4. bass's scales
5. lion's roar
2 1. John and Amy's apartment
2. Edward and Betty's kitchen
3. Selina's and Christine's teddy bears
4. Ken's and Lynn's laptops

Unit 10 p. 27

1 1. the hairdresser's   2. the barber's
3. the doctor's   4. the dentist's
5. the baker's
2 1. Paul's car   2. someone's keys
3. dog's bone   4. company's office
5. today's newspaper   6. week's vacation
7. grandparents' bicycles
8. Mick and Jeri's wedding photos
9. driver's license

Unit 11 p. 29

1 1. Nelly's school   2. name of the ballet
3. Nancy's dance teacher
4. address of the theater
5. price of the tickets   6. Norma's part
7. jury's judgment   8. workers' movement
9. Veasna's VIP card
10. facade of the building
2 1. The cap of the lotion is missing.
2. The vice president of the United Electric Company will visit our new factory next week.

3. The grocery store of Audrey and Lucas is going to open next month.
4. The waiters of the Empire Hotel's Chinese restaurant are well trained.
5. The birthday of my mother-in-law is coming soon.

Unit 12 p. 31

1 1. a whale   2. an eagle   3. a volleyball
4. a first-aid kit   5. a meatball   6. an onion
7. a one-way road   8. an idea   9. an SUV
10. a UFO   11. an astronaut   12. an heir
2 1. a   2. a   3. a   4. an   5. a   6. a   7. an
8. an   9. an

Unit 13 p. 33

1 1. a   2. the   3. the   4. the   5. the   6. a
7. an   8. The   9. an   10. The   11. the
12. the   13. the   14. the   15. the   16. a

Unit 14 p. 35

1 1. /   2. the   3. /   4. /   5. /   6. the   7. /
8. The   9. The   10. The   11. The   12. /
13. the   14. the
2 1. The poor need national health insurance more than the middle class and the rich.
2. The city council has approved several proposals for the welfare of the elderly.
3. The excavation of these sites has revealed the life and culture of the Maya.
4. Opportunities go to the strong, not the weak.

Unit 15 p. 37

1 1. the countryside, the city   2. the cello
3. The mayor   4. the beach   5. The king
6. the Moon   7. The President
8. the airplane   9. The lion   10. the stars
2 1. Bill is climbing the mountain.
2. Lee commutes between his downtown office and his home in the suburbs.
3. Larry is working for the Ministry of Education.
4. In 1990, NASA launched the Hubble Telescope into orbit.
5. John is swimming laps in the pool.
6. Caterina learned to play the flute when she was 12.

Unit 16   p. 39

1 1. a   2. the   3. an, *the*
4. the   5. The   6. the   7. a/the   8. a
9. The   10. the   11. an   12. the   13. the

2 1. Snow   2. Tornadoes   3. the rain
4. the circus, the performance
5. the evening   6. the wind
7. *the Taipei Times*

Unit 17   p. 41

1 1. The Dragon Boat Festival
2. summer, autumn
3. The Songkran Festival   4. June
5. Father's Day   6. noon   7. Valentine's Day
8. Saturday, Sunday   9. night

Unit 18   p. 43

1 1. /   2. /   3. /   4. the   5. /, /   6. /, /
7. the   8. the   9. /   10. /   11. the   12. /
13. /, /   14. the   15. /   16. /   17. the   18. /
19. the   20. the

Unit 19   p. 47

1 1. Europe   2. the United Kingdom
3. the Philippines   4. the Nile
5. The Colosseum
6. The Metropolitan Museum of Art
7. Ridge Street

2 1. /, /, /   2. /, /   3. the   4. /   5. the, /
6. the

Unit 20   p. 49

1 1. the   2. /   3. /   4. /   5. The   6. a
7. a   8. /   9. a

2 1. /   2. the   3. the   4. a   5. /   6. the
7. the   8. /

Unit 21   p. 51

1 1. he   2. her   3. them   4. They   5. we
6. She   7. me   8. her   9. her   10. I am
11. I can't   12. we

2 1. She   2. He   3. she   4. me   5. It   6. he
7. them   8. us   9. him   10. you

Unit 22   p. 53

1 1. it   2. we   3. We   4. It   5. you   6. They
7. They

2 1. It was cold outside   2. It was 10 p.m.
3. It is going to rain
4. It is 200 meters from here

3 1. It is exciting to go down a water slide.
2. It is good for your health to drink soy milk
every day.
3. It is important that we follow the traffic
rules.

Unit 23   p. 55

1 1. her   2. his   3. my   4. their   5. Our
6. mine   7. ours   8. my own   9. her own
10. on my own   11. my   12. hers
13. of my own   14. his own   15. my
16. on his own

2 1. theirs   2. hers   3. Mine, yours
4. his   5. ours   6. yours

Unit 24   p. 57

1 1. himself   2. himself   3. ourselves
4. by myself   5. all by yourself   6. by
7. yourself   8. himself   9. herself

2 1. myself   2. herself   3. yourself/yourselves
4. himself   5. herself   6. themselves

Unit 25   p. 59

1 1. me   2. by herself   3. /   4. ourselves
5. each other   6. one another   7. /   8. /
9. /   10. himself   11. /   12. each other

2 1. each other   2. one another   3. themselves
4. herself

Unit 26   p. 61

1 1. plenty of   2. Plenty of, was   3. are
4. people   5. a great deal of   6. planning
7. was   8. time   9. The number of, is
10. A number of, have   11. problems
12. a number of   13. lots of   14. sand
15. sand castles   16. are

Unit 27 — p. 63

1 1. some 2. Both 3. A few of 4. neither
5. All / All of 6. a few 7. some
8 half / half of 9. some of 10. Most of
11. Many of

2 1. I need some crayons. Do you have any ~~crayons~~?
2. I bought some soy milk. Would you like to drink some ~~soy milk~~?
3. I ate some cherries, but not all of ~~the cherries~~ them.
4. I borrowed some books from the library, but not very many ~~books~~.
5. I've read a few articles in the newspaper, but not all of ~~the articles~~ them.
6. I've run out of printing paper. I need more ~~printing paper~~.
7. I dropped the spoon. Please give me another ~~spoon~~ one.
8. There're five singers in the band. Each ~~singer~~ has his or her own fans.
9. I can't decide which shirt to buy. I think I'll take both ~~shirts~~.
10. I took the whole box of grapes out of the fridge and found out half ~~of the grapes~~ had gone bad.
11. I can't lend you much money. I have only a little ~~money~~.
12. Over two hundred students joined our dance club. Most of ~~the students~~ them are college students.

Unit 28 — p. 65

1 1. are 2. are 3. are swimming 4. has
5. are 6. works

2 1. Does 2. was 3. was 4. his or her
5. their 6. isn't 7. it 8. cost

Unit 29 — p. 67

1 1. some 2. any 3. any 4. any
5. some/any 6. any 7. any 8. Some
9. some

2 1. → We can't take any grapes from the box.
→ Can we take any grapes from the box?
2. → I don't have any lip balm.
→ Do you have any lip balm?
3. → She didn't make any strawberry milkshake in the morning.
→ Did she make any strawberry milkshake in the morning?

3 1. Sue never buys any diamonds.
2. Tanya rarely plays any online games.
3. Sunny hardly cooks any fish.
4. We seldom watch any horror movies.

Unit 30 — p. 69

1 1. many 2. a lot of 3. much 4. plenty of
5. many 6. much 7. much 8. a lot of
9. too much 10. many

2 1. much 2. too much 3. as many
4. too many / plenty of 5. plenty of
6. many

Unit 31 — p. 71

1 1. few 2. little 3. a little 4. A few
5. Few of the 6. a little 7. a little 8. a little
9. A few of

2 1. is poured 2. have solved 3. are 4. is
5. penetrates 6. survive

Unit 32 — p. 73

1 1. both of 2. both 3. are both
4. are athletes 5. Both of you
6. Both / Both of 7. Both concerts 8. and
9. Both / Both of 10. them both

2 1. both love fishing 2. are both violinists
3. are both Russian Blue cats
4. have both passed the exam
5. can both do the freestyle
6. are both the best friends of human beings

Unit 33 — p. 75

1 1. neither of 2. either 3. either of
4. Either 5. Neither of 6. Either 7. Neither

2 1. is flying（正式）；are flying（非正式）
2. is 3. are
4. has made（正式）；have made（非正式）
5. is 6. can make 7. is

Unit 34 — p. 77

1 1. love 2. Do 3. them all 4. All 5. is
6. should all 7. All / All of 8. is
9. that was 10. was all 11. is 12. it all

2 1. I've sold all I had.
2. This lamb chop is all that is left.
3. Do you have all the books I requested?
4. All you've done right is marrying that woman.

5. You will find all you need in this outlet.
6. Did you eat all that was in the refrigerator?
7. I looked up all the words I didn't know in the dictionary.
8. All I read last week was *The Stolen Bicycle*.

Unit 35   p. 79

1 1. Every   2. all   3. Everybody   4. all
5. the whole   6. all the   7. all   8. every
9. Every one of
2 1. every   2. whole   3. All   4. every
5. every   6. whole   7. whole
8. every, all   9. whole   10. all

Unit 36   p. 81

1 1. no   2. None   3. no   4. none   5. no
2 1. no   2. none   3. None of the plates
4. is   5. is/are   6. was/were   7. wants
8. No Smoking   9. was/were
3 1. There is no milk in the refrigerator.
2. She trusts no one but her sister.
3. I have no money with me.
4. There are no rooms available today in this hotel.
5. There is no room for negotiation.

Unit 37   p. 83

1 1. one   2. ones   3. ones   4. one   5. one
6. ones   7. ones   8. one

Unit 38   p. 85

1 1. anywhere   2. somewhere   3. anybody
4. nobody   5. something   6. anything
7. everybody   8. nothing   9. nothing
10. everything
2 1. to drink   2. to read   3. to eat
4. to talk to   5. to play with   6. to go

Unit 40   p. 89

1 1. Do, shave, shave   2. Does, open, opens
3. Do, migrate, migrate
4. Does, come, comes
5. does, return, returns
6. Does, eat, doesn't eat   7. do, drive, drive
8. does, feel, feels   9. does, depart, departs
10. do, check out, check out

2 1. likes   2. prepare   3. lives   4. don't raise
5. Does, study   6. takes   7. finishes   8. pays
9. rises

Unit 41   p. 91

1 1. is getting   2. am sending
3. Are, practicing   4. is applying for
5. is carrying out   6. is selling   7. is going
8. is waiting
9. is bringing（who 當主詞時，視為第三人稱單數，故用 is）
10. is having   11. am flying   12. are enjoying
13. is rocking   14. am writing
15. is growing, am not working
2 1. is always jumping   2. is always working
3. is always messing   4. is always losing

Unit 42   p. 93

1 1. are burning   2. bloom   3. am eating
4. am hiding   5. Is Lonny reading
6. often watch   7. Do you play   8. travel
2 1. is weeding, weeds   2. is raining, rains
3. is checking, receives   4. are taking, take
3 1. consists, (A)   2. am taking, (D)
3. don't eat, (A)   4. is changing, (F)
5. am playing, (C)   6. am attending, (E)
7. orbits, (A)   8. is getting, (F)
9. sits, enjoys, (B)   10. am teaching, (D)

Unit 43   p. 95

1 1. recognize   2. does not like   3. have
4. am thinking   5. Do you believe   6. heard
7. am listening   8. deserves
2 1. doesn't exist   2. cost   3. forgets
4. includes   5. knows   6. owns
7. do, prefer   8. weigh

Unit 44   p. 97

1 1. sounds   2. cannot see   3. looks   4. feels
5. is   6. is having   7. is looking after
8. can't smell
2 1. is looking, looks   2. are tasting, taste
3. is smelling, smell   4. is feeling, feel
5. is weighing, weighs   6. is having, has

Unit 45 p. 99

1 1. was 2. gave 3. hoped 4. worked
   5. played 6. composed 7. earned 8. lost
   9. wrote 10. died

2 1. called 2. went 3. Did, spend 4. saw
   5. Did, get 6. did, buy 7. Did, pick up
   8. bought 9. Did, need 10. needed
   11. did, pay 12. got 13. Did, buy
   14. bargained 15. got

Unit 47 p. 103

1 1. She was hanging the drape.
   2. They were inspecting the bike.
   3. He was installing the tiles.
   4. He was fixing the pipe.
   5. He was washing the car.
   6. They were putting up wallpaper.

2 1. was taking 2. was changing
   3. was studying
   4. was eating, squeezing（前面的 eating 已有
      be 動詞，因此 squeezing 不須再加 be 動詞）

Unit 48 p. 105

1 1. was walking 2. was minding 3. was going
   4. passed 5. was leaning 6. felt 7. looked
   8. was staring 9. raised 10. said 11. walked
   12. ran 13. sprinted 14. stopped 15. looked
   16. slowed

2 1. I was playing football when I sprained my
      ankle.
   2. I was fighting with my sister when Mom
      came home.
   3. I was buying a wedding present when I
      heard you were getting married.
   4. I lost my passport when I was vacationing
      in Italy.
   5. I was sleeping soundly when the alarm
      clock rang.
   6. I was cranking the volume when I blew out
      the speakers.

Unit 49 p. 107

1 1. was always dripping 2. was always jumping
   3. was always crashing 4. is always watching
   5. was always complaining
   6. is always playing 7. are always telling

2 1. is always piling up 2. is always scattering
   3. is always storing up 4. is always drinking
   5. is always crying 6. is always leaving

Unit 50 p. 109

1 1. have read 2. have not been 3. Have, seen
   4. have never seen 5. have been

2 1. Have, used 2. Have, tried 3. Have, seen
   4. have seen 5. have heard 6. have, seen

Unit 51 p. 111

1 1. have planned 2. have invited
   3. has not started 4. has arrived
   5. has left 6. has dried 7. Have, missed
   8. have, thrown

2 1. Lawrence ~~is working~~ has worked at Flying
      Tomato Pizzeria for six months.
   2. Iris ~~stars~~ has starred in a soap opera since
      last year.
   3. Tom ~~is owning~~ has owned this car for
      several months.
   4. How long ~~are you working~~ have you
      worked on this proposal?

3 1. has gone 2. has been 3. have gone
   4. have been

Unit 52 p. 113

1 1. We have already eaten dinner.
   2. We haven't finished our coffee yet.
   3. We have just received her phone call.
   4. The singer has just gotten her first single
      on the top ten chart.
   5. Have you already thrown away your old
      books?
   6. I haven't discussed the problem with my
      doctor yet.
   7. I have never bought anything online.
   8. Have you ever run in a marathon?
   9. I haven't been to Russia before.
   10. This is the most splendid view I have ever
       seen.

2 1. for 2. since 3. for 4. since 5. for
   6. since

Unit 53 p. 115

1 1. have searched, has left 2. found
   3. has changed 4. hit, caused / has caused

2 1. have adopted 2. was abandoned
   3. wandered 4. was brought 5. was
   6. has become

3 1. went to bed at 1:00, has slept since 1:00,
      has slept for four hours
   2. moved in here on July 3rd, have lived here
      since July 3rd, have lived here for a week

Unit 54   p. 117

1 1. did, arrive   2. arrived   3. Have, been
4. have been   5. did, buy   6. gave
7. Have, started   8. have started

2 1. have played   2. Have you ever been injured
3. have had   4. you played   5. played
6. did you hurt   7. hurt
8. Have you ever played   9. played
10. Did you like   11. loved
12. Have you ever been recruited
13. has received   14. have said

Unit 55   p. 119

1 1. It has been raining.
2. We have been drinking.
3. Those people have been chatting.
4. Camille has been wearing high heels.
5. People have been boarding the plane.
6. Have you been practicing your Spanish?
7. Have you been redecorating your house?

2 1. have been arguing   2. has been raining
3. have been washing   4. has been reeling

Unit 56   p. 121

1 1. have you eaten, (D)   2. has been sitting, (C)
3. has cleaned, (C/F)   4. have you realized, (G)
5. have been chatting, (C)
6. has been sending, (B/E)
7. have been working, (E)   8. have finished, (A)
9. have imagined, (G)   10. has traveled, (A)

Unit 57   p. 123

1 1. I ~~have been~~ was out for dinner last night.
2. Roy ~~has held~~ held a party yesterday afternoon.
3. Sandra ~~wrote~~ has been writing her essay since this morning.
4. Larry ~~hasn't gone~~ didn't go home until his boss left the office.

2 1. Jessica and her kids have decorated the Christmas tree for three hours.
= Jessica and her kids have been decorating the Christmas tree for three hours.
2. Emma has taken photos for *National Geographic*.
= Emma has been taking photos for *National Geographic*.

3. Daniel has made trips with a hot air balloon across America since 2019.
= Daniel has been making trips with a hot air balloon across America since 2019.
4. Nicky has stood by the window since 2 p.m.
= Nicky has been standing by the window since 2 p.m.

Unit 58   p. 125

1 1. called, had ended
2. arrived, had already started
3. had proposed, was   4. wanted, had told
5. accepted, took

2 1. talked, had seen
2. hadn't practiced, dropped
3. looked at, had already passed
4. left, was finished   5. had given
6. did not dawn, needed   7. opened, dashed
8. had taken   9. had built

Unit 59   p. 127

1 1. had been playing   2. hadn't been trying
3. had Charlie been cracking
4. had been eating   5. had been smiling
6. had been trading   7. hadn't been living
8. Louise had been planning

2 1. had been eating   2. had been washing
3. had been talking   4. had been preparing

Unit 60   p. 129

1 1. will recognize   2. won't be   3. will sell
4. will serve   5. will have   6. will arrive
7. won't be   8. will, do   9. will be

2 1. won't find   2. will hear   3. Will, finish
4. won't go   5. will buy   6. will eat

Unit 61   p. 131

1 1. am going to rewrite   2. am going to work
3. are going to have   4. are, going to get
5. Is, going to lend   6. am going to buy
7. are going to smash   8. am going to quit
9. are, going to buy   10. are going to win

9

Unit 62 — p. 133

1. 1. will leave 2. am going to take / will take
3. will start / am going to start
4. I'll have / I'm going to have 5. will do
6. will come 7. will begin / is going to begin
8. will grab

2. 1. Edmond will apply for a new job.
2. He is going to apply for a job at a cookie factory.
3. He said, "I'll be the best cookie tester in the world!"
4. He said, "I am going to pass the exam with flying colors."
5. He said, "First, I'll practice testing some cookies."
6. Lou asked, "Are you going to bake cookies as well?"
7. Lou claimed, "You'll burn those cookies."
8. Edmond retorted, "I'll bake some cookies right away!"

Unit 63 — p. 135

1. 1. is performing 2. is cutting
3. is transferring 4. is closing
5. is inspecting 6. is planning

2. 1. is going to leave / is leaving
2. is going to tank 3. is going to fix
4. is going to run out
5. is paying / is going to pay
6. is graduating / is going to graduate
7. is going to have
8. is going to bankrupt / is bankrupting

Unit 64 — p. 137

1. 1. makes 2. washes, leaves 3. picks up
4. does, open 5. opens 6. serves
7. are closed 8. starts

2. 1. will go, goes 2. will sneak out, is
3. will enlist, graduates 4. will tour, visit
5. will stay up, turn in 6. will stay, bring
7. will appear, performs 8. will be, accepts
9. will sing, plays 10. will eat, have put

Unit 65 — p. 139

1. 1. Dr. Edwards will be meeting the committee members at 9:00.
2. Dr. Edwards will be watching the demonstration of sterilization equipment at 10:30.

3. Dr. Edwards will be eating lunch at 12:00.
4. Dr. Edwards will be listening to a panel discussion about childhood disease at 15:00.
5. Dr. Edwards will be presenting a paper about disease treatment plans at 16:30.
6. Dr. Edwards will be touring the city at 19:30.

2. 1. won't be cooking, Can you buy us a pizza?
2. won't be driving, Could I get a ride from you?
3. will be leaving, Would you like to use my computer this afternoon?
4. will be returning, Are you planning to watch it again?
5. will, be walking, Can I walk with you on the Nature Trail?
6. Will, be playing, Can I come to listen to you play?

Unit 66 — p. 141

1. 1. will have moved 2. will have settled
3. will have climbed 4. will have started
5. will have finished 6. will have begun

2. 1. How long will he have been swimming in the ocean by sunset? /
He will have been swimming in the ocean for four hours by sunset.
2. How long will he have been traveling by the time he gets to Buenos Aires? /
He will have been traveling for four months by the time he gets to Buenos Aires.

Unit 67 — p. 143

1. 1. Have you got 2. have got
3. does not have 4. does not have
5. Does she have

2. 1. have / have got 2. have 3. have
4. don't

Unit 68 — p. 145

1. 1. had a fight 2. having a baby
3. have a glass of orange juice
4. has a bowl of soup 5. have a bubble bath
6. have a look

2. 1. (C) 2. (A) 3. (B) 4. (A) 5. (A)

Unit 69 — p. 147

1 1. is 2. was just being 3. was being
4. was / was being 5. was 6. is
7. was / was being 8. is 9. was 10. was
11. was 12. was / was being 13. am

Unit 70 — p. 149

1 1. fruity 2. like raspberry 3. the aroma
4. graceful 5. the most beautiful lady
6. at me 7. my Mapo tofu 8. spicy
9. like a dish 10. cool and hairy
11. my finger 12. red 13. better 14. bigger
15. worse 16. to him 17. the medicine
18. normal

Unit 71 — p. 151

1 1. (B) 2. (D) 3. (D) 4. (A) 5. (D) 6. (D)
2 1. make her go away 2. make the baby cry
3. get him to move over a little
4. get the coffee cup washed
5. have her write an article
6. have the pillowcase changed

Unit 72 — p. 153

1 1. Please don't fire us. ~~Let's~~ Let us stay . . .
2. Let's not ~~to have~~ have . . .
3. Sarah lets her daughter ~~to go~~ go . . .
4. Let's build another sand castle, ~~don't~~ shall we?
5. Let's ~~don't~~ not cry.
6. ~~Let's~~ Let me hang up your coat . . .
7. Father won't ~~let's~~ let us / let me come . . .
8. ~~Let's do~~ Let's make a . . .
9. Let us race to the bridge, ~~do~~ shall we?
10. Let's not ~~entering~~ enter that house . . .
11. Let me ~~to have~~ have a talk with him . . .
12. ~~Don't let's~~ Let's not go to that beach. . . .

Unit 73 — p. 155

1 1. (A) 2. (B) 3. (A) 4. (B/C) 5. (C)
2 1. Driving 2. to roast 3. to compete
4. Stretching 5. Enjoying

Unit 74 — p. 157

1 1. to attend 2. to find 3. to tell
4. to be able 5. to use 6. to play
2 1. how to contact 2. where to find
3. what to wear 4. when to arrive
5. what to watch

Unit 75 — p. 159

1 1. to have 2. to help 3. going 4. to join
5. to go 6. ordered Melvin to attend
7. to calibrate
2 1. Colleen to knit 2. Dolly to accept
3. me not to exceed 4. to drop by
5. the airport to close 6. us to finish
3 1. We were instructed how to key in the code to open the gate (by them).
2. Simon was encouraged to take part in the speech contest by Mr. White.
3. Hal was advised to wear a suit for the press conference (by them).

Unit 76 — p. 161

1 1. eating 2. cooking 3. shopping
4. offending 5. inviting 6. vacuuming
7. reading 8. smoking
2 1. not delivering 2. not watching
3. not using 4. not listening 5. not having
3 1. go fishing 2. does some reading
3. do the painting 4. goes swimming
5. doing the washing

Unit 77 — p. 163

1 1. barbequing / to barbeque
2. heating / to heat 3. to fast 4. to join
5. exercising / to exercise 6. participate
7. to read, play 8. to feel 9. to realize
10. feeling / to feel
2 1. to help 2. to buy 3. to spend
4. to reduce
3 1. ride a banana boat
2. climbing a mountain
3. to relax on a tropical island

11

Unit 78 — p. 165

1 1. to bring　2. lending　3. running
　　4. to send　5. jogging　6. to rest
2 1. to put　2. finishing　3. taking　4. to pay
　　5. to talk　6. to stay　7. hanging
　　8. to drink

Unit 79 — p. 167

1 1. playing　2. to become　3. withdrawing
　　4. canceling
2 1. to discuss　2. to discuss　3. taking
　　4. feeding, playing, loving, abandoning
　　5. walking　6. to lie　7. moving　8. to tell
　　9. not joining　10. recommending

Unit 80 — p. 169

1 1. to drink　2. to help
　　3. We are happy to hear　4. to ask
　　5. clever of you to open
　　6. polite of you to knock on　7. to mail
　　8. to play
2 1. to buy　2. to help　3. to celebrate
　　4. to check　5. to see　6. to update
3 1. visit her daughter　2. keep fit
　　3. reduce paper waste
　　4. cure his eye disease

Unit 81 — p. 171

1 1. on paying（plan on V-ing/V 表示「打算
　　做……」）2. about getting
　　3. for parking　4. before driving
　　5. of listening　6. at finding
　　7. in collecting　8. to traveling
2 1. to hopping　2. to ride　3. to own
　　4. to fighting　5. to navigating
　　6. to moving

Unit 82 — p. 173

1 1. need to set　2. need to buy
　　3. needs fixing（英式）/
　　　needs to be fixed（美式）
　　4. need washing（英式）/
　　　need to be washed（美式）
　　5. needs cleaning（英式）/
　　　needs to be cleaned（美式）
　　6. need picking up

2 1. watching　2. announce/announcing
　　3. leave　4. walking　5. floating　6. rushing
　　7. running

Unit 83 — p. 175

1 1. brushing her hair
　　2. looking at himself in the mirror
　　3. shopping at the department store
　　4. Thinking about buying a pair of news
　　　shoes
　　5. Having purchased a three-piece suit
　　6. Having bought a new dress
　　7. Knowing she had to look sharp for her
　　　presentation
　　8. Having an attractive new hair style
2 1. While eating the glazed strawberries on a
　　　stick, Howard bit his tongue.
　　2. Irene lay on the bed, thinking about the
　　　next day's presentation. /
　　　Lying on the bed, Irene thought about the
　　　next day's presentation.
　　3. Who is that woman talking on a cell
　　　phone?
　　4. Having taken some medicine, Mary started
　　　to feel better. /
　　　After taking some medicine, Mary started
　　　to feel better.
　　5. Having the ambition to win the
　　　championship, John practiced extremely
　　　hard.
　　6. Wanting to have a bubble bath after work,
　　　Trudy bought a cedar bathtub last week.

Unit 84 — p. 179

1 1. turn off　2. put away　3. try on　4. look up
　　5. think over　6. talk it over
2 1. pick her up　2. called it off　3. figure it out
　　4. bring it in　5. write it down
　　6. hung them up　7. turn it down
　　8. made it up

Unit 85 — p. 181

1 1. look after Puffy　2. keep off the grass
　　3. waiting on Table 2
　　4. takes after her twin sister
　　5. came across a stray dog
　　6. applied for a scholarship
2 1. get over　2. pull for　3. is made from
　　4. are made of

12

Unit 86
p. 183

1 1. for   2. in   3. to   4. about   5. over   6. in
7. on   8. at   9. from   10. of
11. of/about（這句用 of 和 about 都正確，
「was thinking of」指「正在考慮」，「was thinking about」指「此刻腦海裡正浮現的事」）
12. of   13. for   14. of   15. on   16. into
17. at   18. of

Unit 87
p. 185

1 1. The wolf came out from behind the tree and blocked the path of Little Red Riding Hood.
2. Gin is staying up to watch *Emily in Paris*.
3. I feel like throwing up. I'll go to the bathroom.
4. The fire broke out in the middle of the night and spread very quickly.
5. I've come up with an idea. Let's start over.
6. My sister is dressing up for the masquerade.

2 1. The fire broke out at 2:00 a.m.
2. The smoke alarm went off.
3. The fire department showed up.
4. The police shouted, "Come out of the building."
5. I fell down while running out.
6. After I got out, I started to shake and then threw up.

Unit 88
p. 189

1 1. fed up with   2. Keep away from
3. looking forward to   4. stand up for
5. keep up with   6. come up with

2 1. Watch out for the banana peel!
2. We will set off for Venice on Friday.
3. Why are you moving out of the apartment?
4. Have you signed up for the bus tour yet?
5. We are running out of tissue paper.
6. Hang on to the buoy! I'll pull you up.
7. Please come over to my office to sign the contract.
8. I don't want you to drop out of the team. We really need you.

Unit 89
p. 191

1 1. calmed down   2. blew up   3. blew up
4. woke up   5. Cheer up   6. cheer, up
7. blew out   8. cheered up   9. calm, down
10. Calm down   11. working out
12. work out   13. blow, out   14. woke, up
15. woke up   16. blew out